Lacy Rose Gardenia

Gets Her Bloom

By
Janet G. Sims

Strategic Book Publishing and Rights Co.

Strategic Book Publishing and Rights Co., LLC
USA | Singapore
www.sbpra.com

For information about special discounts for bulk purchases, please contact Strategic Book Publishing and Rights Co., LLC, Special Sales, at bookorder@sbpra.net.

ISBN: 978-1-68181-107-9

Acknowledgement

I want to thank my husband Jim, my family, and friends because without them my life would be boring.

For the help from my son Mark who shares my humor,

and for Lacy Littlebook who inspired me to write it.

Janet G. Sims

CHAPTER 1

"Bouncing ballerinas! Where are all these cars going?" Lacy shouted out loud, talking to herself. She'd developed quite a habit of doing that. Having overslept that morning and now running short on time, she decided to take the freeway to work.

"I guess everyone overslept this morning. I suppose that should make me feel better, but somehow it just doesn't," Lacy sighed.

The traffic was moving at a snail's pace and sometimes not moving at all—like at this very moment—which made her very impatient. *Oh well*, she thought. It wouldn't be the first time she was ever late for work, and usually it was something out of the ordinary that happened, and she'd have an extraordinary story to tell everyone why she was late. Most of her stories were hard to believe, but since they were being told by Lacy, they had to be true, because she didn't like to tell a lie. And strange things always seemed to happen to her.

Lacy Rose Gardenia worked at a rapidly expanding advertising agency located in Stoneybrooke, a much larger town than Pebblestone, where she lived and which was about twenty miles north. She usually drove the road less traveled, State Route 50, when she wasn't running late, but this morning, when her alarm clock hadn't gone off because she'd forgotten to set it, she got up later than usual and decided not to have her coffee until she got to work to make up for lost time. *Note to self: learn how to set the alarm clock in my phone.*

As she rushed out the door, she heard strange noises coming from the front of her car. Quickly popping the hood, she discovered that the neighbor's cat, Tom, had managed to climb under the hood and get tangled up in wires hooked to the motor of her car, which she had forgotten to put in the garage the night before.

"Flying felines," Lacy gasped. "You are one dumb cat, but lovable. If you wanted a ride you could have waited for me to come out and just asked me." *Oh! I must be dumber than the cat.* "Here, kitty, kitty. Let me help you get out of there."

Finally managing to get the cat loose from all the wires that had captured it, all the time she'd saved by not having her coffee was lost. But Tom was safe and happy again, and she hoped he'd learned a good lesson about climbing under the hood of her car. And she hoped her car would start. It did, and she was on the freeway, again trying to make up the lost time.

The cars had started to move forward again as she was reliving her heroic act of saving the cat. She could hear the horns of the other impatient drivers behind her. She took her foot off the brake and stepped on the gas, finally moving forward.

"Dingy dogs!" she cried, stomping on her brakes. A puppy had somehow managed to get onto the freeway and stopped smack dab in front of her car. She heard the screeching tires before feeling the car behind her smash into the rear of her car and realized she had just been rear-ended.

"Oh. Wonderful! Today must be the curse of the animals."

Before she could open her door, an angry man was standing beside it, banging his knuckles against the window.

"What happened?" she asked him, pushing the door open to get out of the car.

"What do you mean what happened?" *Has this woman lost her mind?* the man thought. *She must have hit her head on the steering wheel.* "You tell me what happened, lady. Why did you pull a brake job on me?" *She must be a lunatic.* "Were you trying to make me hit you?"

"Of course not!" she shot back. He's a mean, crazy man. At least I managed to miss the little puppy. Why couldn't this mean-looking man try to miss my big car?

Lacy pushed past him to run to the front of her car to make sure she'd stopped in time to miss the puppy, but she didn't see it anywhere. She was down on her knees looking.

The man said, "What are you looking for?" Now I know for sure she's lost her mind.

Looking up at him while still on her knees, she sweetly replied, "The puppy that was sitting in front of my car. The one I was able to keep from hitting."

Cars were trying to make their way around the two angry

drivers who were outside of their cars in this traffic jam, yelling at each other, while horns were blasting all around them.

"What puppy? I don't see a puppy." Now she appears to be seeing things. I better leave before I catch what she has.

"Of course you don't see the puppy because it got away safe." *Unlike you, I missed it.*

"Okay, whatever you say. We can't stand around in traffic waiting for the police to come, so give me your information, and I'll make sure my insurance takes care of your car. There doesn't seem to be too much damage done to the cars, since you only moved a couple of feet before slamming on your brakes to miss the puppy," he said, dragging out the last two words.

"How do I know I can trust you? I don't even know your name."

As a car came around their cars, just missing them by inches, he blurted out, "My name is Jay. Now before we both get killed, will you please give me the information I asked for? I'm late for an important meeting, and I need to get going ASAP."

"Okay, I'll give you my card, but only because I'd hate to see you get killed by a passing motorist." *That would be an awful thing to see, even if it is this mean, angry man.*

Lacy climbed into her car and pulled out one of her business cards and handed it to Jay. He took it from her hand, then turned to walk back to get into his own car without even saying goodbye.

"Goodbye, Jay. I bet I never see you again. The way you were in such a hurry to get away, I bet you don't even have car insurance. And I bet your name isn't Jay either," she mumbled to herself as she put her car into drive and took off.

Lacy really was going to be late now. She wondered if she should try to come up with a more sensible excuse, because no one in his right mind was going to believe all the tales she had to tell this morning. If she hadn't just experienced this, she'd find it hard to believe herself.

Reaching her exit, Lacy turned right and was finally nearing her destination. Before getting out of her car, she reached down to get her briefcase sitting on the floor of the passenger side. As she lifted the briefcase, Lacy let out a cry of disbelief. "Slippery suckers!

Where'd you come from? No, I mean, how did you get into my car, you little bundle of trouble?"

There sat the little puppy that had been standing in the road in front of her car. It must've climbed into the car after she opened the door to go look for it, and she hadn't closed the door completely. Neither she nor Jay had seen it move out of sight under her car and crawl inside.

"Aren't you cute? Look at those adorable, big brown eyes. You look like a tiny bear cub with your black fuzzy coat. Well, I'd like to stay and play with you a while, but I've got to go to work now. Oh no! What am I going to do with you? I can't leave you alone in my car. Think, Lacy. I know. I'll take you inside and hide you until I can figure out what to do with you. Is that okay with you?" *Crazy is what you are for asking a dog what it wants to do.*

Looking behind the front seat, she spotted her gym bag. She kept workout clothes in her car so that, on a moment's notice, she could go to the gym after work with her friend, Stephanie. She emptied the contents of the bag onto the back seat, gathered the little puppy with his big brown eyes, and shoved him into the bag. The puppy wasn't very happy with her decision. He started whimpering and trying to crawl back out.

"No, puppy. You must stay inside until I find a safe place for you. Okay?"

Closing the bag but leaving a small opening to let in air, she headed for the front entrance of her building. She walked inside and entered an almost-full elevator with people going up. She could feel the puppy moving inside the bag, which she'd pulled against her side to protect it from being squashed.

Suddenly the puppy began to whimper again. As everyone turned to stare at her, she placed her hand on her stomach and started to cough and clear her throat, hoping they'd think it was something she'd eaten. Was it just her imagination, or did it seem to her that when the doors opened everyone was exiting the elevator rather quickly? They must've thought the next sound they would hear would be the passing of gas. She would've been embarrassed if she hadn't been laughing as hard as she walked off the elevator.

Lacy managed to reach her office without another incident.

She'd made her greetings to all her fellow workers and then ducked into her own office. She placed her briefcase on her desk, set the gym bag on the floor, and opened it up to free the puppy. It was so happy to be free from the bag that when she picked it up, it began to lick her face, making her giggle.

"You're so cute and cuddly. What am I going to do with you? I suppose I should give you a name while you're staying with me. Let's see. You appear to be a little boy. What if I call you Samuel Ace? Do you like that? And I'll call you Sammy for short."

Her phone rang. It was her boss, and she was forced to put Sammy down on the floor to answer the call. It only took a few minutes before the puppy managed to tip over her trash can and begin tearing up paper. Fortunately, her boss just needed to remind her of a meeting, and she hung up and went for the dog.

"What've I got myself into?" No sooner were the words out of her mouth before Sammy squatted to pee on the rug. "No, Sammy! Not on the rug, please." But by the time she got to him, he'd already done the deed. "Well, I'd better find some newspaper for your next little trick, huh, buddy?"

Lacy put Sammy in her closet and closed the door to go look for some newspaper. Halfway out of her office, she heard him begin to whimper. This was going to be a fun day if she survived it.

A couple of hours later, Lacy was sitting at her desk working on her computer, trying to get caught up on some of the time she'd lost this morning. She'd been lucky when she found a large cardboard box to put Sammy in, and she lined the bottom with newspapers and cut a hole in the side so he could see her as she sat at her desk. As long as she spoke to him every now and then and kept a radio playing softly, he was quiet.

She also found a small plastic bowl to put water in so he could have a drink. She knew it wouldn't be long before he'd be hungry. She'd fed him some of a doughnut that she'd had with her morning—or mid-morning—coffee. No one was allowed to enter her office. She'd go outside her door to speak to all visitors. When they gave her a funny look, she'd tell them that she didn't want them to wake her new puppy and laughed. They thought she was kidding and laughed too—about the strange way she was acting.

When lunch time came, Lacy stuffed Sammy back into her gym bag and, using the stairs this time, headed for her car to go to a fast-food restaurant, where she bought sandwiches for two. She also bought a bottle of water. She drove to a park nearby so they could enjoy their lunch together.

"Well, Sammy, this isn't the way I thought I'd be spending my lunch today. But I've got to say it's very nice." Pulling him free from the gym bag, she set him down on the grass, which made him very excited and happy. His first act was to squat and do his business.

"I guess that was another good reason for us to have our lunch outside in this nice park, cutie pie."

Finally it was time for Lacy to go back to work with Sammy safely hidden away inside the gym bag. Being tired from all the excitement, plus having a full tummy, caused him to fall asleep as soon as he entered the bag. "What a little angel you are," she whispered.

Just as she was about to take hold of the front door handle of the building where she worked, a big hand came from behind and grabbed the door, bumping into the back of her. She turned her head quickly to see who it was.

"Rushing rhinos!" came spilling out of her mouth. There stood Jay, the man who'd rear-ended her that morning. "Good grief. Do you have a habit of running into women from behind?"

"No. Not really. Not until you came into my life this morning." *I just wish you'd disappear.* "Do you have a habit of stopping quickly as well as a habit of talking to yourself?" *Did I say that last part out loud?*

"Are you talking to me or about me?" *You're angry, mean, and weird.*

"What are you doing here?" Jay chose to ignore her last question.

"I work here. What are you doing here, Jay? Did you come here to tell me that your insurance is going to fix my car?" *If you really do have insurance?*

"No. I came for a meeting this morning, and I'm just getting back from lunch. Speaking of your car, did my insurance call you?"

"No, they didn't." And with my luck, they never will.

"I'll get hold of them today and make sure they do." I've got to get this woman out of my life and real soon.

Jay went through the door, leaving her standing there, again without saying goodbye or giving her a chance to respond.

"Okay, Jay. I bet you'll get right on that today. Right after the fire you're rushing to put out. Maybe my deodorant failed or the puppy is making me smell bad. Sammy, we'll both get a good bath tonight."

The rest of the day was a repeat of the morning, except Jay didn't run into her again. She'd managed to keep Sammy from being seen by the other co-workers and knew they thought she was acting crazy. They'd all laughed at her when she told them why she was late, leaving out the part about Sammy climbing in her car and hiding in her office. That story would be told at a later date. Jay's insurance hadn't called all day, and she realized that she hadn't checked her car to see if it had any damage. That would have to wait until she got home and decided what to do with Sammy.

Lacy didn't take the freeway home. Her day had been very exhausting, and she didn't want to risk having any more excitement like she'd experienced this morning. Sammy was lying in the passenger seat watching her as she drove. He seemed to be very happy to be out of the box and in the car with her.

"Well, sweetie, what am I going to do with you? I'd love to have a puppy, but right now isn't a good time. I have to work to pay for my house and all my bills. Who's going to stay with you while I'm away?"

Lacy had bought a house in Pebblestone that had sat vacant for over a year and needed a little work to turn it into her dream home. The house was located a few blocks from the main street in town. The senior citizen building was to the right of her house and only two houses were on the left. The road ended a little past the senior center building and led to a house on the other side of the street. The Pebblestone County Fair Grounds, across from her house, stretched almost the entire length of that block and was situated between two houses. One section of the lot was a fenced-in empty field that was used for parking for big events. From her house, she could see where the bleachers were and could hear music from special events. She also could see the horses with carts being exercised on the race track almost every day. The fair was one of four that was open all year round.

Lacy pulled into her driveway, parked her car, and made a mental note to make sure to park it in her garage later that night. She grabbed Sammy and put him down in the grass while she picked up her briefcase. Sammy was running around in circles to find the right spot to *go*. She walked around to the back of her car and was surprised to find very little damage to her bumper.

"Wonderful! I may not have to set eyes on Jay again. Even if he does have insurance," she sang out rather loudly while doing a little dance, which scared the puppy. "I'm sorry, boy. Mommy's happy because her bad luck may be changing to good luck."

She picked up the puppy, unlocked the door, and went inside, kicking off her shoes. The phone was ringing, so she put the puppy down and went to answer it.

"Hi, Lacy. How was your day?" It was Spence.

"Well, do you mean after the cat rescue, after I got up late, or the traffic jam where I almost hit a puppy, or the accident where I met the mean, angry, weird Jay? Would you like to hear the rest of my day?"

"No. But maybe you could tell me more about the weird guy named Jay." *It sounds like she had one crazy day.* "Did I hear you say accident?" Spence asked, starting to feel a little apprehensive.

"Yeah, I had a fender bender because I had to stop suddenly to miss Sammy, and the weird man named Jay didn't stop in time so I was rear-ended."

"So you're telling me that this Jay ran into your car because you stopped suddenly to miss Sammy. Who the heck is Sammy?"

"The puppy I almost hit when he came walking out in front of my car while I was driving on the freeway this morning. I was driving on the freeway because I was late, because the alarm clock was not set to go off. And Tom was stuck up under my car engine this morning because I forgot to put my car in the garage last night."

"I think I'm going to be sorry for asking, but who is Tom?" *Maybe she has started taking drugs.*

"You know who Tom is. He's the cat next door, silly." *Men! They just don't pay attention.*

"Oh. Of course! He's the cat next door. And I should know this because ...?"

"Because I told you his name was Tom when he came into the yard a couple of weeks ago when we were outside grilling."

"And I was expected to remember his name?" *That's a lot to ask of any man.*

"Listen, Spence, were you calling for a reason? I've had a really long day, and I just got home from work. I need a long relaxing bath before I sit down and eat my dinner."

"Dinner that we have plans to eat together tonight?" *It looks like her memory isn't much better than mine.*

"Oh, leaping lions! I'm sorry. I forgot. I've had a super bad day."

"You didn't get hurt when you got rear-ended by this weird, mean, angry man named Jay, did you?"

"I don't think so. My head hurts a little, but that may be from all the stress I've been under all day."

"How'd you like it if I brought over a pizza while you take your bath? Then you can tell me all about it, or not." *I think I might have heard most of it already*

"That sounds like a plan. Then when you get here you can meet Sammy. Bye." She hung up quickly so she wouldn't have to explain what she meant.

Lacy knew she didn't have a lot of time to waste, because Spence was a man who didn't let any weeds grow under his feet. He was probably already in his car headed for their favorite pizza place with his cell phone on his ear calling in the order. If she was going to get her bath, she'd better start moving now. Not knowing what to do with Sammy, she took him into the bathroom and let him play with an old stuffed teddy bear she just couldn't throw away—she knew it would come in handy one day. And now it had.

Spence Edward Taylor had met Lacy Rose Gardenia for the first time when they'd been enrolled in the same kindergarten class at the age of five. From that day forward, they were best friends. They'd grown up a couple of blocks from each other in the town of

Stoneybrooke—their parents were friends—and had spent most of their childhood together.

Spence's dad, Spencer Taylor, was a lawyer who worked with a group of well-known lawyers, and his mom, Janey, owned a popular hair salon in Pebblestone. After graduating high school, they both attended Stoneybrooke University. Spence had majored in journalism while Lacy majored in advertising. Not long after graduating, she'd been hired by J.S. Bloom Advertising Agency, which was rapidly expanding, while he landed a great spot at the *Stoneybrooke Hometown Newspaper.*

At the beginning of Lacy's junior year in college, she'd moved to her grandparents' 295-acre farm in Pebblestone where her father had grown up. She lived in a one-room apartment with a bath in the top of the big red barn. Her grandpa, Robert Lester Gardenia, had made the room for his son, William, when he became a teenager, because he wanted more privacy—William was the eldest of the five children (four boys and one girl). William had lived there also while going to college to become a doctor, where he had met and married his wife, Samantha Suzanne Martin, who was studying to be nurse.

Lacy loved living there and found it very peaceful. She was able to study without many interruptions. When she wanted company, Grandpa Robert and Grandma Lily Rose were nearby in the big farmhouse. Spence came to visit her as much as possible and loved it too.

When she wasn't taking classes or doing homework, she worked with her grandpa in his grain business, which was considered the largest and best one in the area, and she was well paid. She also lived in the barn apartment rent-free and didn't have to pay utilities, so she was able to put most of her wages in the bank.

Lacy's grandfather had taught her how to plant and harvest corn and soy beans. He also taught her all the other jobs required to run the farm. He'd laugh and tell her she'd turned into a good little farmer, which made her feel useful and loved.

Her grandma had taught her how to cook, using all the vegetables grown in her garden, which she worked in every day during gardening season. Lacy loved helping her with it when she had time. She didn't want to leave the farm after graduating and starting her job, but one day she'd seen her dream house on the market and used her savings as a down payment on the house. She knew she could go back to visit the farm and her grandparents whenever she wanted.

When Lacy finally climbed out of the bathtub and was wrapped in a large towel, she threw Sammy into the tub as promised. She didn't want him smelling bad when Spence got there with the pizza. Sammy seemed to love the water and kept splashing it in her face. After drying Sammy off with her towel, they both went into her bedroom so Lacy could get dressed. Sammy went back to get his teddy bear. The doorbell rang as she pulled her T-shirt over her head and down over her jeans. She slipped on her sandals, picked Sammy up with the teddy bear in his mouth, and went to welcome Spence.

"Hi. Oh, that pizza smells delicious. Come in while it's still hot."

"I'm glad to see you too. What are you doing with a puppy in your arms? I can make an educated guess: that's the puppy you said you missed hitting on the freeway this morning. So, this must be Sammy. I'm so glad to meet you, I think." *He's so cute. Should I be jealous?*

"When I got out of my car to see if I'd really missed hitting him, he'd somehow climbed through the open door and hid behind my briefcase sitting on the floor on the passenger side. Can you imagine what I thought when I found him there?"

"No. But I can tell you what you did after you found him. You decided to name him, bring him home with you, give him a bath— and, by the way, he smells as good as you do—and now you're thinking about keeping him. Have I got that all right?'

"Well, yeah. I guess I'd like to keep him. We kind of bonded while he was in the box in my office, and we had lunch together in the park today. Sammy is awfully cute, isn't he?"

"Yeah, he's real cute. Don't you know the rule? You never name a lost puppy, because once you name it, you own it. You actually kept him in a box in your office and went out to lunch with him in the park? What did your boss say? 'You're fired!'" *You had lunch with a puppy and forgot about our dinner tonight?*

"I didn't tell anybody that he was in my office, and I wouldn't let anyone come in. He had to go to potty, so I took him to the park for lunch. He was a really good puppy after I cut a hole in the side of the box so he could see me, and I played some music so he didn't whimper."

"Should I ask how you got him into your office without anyone seeing him?"

"Oh. That was the easy part. I put him in the gym bag I leave in the car and carried him up." *I'm not as dumb as you think I am.*

"Oh. I see." *She's not as dumb as I thought she was.* "Well, shall we eat now before the pizza gets cold?"

"That sounds good to me. I'm starving to death. Bring it to the kitchen and open it up while I get the drinks and find something for Sammy."

They worked together getting everything ready to sit down and eat their pizza. Lacy gave Sammy some cereal with milk, and knew she'd have to go to the store later to get some puppy chow. The big question now was what was she going to do with him tomorrow?

"Seriously, Lacy, are you really planning on keeping Sammy? I know you think he's cute, and you're right about that, but he'll be a big responsibility. He'll need a lot of care while he's in the puppy stage, and he'll get bigger. He looks like a black Lab, so he'll get bigger."

"I know, but like you already said, I gave him a name, and we've bonded. I don't think I'll be able to find out where he came from, because there are no houses on that stretch of the freeway. And don't tell me to put an ad in the newspaper, because anyone could claim him, and it may not be the one who lost him."

"Oh, my sweet Lacy, you made up your mind to keep him from the first moment you laid eyes on him, didn't you? You'd better make arrangements tonight for someone to keep him tomorrow. I don't think your boss will be happy to find him in a box in your office, do you?"

"How about if I bring him to your office?" Lacy asked jokingly.

"Yeah, that'll work. He can fetch files for me all day. And when I go out for a big story, he can be my photographer and go potty at the same time."

"I know! My grandma can keep him on the farm during the day, and I can pick him up when I get off work—just until I can put up a kennel and get a dog house and fence in my backyard and put in a doggie door."

"Did you just think that up or have you been planning that all day?"

"Yep, it just popped into my big empty head. But it sounds like a good plan to me. No! Sammy, you have to go outside to do that kind of stuff." Picking him up, she raced to the door.

"Good luck," Spence shouted as Lacy disappeared through the back door. "Well, I guess those two can grow up together, and when he's bigger, he'll be able to protect her since she's living here alone. I guess this is one of those times when the puppy got to pick its owner."

"I can hear you through the open door. I'm just out of sight, not out of hearing distance. But I agree with everything you just said. Thanks for understanding. That's why I keep you in my life."

"Thank you. And here all this time I thought you just kept me around to do your dishes, cut your grass, change your oil, fix this, fix that, and because you love me just a little."

"You know I love you just a little," she said, walking back into the kitchen, laughing as she went to stand next to him. And to prove it she gave him a big kiss.

"Well, that makes me feel much better. But what can I do to make you love me more than just a little?"

"I know. You can come to the farm with me and help me talk my grandma into taking care of the puppy. Then later you can help me put up a kennel for him. Please?" *He can't resist me when I beg.*

"I've got to turn you down on your first request, but I'll consider the second one and get back with you." He couldn't resist her pretty little face when she was begging so sweetly. "Of course I'll help you with the kennel, but I do need to go on home tonight to work on a piece that needs to go to the printer early in morning."

Lacy had been a pretty little girl and had grown into a beautiful young lady. She had light blue eyes that darkened with excitement, and her natural blonde hair was long and full of curls. She'd been blessed with a flawless, creamy completion and a small, perky nose. Her mouth was small, shapely, and very kissable. She always was smiling, which showed her perfect set of pearly white teeth. She had a tiny, curvy figure that any model would envy. Lacy wasn't aware of how beautiful she really was, because being vain was not part of her virtue. She stood a full five feet three while barefoot, but always thought of herself as being taller. She was always full of energy and moved in one speed: fast.

Spence was, in some ways, the opposite. He had shiny black hair and dark brown eyes that got even darker when he was emotional, which was often. He was downright handsome and blushed when someone told that to him. He had a perfectly shaped nose for a man and a soft but sensual mouth. He had a great sense of humor, much like Lacy. Both were kind hearted and easy going.

Spence had managed to make it through school without picking up any of the bad habits most guys his age did, thinking it made them look macho. Getting drunk, smoking, and cursing all the time were things he'd thought were stupid. He had wanted no part of it and stayed away from the guys who did. He was always a gentleman and didn't care what others thought of him. His parents had brought him up this way, making him a great catch for any girl.

"Well, I guess I'd better go home so you can make that visit to the farm and see if your begging for help is going to work. Give your grandma that sad little face when you ask her, and she'll agree to anything. Goodbye, sweetheart."

"Thanks, honey. And thanks for bringing the pizza. I'm so sorry I forgot about dinner."

"Well, I'll let you get away with blaming it on Sammy this time, but don't think it's going to work every time. Okay. See you tomorrow. Call me later, and let me know what happens. Goodbye, Lacy." Spence hugged Lacy and gave her a kiss before leaving for his house, also in Pebblestone and located nearby, because he wanted to be close to her.

"Okay, little man. It's time to go meet your grandparents. Let's go get it over with. Then I've got to buy some puppy supplies. I'm afraid you're going to be very expensive. I've also got to find a good vet to take you to for your shots, and maybe find out your age.

You're going to be a lot of work, aren't you? But I think you're worth it, because I already love you so much."

Lacy was wiped out by the time she returned home, but was very happy because her grandma had fallen in love with Sammy on first sight and said she'd help with him. Even her grandpa liked Sammy and said he thought he was going to be a very smart dog. Now she'd have to get up a little earlier in order to drop him off before going to work. But still she planned to have a kennel installed as soon as possible so he could stay home, although she'd give him a little more time to get bigger, because he couldn't be much older than six weeks.

There was a message on her answering machine when Lacy got home. She figured it was Spence calling to find out what happened. She pushed the button and a man identifying himself as Jay's insurance man had left a message for her to call him back at her convenience. She took down the number that he'd left, and was surprised that he really had called.

"Well, my convenience will have to be tomorrow, because I'm too tired to deal with it tonight. I can't wait to get this matter settled so I don't ever have to hear from Jay again. He's a mean, angry, weird man. Don't you agree, my furry little bear cub?" Sammy made sounds in his throat like he was trying to agree with her, which made her laugh.

Before she went to bed, she called Spence to tell him that her begging had worked. She also told him that she'd used her little sad face, but just seeing Sammy had been enough. Her grandparents had both fallen in love with her little stinker.

Chapter 2

Lacy bought an extra-large crate for Sammy, because she didn't want him running loose in the house, especially since he wasn't potty trained yet. She'd bought the biggest one, since Spence told her that he'd grow to be a large dog, and she didn't want to be forced to buy a larger one later. She turned on a nightlight that she kept in her bedroom and put Sammy into the crate with his teddy bear and a cozy little blanket. But as soon as her head hit the pillow, the whimpering began.

Lacy raised her head to take a look at Sammy in the crate that she'd set up in her big bedroom. "Oh. Sammy. Mommy is so tired. Please go to sleep. Pretty please. I'll take you to see Grandma tomorrow."

Sammy looked at her with his big brown eyes and tilted his head while as he listened to her speak. He'd stopped whimpering and was sitting there waiting for something to happen. Because he'd quieted down, she lay her head back down on her pillow. She knew he didn't need to go outside because she'd taken him out just before putting him in his crate and lying down.

Round # 1: Sammy wins paws down.

The whimpering began again within seconds of her head touching the pillow. "Okay, Samuel Ace, you win, but only because I need to get some sleep tonight." *I hope that I didn't make a bad choice in keeping you, you little trouble maker.*

Sammy was very happy to be in bed with Lacy, wrapped in his new blanket, his head on a pillow, and his new friend, the teddy bear, lying next to him. Little did Lacy know that this was only the beginning of this sleeping arrangement for many weeks to come— or at least until he got too big to sleep on her bed. But for right now it worked, and Lacy only had to get up twice during the night to take him out to go potty.

Surprisingly, the morning went very smoothly. While the puppy ate breakfast, Lacy sipped her coffee and nibbled on a piece of toast. The she gathered all the puppy's things to take with them to the farm—she felt liked she'd just adopted a new baby.

After dropping Sammy and his things off, she drove the back roads to work that morning and sang along with the radio, listening to her favorite station.

At work she smiled at everyone she walked past before she entered her office. The door to her office was unlocked and stayed that way, because her co-workers always needed something in there. This way they could go in and help themselves. They knew they could find what they needed in her office, which was fine with her as long as they brought it back or replaced it if they used it up.

"Creepy cats! What are you doing in my office?" *Just who do you think you are, and why do you think you can just walk into my office without being invited even if my door is unlocked?*

"Good morning to you too," Jay said. *"Creepy cats"? What kind of language is that?* "I have another meeting here this morning and thought I'd meet with you first. I was going to knock but your door was slightly open so I came in to wait for you. My insurance man told me he called you last night and left a message to call him back, but he still hasn't heard from you."

"It's still early and, as you can see, I just walked into my office. I was out late last night when he called, and he said to call him back at my convenience, if that's okay with you." *Oh shoot, I didn't mean to ask his permission.*

"I just thought you wanted to get your car fixed right away. I guess I thought wrong. Excuse me." *You must've crawled out on the wrong side of bed this morning, and maybe not your own.*

"I'll leave you alone now, but please call soon so we can get this matter resolved quickly."

"I'm sorry, I just didn't expect to see anyone in my office, especially you. Oh! I'm sorry again. Yes, I'll call this morning, but I didn't see much damage to my car, so I don't think it needs very much work done. Did your car have any damage?"

"No, actually, it didn't. Why don't you let me take a look at it first, and if it doesn't look like it will cost very much to fix, I'll pay for it without involving my insurance company?"

"That's fine with me." *Maybe he isn't so mean after all.*

"How about if I come by your house tonight and check it out?"

"I have to go to my grandparents' farm first to pick up my puppy before I go home. Their farm is in Pebblestone, about ten miles from my house."

There she goes talking about a puppy again. "You have a puppy?"

"Yes, I do now. It's the same one that ran out in front of me. Somehow it climbed into my car when I was looking for it and hid on the floor behind my briefcase."

"And you decided to take it home with you?"

"Well, of course I did. I couldn't just throw it back out on the road again, could I?"

"I guess not. Okay, I'll come to your house later tonight after you get home, if's that okay with you? I have some business to attend to in Pebblestone tonight anyway." *I do if you say it's okay,* Jay said to himself, because he really wanted to see her again. He hadn't realized what a beautiful lady she really was until right now, and he liked what he saw. And he'd like to get a chance to see her again and maybe get to know her a lot better.

"I guess that'll work. You already have my card, and it has my address and phone number. Call before you come by, okay?"

Lacy had some business cards printed that included her home address to give to those clients she took on outside the agency. These were little projects the agency had to turn down because of the volume of clients the agency had already accepted. Her boss, Jason Smith, had encouraged her to take them on. He said it would be a great way for her to gain more experience and often gave her advice when she needed help.

"See you later, Jay," Lacy spoke over her shoulder as she began walking to her desk to sit down.

"Goodbye, Miss Flower," Jay said as he walked out the door.

It'd taken her a couple of seconds to realize what he'd said. "Miss Flower! That's Miss Gardenia!" Lacy yelled after him, but the doors had already closed on the elevator he'd entered.

"Pickled pigs! What've I gotten myself into? Why didn't I ask him to go look at my car in the parking lot? Why does he have to come to my house?" She started to panic and called Spence.

"Good morning. Spence speaking."

"Good morning, sweetheart. What're you doing after work tonight?"

"Don't you remember I had asked you to go to the baseball game with me, since I had been given two free tickets, but you told me to ask Mitch, who said yes? You didn't change your mind, did you?"

"Oh, no. I knew that. I was just wondering if you were going to come by before you went to the game." *Good save, Lacy.*

"Ah, no. Did I tell you I would?"

"Nope, I just wondered, that's all. You and Mitch have fun tonight."

"Is everything okay, Lacy? You sound a little upset."

"No, I'm fine. I'm having someone look at my car tonight to assess the damage done from the accident. There really isn't much damage from what I could see."

"Do you want me to swing by tonight? What time will that be?"

"No, I can handle it, so don't worry about it. But thanks for saying that you'd do that for me. You're a keeper."

"That's what I keep trying to tell you. Goodbye, honey. I have to go now."

"Goodbye, and have fun tonight."

Lacy decided she'd better get started on the work on her desk. Ten minutes later, in walked her best friend, Stephanie.

"Lacy Rose, what was going on yesterday? I heard you were acting a little strange, or should I say even more strange than usual, and you didn't even ask me out for lunch. I know I could've asked you, but my boss kept me very busy yesterday. I was going to call you last night, but I had to go to my brother Zack's house for a family dinner. That was fun."

"Stephanie Louise, you're just the person I needed to see today. What're you doing after work tonight?"

"Today is Friday! We're going shopping for all the party supplies you need for your party tomorrow, remember? What's wrong with you? You're still acting strangely. And don't call me Louise, please." *Gee whiz, already.*

23

"That's right, you remembered. Yay! I just wanted you to know that I have to go to my grandparents' farm right after work. I won't be there long. I just have to pick up something. So don't be late, okay?"

"Yep, and don't you be late either."

Stephanie Louise Baker had followed in her best friend's footsteps by buying a house only two blocks down the street from Lacy. It was a little smaller than Lacy's and had needed very little work. Lacy had met Stephanie in first grade, after her parents had moved from Pebblestone to Stoneybrooke. Her dad, Harold "Harry" Baker, had been promoted to assistant principal at Stoneybrooke High and had moved his family there to be closer to the school. Her mother, Rebecca, a teacher, had been able to fill a vacant position at the high school at the same time. Stephanie had cried, because she didn't want to go to a new school, but when she met Lacy she was very glad they'd moved.

Stephanie stood a little taller than Lacy, at five-feet-four, and had the same long, naturally blonde hair, but it was not as curly. She had pretty blue eyes with green specks, and a cute little nose and mouth. She also was very beautiful. People who didn't know them thought they might be twins, or at least sisters. Like Lacy, Stephanie was able to find a job at the advertising agency as a secretary. Both women had submitted resumes at the same time. Stephanie's parents had put away money for her college education. She'd attended the same college as Lacy, but had majored in business with the dream of starting her own business someday. For now, though, she needed to work in an office to get more experience and maybe work her way up. She'd worked small jobs while going to school and had lived at home with her parents. She also had saved enough for a nice down payment on her house. Her brother, Zach, was four years older and married to Andrea; they had one son, Timmy, who was a year old. Stephanie also loved visiting Lacy when she had lived in the barn.

"See you later for lunch," Lacy reminded her.

"Okay, but if I forget to tell you later, tell Grandma Lily Rose that I said hi. And tell Grandpa Robert too."

"You know I will. Now go to work, woman."

Lacy was relieved that she wouldn't be alone when Jay came by. She wasn't afraid of him, but there was something about him that made her nervous. She'd just noticed today when he was in her office that he was a very good looking man, a fact she hadn't realized in all the times he'd literally run into her, which she hoped he'd stop doing—or maybe not. He had a way of making her heart race and her thoughts run wild at the same time. That couldn't be a good thing, could it?

"Oh, stop torturing yourself, Lacy. He's still an angry, weird, mean, tall, dark, and handsome man who's coming to my house to check out my car. Lord, give me strength."

The rest of the day kept her so busy she'd had no time to think about the situation until her drive home. She turned the volume on the radio up loud to try and drown out her thoughts. Thinking about seeing her puppy again helped a little. She'd really missed the little creature. He'd crawled up close to her in the middle of the night and slept by her side. Maybe he was missing his real mommy. Well, she was his mommy now.

Lily Rose Gardenia was happy to see Lacy when she arrived at the farm. She told Lacy that she'd really enjoyed having Sammy with her today, the he was such a gentle, sweet, and loving little puppy. Even Grandpa Robert made the comment that he was surprised Sammy was such a smart little thing for being so tiny, and that if for some reason Lacy wasn't able to keep him, then Sammy could stay with them. That was quite a big statement coming from him, because he always tried not to get attached to animals, especially dogs. Lacy was sorry she was in such a hurry to go home and didn't have more time to visit, but she had to get home. She relayed Stephanie's greeting to both of them, then put Sammy in the car to leave. She left all his stuff there so she wouldn't have to pack it again on Monday. When she'd gone shopping she decided to buy two of everything except the cage. They already had a small fenced in area for their bulldog, Oscar, when he'd been a puppy, but now that he was older he stayed in the yard around the house when he wasn't inside. The two dogs got along great.

When she got home, she quickly took Sammy out of the car, gave him time to potty, and then ran into the house, with the puppy running after her. She wanted to change out of her office clothes and put on something more comfortable. She didn't know when Jay would get there, since he hadn't called yet, but she hoped Stephanie would get there first. When her phone rang, she knew it was Jay even before she answered.

"Hello, Miss Petal. It's Jay, and I'm calling to say I'm on my way. See you soon." Before she'd had a chance to say hello, he'd hung up.

"Jay, I'll have to add rude to your growing list of bad habits, and why can't you get my name right?" Lacy said to herself, rather loudly. "Gardenia is not that hard to remember!"

As soon as she'd said that, the doorbell rang and, as she was opening the door, she said, "Thank goodness it's you. I was afraid you were going to be—" Lacy stopped talking when she realized the person who was standing there was Jay. She was about to belt out one of her many phrases that she was so famous for, but her mind was blank as she stood there, her mouth wide open.

"Yes, it's me. Were you about to say something about crazy felines? What were you saying to me about 'going to be'?"

"Um, no, I was just saying that I thought you were going to be . . . uh . . . upset when you saw my car." *He must've been standing on my porch when he called and heard what I said.*

"Should I be? It didn't look that bad when I drove up behind it in your driveway."

"Oh! That's a relief. That makes me feel a lot better." Yeah, right. My hands are sweating, and my brain has gone stupid on me.

"Well, let's take a closer look at it, shall we?" *I would love to take a closer look.*

"Let's," was all she could think to say.

They walked out to her car, and Jay bent down to take a closer look at the back. Lacy just stood there watching him, wondering where the heck her friend was—although she didn't know what Stephanie could do to help her, except be there and watch her make a fool of herself.

Jay stood up and turned to look at her. "There's a big dent in the middle of your bumper that needs attention. I know a great body man who can take care of that for you." *And I know someone who can take care of your car as well.*

"I bet you do . . . uh . . . I mean, that would be great." *Good grief, Lacy, have you lost your mind? Just say thank you and walk away.* "Thank you for coming by. Let me know when you want it, I mean, when you need me . . . that is . . . to drop off my car. Just let me know when and where. Oh! And I'll need some . . . um . . . transportation to get around. Is that okay with you?" *Now just go into the house and pull your foot out of your mouth.*

"I'll set it up and get back with you soon. Is that okay with you?"

"Yes, that'll be just fine."

Jay looked deep into her eyes. "Then it's a date. I'll be calling you soon. Goodbye, Miss Daisy." Then he turned, and she watched him walk to his car. He was gone before she realized what he'd said.

"My name is Gardenia! *Miss* Gardenia!" she yelled.

As he was driving away, she saw Stephanie walk up her driveway. "Who was that man pulling away from your driveway?"

"The man who rear-ended me yesterday—not once, but twice," Lacy explained.

"What do you mean 'twice'?"

"It's a long story, and I'll have to fill you in when we're in the car, but first I have to make sure Sammy is okay and put him in his crate."

"Who the heck is Sammy, and why are you putting him in a crate?"

As much as she dreaded it, Lacy was going to have to tell Stephanie everything about yesterday, starting with forgetting to set her alarm clock and leaving her car outside on the driveway. She'd tell her all the facts, but leave out the way she felt while talking to Jay.

Stephanie was introduced to Sammy as soon as she entered the house, but was told she'd have to wait to get an answer to "Where'd the heck did he come from?" Lacy wanted to wait until they were in the car to explain what had happened the day before and only wanted to explain it all at one time, including the part about who that man was pulling away from her driveway.

Stephanie listened intently as Lacy began telling her story once they were in the car. She tried to ask questions, but Lacy wouldn't give her a chance until she had finished.

"No way! Lacy, you've got to be kidding me. You mean to tell me that all of that happened since yesterday morning? No wonder you were acting so strange. Is Jay good looking?"

"Stephanie Louise! I guess you could call him good looking. But that doesn't matter to me. He's just going to fix my car and nothing more."

"Oh really? Then why are you blushing? I want to be there when he comes back."

"If you hadn't been late today you would've met him already."

Lacy pulled into the parking lot and found a spot to park her car. She checked to make sure she had her list of things she needed to buy for the party she was giving for her parents tomorrow evening. They'd been on a month-long trip. She'd invited some family members and a few friends to welcome them back. She told her parents that it was only a cookout with her and Spence, and they'd agreed to come. They lived nearby, so it wouldn't be a long drive for them, and they really wanted to see their only daughter after being away for so long.

After the two friends entered the store, Lacy headed off to the grocery section while Stephanie went in search for a new pair of flip-flops.

"Stephanie, step on it because we don't have much time to get things done before the party tomorrow."

"Don't forget the pickles," Stephanie shouted out to remind her.

After filling her cart with all the needed supplies, she realized she still needed to get pickles. She went to get some, and then headed toward the front of the store. Stephanie caught up with her and decided to check out first. Lacy placed all of her items on the counter, one by one, the pickles being the last thing out of the cart. She grabbed hold of the top of the jar and lifted. The jar slipped from her fingers and hit the floor, where it shattered and spilled the pickles all over, causing a sticky mess.

"Oops, I'm sorry. I had the jar in my fingers, but it just slipped out," Lacy apologized.

"We need cleanup at express lane number one, and we need a broom and a mop," the lady at the register said over the loud speaker, not once, but three times.

Stephanie couldn't keep herself from snickering, and Lacy gave her a stern look. A woman who worked with them walked by and said, "I bet I know who did that." It made both of them giggle, although the clerk didn't seem to share in their amusement.

"I'd better run back and get another jar of pickles so I don't hold up the line," Lacy said to anyone who'd listen and raced off to get another jar.

After Lacy had paid for everything and all was in bags, a young boy showed up with a broom, a bucket of water, and a mop. As the two women were exiting the front door, a man was entering, pushing his wife in a wheelchair. They heard him say, "Oh, look, honey, there's a pickle emergency," which made both Lacy and Stephanie howl out loud with laughter on their way to the car.

When they got back to Lacy's house, they carried the bags inside. Sammy began to whimper when he heard them, so Lacy went to get him out of the cage to take him outside. "Yay, no mess. You are such a good little thing, aren't you? And smart too. You'll get an extra treat for waiting for me."

After Stephanie left, Lacy began preparing the dishes she was going to serve tomorrow, stopping long enough only to take the puppy out, because he was still in the potty training stage. She kept thinking to herself that so far everything was going fine.

Spence called her as she was about to retire for the night to tell her about the baseball game. His team won, and he was still excited.

"I'm so happy to hear our team won, and that you and Mitch had such a great time. Steph and I went to the store and picked up stuff for our cookout. I can't wait to see Mom and Dad."

"I can't wait to see them either. How are Billy Bob and Sammy Sue?"

"Please don't call them that when you see them. I don't think they like being called that. No, I know for a fact they don't like it because of being teased at school. But they do sometimes call each other that. But you know all that already, right?"

"Right, I'm going to say good night now. I'm tired, and I know you are too. Oh, wait a minute. How'd your meeting go with weird Jay?" *She didn't say it was him, but I bet it was.*

"He came by, looked at my car, and said he would pay to have it fixed. I said that would be great and asked him to get a rental car for me to drive until mine is fixed. Then he left," Lacy said without explaining the small details.

"Sounds like you handled that just fine without me. Goodbye, sweetheart."

"Thanks. Good night, Spence."

Lacy turned to Sammy. "Let's try this one more time, boy." She put him into the crate and closed the door. She laid down on her bed and gave a sigh of relief when she heard no whimpering. It was when she turned over to get comfortable that the whimpering began.

Round #2 goes to Sammy.

Chapter 3

Lacy was up early the next day. One of the reasons was to finish up for the party and the other was because Sammy woke her up licking her check. He was an early riser. He had gone out only once last night. Spence would be coming over later to help get out the grill that he'd bought for her as a house-warming gift and get it ready to use. She'd bought some steaks for the ones she knew would eat one, and hamburgers and hot dogs for the rest. It wasn't going to be a large group because she knew her parents would be tired after their trip, and she didn't want them to be overwhelmed.

Stephanie was coming over this morning after breakfast for their trip to the mall. Lacy was going to buy her dad his favorite cologne and her mom a box of her favorite chocolates for a homecoming gift. Lily Rose had called to ask how Sammy was doing and said she missed him, so Lacy said she'd drop him off since they would go past the farm on the way to the mall. So far, her plans for Sammy were working out fine, although they didn't include her grandma keeping the puppy on weekends. As soon as he was a little older, potty trained, and had a kennel and fence installed, he'd be able to stay home except when she took him for a visit. That was the plan.

Lacy heard Stephanie knock on the door and then open it and come in. "Lacy, are you ready to rock and roll? Get the lead out. Oh, hello, Sammy, you little darling. He's so cute. No wonder you decided to keep him," she agreed, picking him up to cuddle him.

"Hi, Steph. Could you take him outside for me so I can put on my shoes and grab my purse? We have to drop him off at the farm before we can shop."

"Yes, I can handle that."

It didn't take long to reach the mall and park the car. As they were entering the door, Lacy said, "Do you mind if we pick up the gifts first? Then we can spend some time looking in the rest of the mall." Lacy wanted to make sure she got what she'd come for before running out of time.

"That's the only reason we came, isn't it? But if I see something I just can't live without, I might be persuaded to part with some of my hard-earned money. Maybe," Stephanie said with a smile.

"Well, don't let me talk you out of buying something you need, or may not need. I might just do the same thing. Let's shop!" As it turned out, they both found an outfit to wear that night that was *to die for*, and they just couldn't do without.

Back on the highway and driving the speed limit of fifty-five, Lacy kept a safe distance between her car and the car in front of her—she always tried to be a careful driver. In one split second, however, the car in front suddenly stopped. The driver then put on a left turn signal. It took her brain a couple of seconds to register that the car was no longer moving. Fear began to rise inside her as she slammed her foot down on the brake and realized that her car was not going to stop in time to keep from slamming into the back of the other car. With her mind racing, she took her foot off the brake, steered her car onto the side of the road, and safely drove around the other car. Thank goodness there was room enough for her car to make it around safely.

Lacy experienced a great feeling of relief until she remembered that Stephanie was in the front seat next to her. Turning quickly to ask her friend if she was okay, Stephanie, with a big smile on her face, held up her little finger and said, "Look, I broke my nail. Look how weird it looks!"

"Aw, you broke your nail. I'm so sorry," Lacy told her, and continued driving.

The rest of the trip went smoothly, and they managed to make it back safely to Lacy's house with Sammy. Stephanie went home as soon as they got there and promised she'd come back early to help Lacy set up.

Lacy was in the kitchen taking out the baked beans when she heard the doorbell ring, and before she could set the hot dish down, in walked Spence.

"Hi there, gorgeous. Boy, those beans sure do smell good. Did you make your famous potato salad?"

"What do you think? It wouldn't be a cookout without it, now would it?"

"You're right, partner. What can I do right now to help you?"

Spence asked, putting his arms around her and beginning to kiss her.

"Exactly what you are doing right now," Lacy said before kissing him back. "Did I ever thank you for the nice grill you bought me?"

"Yes you did, over and over and over again. It's a very nice grill, if I do say so myself."

"Well, then, let's get this cookout set up before my parents get here."

Spence and Lacy decided to stay inside the house when it was time for her parents to arrive. All the other guests were waiting in the backyard. They'd parked their cars in the senior citizen parking lot next door.

Lacy and Spence heard her parents' car pull into the driveway and met them at the front door, opening it before they could ring the doorbell.

"Welcome home, William Robert and Samantha Suzanne," Spence announced, shaking hands with Lacy's dad while she was hugged her mom. Lacy shot a mean look over her shoulder at Spence to let him know that she knew he'd done that on purpose to tease her, but at the same time she was glad he hadn't used the other names. He just winked at her to let her know she was right.

When her parents reached the backyard, they were surprised to see everyone who'd come to welcome them home. Stephanie had taken over the grill while Spence was inside and was only too happy to let him take it over again. After all the greetings, everyone sat down to enjoy the meal. Lacy was sitting at a table talking to her mom when she heard her phone ring. She went inside to answer it, wondering who it could be.

"Hello, Miss Petunia. This is Jay. I was calling to see if it'd be a good time to bring you a rental car and to take your car to the shop to be fixed." While he was speaking, Lacy had decided to open the front door to make sure he wasn't sitting in her driveway. Good, she didn't see another car. She was just about ready to close it when she saw him pull up and park a car in the grass across the street.

"I guess it's too late to say no, isn't it?" Lacy clicked off the phone and waited for Jay to get out of the car. He came walking up to the door, holding a bouquet of gardenias, which made her laugh because, after all the frustration he'd put her through about her last name, she realized that Jay had been messing with her the whole time.

"Did you say it was okay for me to come by?" *Come on now, you have to say yes.*

What am I going to do with this man? Nothing! "I'm having a cookout at the moment."

"Hey, Lacy, where'd you go, sweetheart? Oh, there you are. Who are you talking to?" Spence asked, walking up next to her.

"It's the man who rear-ended me the other day," Lacy answered. *And he won't go away.*

"Oh, you mean w—Jay?" That was close. I almost called him weird.

"Yes, it's Jay. And look, he brought me a rental. He wants to take my car to the shop to get it fixed tonight." *Jay, you think you're so sweet, don't you?*

"Did you tell him that you're having a family get together this evening?" Spence returned, wondering why he'd come by now, and why he was carrying flowers.

"Yes, she did. And she was just about to invite me to join all of you." *Right back at you, big boy!*

Lacy looked at Spence and raised her eyebrows as if to say "What should I do now?" When he didn't say anything, she turned and invited Jay to join them in the backyard. Jay came in and handed her the flowers. She told him thanks before he walked past them. Spence gave her a look implying that he couldn't believe she was letting him join the party. All she could think to do was hold her hands up in the air as he went back outside.

She put the flowers in a vase near the sink and went back outside. Lacy didn't know how she was going to survive the evening with Jay hanging out in her backyard.

When she stepped through the back door, she saw Jay standing next to Spence, waiting for her to join them. Should she ask him if he was hungry, or take him straight to the garage where her car was parked? She didn't have to make that call herself.

"Lacy, who's your friend? Give him a plate so he can get

something to eat," Samantha instructed as she got up from the table and walked toward her daughter.

"Mom, this is Jay. Jay, this is my mom, Samantha. The man walking toward us is my dad, William, and you have already met my friend Spence." *Friend! He's not going to like me calling him my friend.* "Spence and I—"

"I'm glad to meet you, Jay. A friend of my daughter's is a friend to both her mom and me," her dad replied, reaching his hand out for Jay to shake.

"I'm so glad to meet the two of you. Oh, and you too, Spence. Thank you for inviting me to your party, Lacy. I'm sorry I'm late. Where are the plates?" Taking Lacy by the elbow, Jay guided her to the table that held the food. She was afraid to look at Spence as they walked away.

"You were about to say something about Spence when your father interrupted. Do you want to finish what you were saying now?"

"No. I don't remember what I was going to say. I'm sorry."

"That's okay. You have nice parents. I'm glad I got to meet them. Oh, I didn't know how hungry I was until I smelled all this delicious food. I'm so glad you invited me to join your little party."

"I—" *Didn't invite you, Jay. You invited yourself.* "I'm so happy you could join us. But I got the impression that you were in a hurry to pick up my car." *And then just disappear.*

"No, I didn't make any other plans tonight, so I can stay as long as I want." *Or stay as long as you'll let me stay.*

"Won-der-ful. Help yourself. I'm going back to sit with my mom, if that's okay with you?" Lacy moaned.

"Sounds like a good plan to me."

Lacy walked back to the table where both her parents sat talking to Spence. How was she going to explain to him what had happened when she couldn't explain it to herself? As much as she was enjoying this get together and seeing her parents, she was starting to wish that everyone would go home, with Jay being the first to leave. The last few days had taken a lot out of her, and she felt very tired.

Jay came over and sat at her table to enjoy his meal. Lacy was glad he had his mouth full most of the time and didn't join the conversation. After he finished eating, her mom suggested she take him around and introduce him to the rest of the family and their friends, which she didn't want to do, but she decided to go ahead and do what her mom asked.

Lacy led Jay around her backyard, introducing him as they walked around. When they walked up to Grandpa Robert sitting on the wooden swing, he said, "Who is this good looking fella with you, Lacy Rose?"

"Grandpa, this is Jay. This is Grandpa Robert, Jay. He owns the large farm on the south side of Pebblestone and runs the R&L Grain Mill. He's my favorite grandpa."

"I'm very pleased to meet you, Robert," Jay said, reaching out his hand to shake Grandpa's. "I've bought grain for my horses from your grain mill. You have a well-organized mill, and I bet you do good business around here."

"I do, and it also brings in buyers from other counties around this area. I also ship to other states. It keeps me busy and helps me make a good living."

"You sound like a hardworking man with a plan. Does your wife help you with the business?"

"Yes she does, and so did my granddaughter when she lived in our barn apartment and was going to school. She's a darn good little farmer girl. She still helps us when she can spare some time. She'll make someone a great wife someday."

"Grandpa, he's not interested in hearing all that stuff about me!" Lacy exclaimed, red-faced and starting to feel a little uncomfortable with the way Jay was looking at her.

"You're wrong," Jay responded to her statement. "I find that very interesting. So, who'd think you were a farm girl? I bet you even felt comfortable living in a barn."

"Yeah, she loved living there. She was there for over two years rent free."

"Is that a fact? No wonder he's your favorite grandpa. You let her live in your barn and didn't even charge her for it. Wow!" he chuckled.

"Oh, I see Grandma sitting over there. Do you want to meet her too?" Lacy glared at Jay for the remark he just made and trying not to laugh. She knew he was teasing her again.

"Yes, I'd love to meet her," Jay said, following Lacy.

"Grandma, this is Jay. Jay, this is Grandma Lily Rose."

"Hello there, Jay. I'm so glad to meet you. So, do you have a last name? Where've you been hiding him, Lacy? Have you met her new puppy yet?"

"No, I haven't but I've heard a lot about him," he said to Lily Rose, while turning to wink at Lacy. "I guess I'll have to go meet her little puppy."

"He's in his crate over there by the garage. He's such a cute little thing!" Lily Rose exclaimed.

"Oh, I see him now. He *is* very cute." *Just about as cute as his owner.*

Jay walked over and bent down so he could get a better look at the puppy. Lacy had followed him over and arrived in time to hear him whisper, "Thanks, my little buddy. If you hadn't run out in front of her, I wouldn't have met your new owner, and I wouldn't be here now enjoying this great party with her." Jay turned his head slowly and looked up at her. Her heart skipped a beat.

Spence had been following the two of them around, trying to remain unnoticed. He also overheard what Jay said and saw the way he now was looking at Lacy. He decided it was time to step in and rescue her. He walked over and put his arm around Lacy's waist and asked Jay if he was enjoying himself. Jay assured Spence that he was having a great time. Lacy was so confused by the situation that she excused herself and went to look for Stephanie, but couldn't find her anywhere. When she asked her mom if she'd seen her, her mom told her that Stephanie had left after she'd eaten because her brother Zach had called saying he needed her to watch Timmy. The babysitter had called to cancel at the last minute, and they'd been invited to one of their friend's weddings.

Feeling a little defeated because her friend had left without telling her, she decided that Jay had to leave. Lacy went into the house to get her keys and then went to the garage to back out her car. Spence realized what she was doing and asked Lacy's dad to back his car out of the driveway so he move his own. Lacy backed her car out and parked in front of the house as Spence and her dad parked their cars back in the driveway. She thanked them and went to find Jay. He was sitting at the table talking to her mom.

"Jay, I'd like to have a word with you, please," she said sweetly.

"Okay. It was very nice meet to meet you, Samantha, and your family and friends."

"Well, it was nice to meet you too, Jay. Hope to see you again real soon," her mom said, reaching her hand out, which Jay accepted, kissing the back of it.

Seeing Jay's actions made Lacy want to knock a knot on his head. *How dare you kiss up to my mom in front of me like that!* "Let's go, Jay." She took hold of his arm and led him to the front of the house where her car was parked.

"I think it's time for you to leave now. Thank you for the rental," she said, reaching her hand out for the key.

"Thank you for inviting me to your family cookout. I really enjoyed myself, and the food was delicious. You have a nice family. I'll be seeing you soon."

"I don't think so! Um . . . I mean, have the shop call me when my car is fixed so I can pick it up, please."

"You don't have to worry about that. I'll take care of that for you." *And I'll take care of anything else that you might need taken care of.*

"I can do it myself. Thank you." *Just leave me alone.*

"Thank you again for a nice meal and a good time, Miss Snapdragon. See you real soon," Jay promised as he climbed into her car and drove away smiling.

"Ooh, Miss Snapdragon! I'll show you a real snapdragon the next time you show up at my front door."

Lacy headed to the backyard to enjoy what was left of the evening. Spence came up to her as soon as she rounded the corner. "Lacy, what are you smiling about?" he asked.

"I'm just happy he finally left. Once my car is fixed, everything will be normal again." *If I can remember what normal means.*

Lacy went into the house to get her parents' gifts— she knew they were tired and would want to be going home soon. They were surprised, but happy, with the gifts, and they thanked her. After that, they decided it was time to go home. Hugs and kisses were exchanged all around, with many thanks for the meal and the good time.

Everyone left except Spence, who stayed to help Lacy clean up. Most of the cleaning had been done by everyone before they left. Spence was a little quiet as he cleaned and then put away the grill. She couldn't blame him if he was upset because of the way Jay invited himself to the party and made himself at home with her family.

She was finishing up in the kitchen when Spence approached her. She'd put the gardenias in her bedroom, out of sight from Spence—no sense making him more upset than he already was, and she didn't have the heart to throw away the flowers. *Boy, life has gotten a bit crazy since Jay smashed into my rear end.*

"I think I'll go home now," Spence said, coming into the kitchen. "I've cleaned the grill and put it away. I loved your potato salad, and I had a good time. Thanks."

"Spence, I know you're upset with me, and I'm sorry. I didn't know Jay was coming by tonight. He called me on his phone as he was driving down my street, asking if he could come by. I didn't have a chance to say no."

"Why *did* you invite him to stay? He said you were getting ready to invite him to stay. Did you really want him to?"

"That's right! He said I was going to ask him, but I didn't say anything of the sort. I was just standing there surprised that he'd just showed up. If he'd called before getting the rental, I'd have told him it wasn't a good time to come. But no, not Jay, he just shows up and invites himself."

"That's when you should've told him no."

"You were standing there. Why didn't you tell him no?"

"It wasn't up to me to tell him he couldn't stay, since I'm only your friend. I think it's time for me to go home now," he said, giving Lacy a kiss on the cheek and then leaving. He was gone before she knew what to say.

Lacy was so upset with the whole thing. She and Spence always got along great and were seldom angry with one another. Although they didn't agree about everything, they always respected each other's opinions. They hadn't argued like this since they were much younger and in school. They'd grown up and learned to care about each other's feelings. They'd also learned how to talk things over before jumping to wrong conclusions. And this was a wrong conclusion.

"Crazy crocodiles! Sammy, I hope you aren't mad at me too for keeping you crated. I think I'm going to call Mom and talk to her before we go to bed." Lacy picked up the phone and called her mother.

"Hello, Lacy. Thank you for the nice welcome-home party. Your dad and I already have started eating the candy you gave me. I think your puppy is so sweet, but he's going to be a lot of responsibility. Tell me everything that happened after we left. And what had you so upset tonight, Lacy?" Samantha always knew when her daughter needed her.

Lacy told her everything, including her argument with Spence over Jay. Her mom listened intently and then began asking questions. She asked her how Jay made her feel, how she felt when Spence left upset, and if there was going to be a situation between the two men that needed to be worked out, to which Lacy had no real answers at this time. She told her mom that Spence hadn't tried to listen to her side, and it wasn't fair that she was left to defend herself. She also told her that she thought Jay was being overbearing and seemed like he went out of his way to make Spence mad. But how could that be when she'd only seen Jay a few times, and he'd only just met Spence? The whole thing seemed crazy to her. Spence was her whole world, and Jay was just a man who had come crashing into her life. She hadn't been waiting for him to enter her life, and she knew in her heart that she wasn't willing to give up Spence. He was her life, and she loved him dearly.

"Lacy, I know you and Spence have been together for most of your life, and I know that you love each other very much. You two are best friends, and everyone expects you two will get married someday, and that'd be great, but God has a way of putting obstacles in our way to test us. You say one minute that Jay frustrates you and the next minute he causes your hands to sweat. Maybe fate is stepping in to test you to see how strong your love for Spence really is. I'm not saying to dump Spence—he's a keeper. I'm just saying to keep your mind open to this situation, but let your heart make the decision for you. Don't go out and try to make yourself fall in love with Jay, but don't ignore the little fire you feel inside when he's around. Let fate work its magic for you. Do you understand what I'm trying to tell you, sweetheart?"

"Yes, I think so. You're trying to tell me not to close one door before I open another, and to open my heart to new experiences," Lacy explained to her mom.

"Yes, that's right, but why did I use so many words to say all that? I always told your dad that you inherited your brains from me."

"Thanks, Mom. You always know when I'm upset and know just what to say to cheer me up and make me feel better."

"That's what a mother is for. Good night, Lacy. I love you."

"Good night, Mom, I love you too. I'm so glad you're both back home."

Lacy decided to take her mom's advice and just forget about everything for a while. She ran a nice warm bubble bath and relaxed in the tub. Afterward, she made a cup of hot chamomile tea and curled up in her bed with a romance-suspense novel she'd picked up in the mall. Sammy was curled up next to her on the bed. It took her a while to get into the plot of the story, because her mind kept going back over what Spence had said to her.

"Stop it, Lacy. Just let it go and relax," she said to herself, and she took a deep breath before she started reading again. The story was about a young woman who had been in an accident and woke up in a hospital with amnesia. The poor thing didn't even know her name. She began to dream about a man she didn't recognize, and, after a few dreams, began to fear the man. After waking up from one of these dreams, she saw the man standing by her door.

Suddenly Lacy's phone rang. It scared her so much she threw the book across the room and it made Sammy bark. "Bucking bulls! That scared me to death." Thinking it might be Spence, she grabbed the phone and answered it.

"Hello, Lacy. It's Dad. I just wanted to thank you for the great party and the cologne. I also wanted to know if you were okay. I heard your mom talking to you and wanted to see if there was anything I could say to help. What's up with Jay?"

"So you talked with Mom? I'm feeling better since I talked to her. I didn't like that when Spence went home he was upset with me because of Jay. I tried telling him that I didn't have a chance to tell Jay not to come by tonight because of the party, but he was already coming down my street when he called me. Since he was already there, I didn't want to be rude, so I asked him to join us, which upset Spence."

"Listen to your dad, Lacy. I know how men think. We say a lot of things without really thinking. It just comes out our mouths and lands us in the dog house. Ask your mother how many times she's put me there. We see a situation that we don't like or understand, so we think we have to stop it before it gets out of hand. If we just had enough sense to think before opening our mouths, we could save ourselves a lot of heartaches and misery. But making up afterwards can be a lot of fun."

"Thanks, Dad, but what if he doesn't want to make up? I don't know what I'd do if he broke up with me. Life without Spence scares me."

"He's a smart man, Lacy, and he has spent most of his life with you. He won't do anything stupid like that. He's probably at home using his brain right now to figure out how to make things better again."

"I hope so. Good night, Dad. I love you."

"I love you too, angel. Sweet dreams."

Lacy hoped her dad was right about Spence. Maybe she should call him and save him from having to use his brain to figure out he was wrong. If what her dad said was true, there might just be a certain limit on how much time a man had to use his brain. She didn't want Spence's brain to run dry before his time.

She reached for the phone and dialed his number. It rang and rang, and he didn't answer it.

She hung up the phone before the answering machine could pick up. Well, if he was using it, his brain was telling him to do the wrong thing again. Or maybe he wasn't home. Where was he? Or maybe he refused to answer because he knew who was calling.

"Lazy lizards! What is the matter with you, girl? Calm down and try to relax. When Spence is ready to talk, I'm sure he'll let me know. I know I can trust him."

Lacy read her book for another thirty minutes before putting it down. She set the puppy on the floor and made him follow her to the door. Tonight she made him go outside by himself while she stood by the door and encouraged him to go potty. She didn't give in this time. At first he just stood there looking at her, and then he went to the middle of the yard to do what she wanted him to do. She wanted him to learn to do this without her.

Round #3: Yay! Lacy finally wins one.

Sammy ran back inside, wagging his tail. Lacy was so happy with her little bear cub, and he was enjoying all the attention he was getting from her. She was about to give him an extra treat, but decided that if she started doing that now he'd expect it every time. After all, he'd only done what every other little puppy learns to do: go potty on his own.

"I think I'm finally getting the hang of being a new pet owner. Let's go to bed, because I'm so tired now and my brain has been working overtime."

Chapter 4

Lacy had no real plans after church, so she decided to have a lazy day. Spence had attended church that morning, and even sat next to her, but he was quiet and still seemed upset with her. After the service, he asked her why she had called him the previous night and asked why she hadn't left a message when he didn't answer—he hadn't been home. She told him she'd called to tell him good night and wanted to say it to him personally, not to a machine. He didn't volunteer to tell her where he'd been, nor did she go out of her way to ask him. If he wanted her to know, he'd tell her. He kissed her on the cheek before he left the church, and they went their separate ways, which was fine with her. They didn't spend every Sunday together; sometimes they wanted to spend time with their families or friends or just have free time. Today was one of those days.

"Well, my little puppy, I guess he hasn't used his brain enough yet. What shall we do today? Maybe I could teach you to sit."

Lacy was out in her swing reading her book when her cell phone rang. She knew it wasn't Spence, because of the way he'd been acting, and she answered the phone without looking to see who was calling before she said hello.

"Hello, my friend Lacy Rose. What's happening today? Did your parents enjoy their party and gifts?" Stephanie asked.

"Oh, so you think you're still my friend. I think you were rude yesterday when you left the party without telling me first. I needed you, and you weren't there. Don't you think I should be mad at you?"

"Yeah, you can be mad at me. I'm here now, so tell your good old friend what hurts, so I can kiss it and make it feel better. What happened?"

"Well it all started when Jay decided to stop by without calling me first. Well, actually, he was calling me while he was parking the rental across the street in front of my house."

"Are we talking about the same man who ran you down, the one I missed seeing the other day?"

"Yes, that would be the same man. He was asking me if it was a good time to come by, but he was already there."

"Oh darn. I wanted to be there when he came back. What happened then?"

"Spence came to the door while Jay was standing on the other side with a beautiful bunch of gardenias in his hand, and told Spence that I was about to invite him to the party. But I hadn't been about to invite him."

"And Spence got mad at that?"

"Yes. At that and the fact that I introduced Spence as my friend." She groaned.

"You didn't. I think I'm a little mad at you too. Maybe I shouldn't ask, but what made you do that?"

"Jay made me do it. No, I mean, he makes me nervous when he's around, and my brain gets confused. I don't know what comes over me, but I don't act right. So, not knowing the right thing to say, I asked him to stay. But I also made him leave after he'd eaten, and I introduced him to the others, but only because Mom asked me to. Then he took my car and left."

"Took your car? Oh wait, you said he parked a rental across the street. So he was coming by to get your car. Oh, boy! Sounds like you have a lot of making up to do for that."

"Me? The only thing I did wrong was the friend thing, which technically is right, because that is what he really is. I mean, we aren't engaged."

"Lacy Rose! Shame on you. I think you'd better stay away from this Jay or you may do some damage to your relationship with Spence. Or at least don't let Spence know when you're in contact with Jay again."

"Are you telling me to lie to Spence?" *You know I can't lie to him.*

"No, silly, just don't volunteer any information unless you get caught."

"Oh, thanks. That's one sure way of breaking up, which I don't want to do."

"Is there anything else I can help you with?"

"Yeah, get over here, and we'll go get something to eat for lunch. Let's eat at the park so I can take my little pooh bear for a walk. Then I have to go buy a kennel for him."

"I'll be right over. Behave yourself until I get there, okay? I can't leave you alone for a second, can I?"

Lacy and Stephanie bought their lunches and went to the park as planned. Lacy brought along a bowlful of puppy food for Sammy. The sun was out, shining all around the park, and there was a cool breeze gently blowing. They sat at a table under a shade tree. After they ate and cleaned up, they began their walk.

They had walked only a short distance when Lacy saw Spence a little farther ahead, standing with his back to them. Before she could call out to him, she saw him walk toward a beautiful young lady who was walking toward him and smiling. Spence reached out his hand to take hers, and then he put his arm around her shoulder as she turned, and they began walking in the direction from which she had come.

"Do you see what I see?" Stephanie asked, turning to ask Lacy as they continued their walk, going in the same direction as Spence and the woman, but leaving distance between them.

"Are you talking about the squirrel running up the tree with a nut, or the one Spence is walking with?" Lacy answered without taking her eyes away from the two walking together across the park in front of them.

"Yeah, that's what I'm talking about. Do you happen to know her?"

"I don't think I know her, but he doesn't know everyone I know either. Could be a cousin I haven't met yet, or a co-worker that he hasn't introduced me to. Or it could be his new girlfriend. Oh, Steph, he must still be mad at me. I tried to tell him I was sorry, but he left mad and he is treating me like he is still upset. What do I do now?"

"Call him right now and ask him to go to a nice restaurant tonight for dinner. Then you kiss his feet and try to make up with him. Treat him so good that he forgets the other nut. I mean *her*. Do it now before he makes plans with her."

"But lately we haven't been spending our Sundays together. You don't think he spends his Sundays with her, do you?" Before Stephanie could answer, Lacy pulled out her phone and dialed his number. It only rang twice before she saw him put his phone to his ear.

"Hello," Spence said.

"Hi, Spence. I was getting bored, so I thought I'd call and see what you were doing today."

"Oh, I'm, uh, doing some research for an article I've been working on all week. Isn't the puppy keeping you company?"

"Yes, he's a lot of fun and doing great, but I was hoping the two of us could eat somewhere nice tonight. I was thinking of the Grilling Steak House where we could enjoy a really good meal together."

"That sounds nice, but I'm sorry, I can't make it tonight. I'll be tied up all evening. Maybe we could do that one evening this week?"

"Yeah, okay. Call me and let me know when you're not tied up. Bye, Spence." Lacy hung up before he could say goodbye.

"That didn't go the way you hoped, did it?" Stephanie asked.

"No, it didn't. He just lied to me. He said he was doing *research* at the moment and would be tied up all evening. Can you believe that?"

"Oh, that sounds a little kinky, doesn't it? I'd never have thought that about Spence. I'm sorry, Lacy. I shouldn't have said that to you. What are you going to do now?"

"Nothing. There's nothing I can do, so I'm just going to enjoy the rest of the day if it kills me." Just as soon as the words left her mouth, a football came flying through the air, striking her near her right temple and knocking her to the ground. Sammy ran over and began licking her face.

"Muddy monkeys, what was that? I've been struck again," Lacy said, slowly getting to her feet as a teenage boy came running up to her, apologizing for hitting her, and to retrieve his football.

"Lacy, are you okay? I think we'd better get you back home." Stephanie grabbed the puppy's leash, took hold of her friend's arm, and led her back to the car.

"But I still have to go buy a kennel," Lacy moaned.

They dropped Sammy off at the farm before going to Lowe's. As they were looking around in the store, a good-looking young man with sandy hair and green eyes approached them and asked if they needed any help. Stephanie made a remark about her friend needing a lot of help and that she also needed to buy a kennel for her dog.

It didn't take her long to pick out a large one: ten feet long, ten feet wide, and ten feet high. It came folded in a box, so all you had to do was pull it out, stand it up, and spread out the sides. It seemed simple and it was affordable. Lacy noticed that while she had been inspecting the kennel, her friend had been doing the same thing with their salesman. She'd even heard a little flirting going on behind her back. After she paid for the kennel, she called her dad, who agreed to pick it up in his truck and drop it off at her house before they headed back home.

"Well, Steph, did you get a name and number and confirmation that he's single while you were flirting with the nice-looking young man?"

"What do you think? Of course I did. His name is Andrew Rhymes. He's single, twenty-three—a year older than I am—and he lives within walking distance from my house. He's listed in the phone book. Lowe's is his part-time job—he started his own business. And, yes, I gave him my phone number. Do you need to hear anything else?"

"That about covers it. When's the wedding? And am I going to be your maid of honor? Boy, you move fast!"

"There's no use letting grass grow under my feet. Boy, I hate to cut grass."

Lacy just laughed at her friend and wondered why she didn't have a steady boyfriend. She was such a great person, as well as a great, loyal friend, and she hoped they'd remain friends forever. Looking back over the years, she realized that Stephanie had had many boyfriends, but didn't stay with them for long. Maybe this one would turn out to be the one she'd been looking for.

Glancing at her gas gauge, she noticed it was below half-full and thought she should fill up. Jay must have rented the car in Stoneybrooke and then driven it to her house, because she hadn't driven the car enough to have used that much gasoline, and most car rentals filled the tank when you rented one. She decided she'd stop and fill up the tank when she reached a gas station, because she didn't know when she'd get her own car back.

She drove the car with the passenger side next to the pump like she always did, turned the motor off, and got out of the car to slide her credit card in the slot. Then she realized that this car's tank was on the driver's side.

"Dirty donkeys! Why don't they make all cars with gas tanks on the same side?" She looked for a cancel button but wasn't sure which one to push. "Now I have to turn the car around."

"Are you okay?" Stephanie asked.

"Well, I do have a headache, but I'm okay." She explained to her friend what she'd done, and they both had a good laugh. She wasn't used to driving this car yet, so it really wasn't her fault. She started the motor and began driving the car forward, then made a circle and was almost in front of the pump when another car pulled in front of her car, blocking her way.

She got out of her car crying, "Crazy crocodiles, who's trying to steal my gas?" She saw the door of the car in front of hers open and Jay get out of the car. *I should have known that you'd show up at some point today and make my day worse.*

"Crazy *what*? What kind of language is that? And what makes you think I'm trying to steal your gas?" Jay said, trying not to laugh at her.

"I use silly phrases when I get upset, excited, or mad, instead of using nasty words. I picked that up when I was attending college, because I didn't want to develop a bad habit of cursing, drinking, or smoking, like all the other girls had, because once you do, it's hard to stop. Now, could you please back your car up so I can get my gas?"

"I was here first, so why don't you back up and let me put gas in my car?" Jay said, hoping she would use another silly phrase.

Lacy didn't want to explain to him what she'd done, but couldn't think of a way to get out of it, so she just told him, "I'd already put my card in before I realized that the gas tank was on the other side this car, and I didn't know how to cancel the transaction, so I had to turn the car around to bring the other side around in front of the pump. So, could you please back up and let me get my gas? There should've been a full tank in this car already."

"Of course I will, especially since you asked so sweetly." Jay climbed back in his car and backed up enough for her to pull forward. Then he got back out to stand next to her, which made her nervous. She motioned for Stephanie to get out of the car. When her friend finally reached her side, Lacy introduced them.

"Jay, this is my friend Stephanie. Stephanie, this is my . . . this is Jay." I almost called him my friend. That's funny—when I called Spence that, he got mad.

"Hi, Jay. I've heard so much about you," Stephanie said in a sweet little voice.

"That's nice to hear. All good I hope." *I might be making some progress.* "I'm glad to meet you, too. Were you at the party the other night?"

"Yes, but I had to leave early because my brother needed me to watch my nephew."

"Are you two going somewhere?" Jay asked.

"No, just getting back from Lowe's, and Lacy was about to drop me off. She has no other plans tonight," Stephanie explained.

"Oh, is that right, Miss Gardenia? How'd you like to go out to dinner with me? I don't have any plans either."

"I don't think—" Lacy started to say when Stephanie interrupted.

"Remember the squirrel with the nut, Lacy?"

"Yes, I do remember. That's going to be hard to forget. Okay, Jay, I'll have dinner with you. Meet me at the Grilling Steak House around six."

"You won't let me pick you up?" I need to show her that she can trust me.

"Nope, see you there. Don't be late." Lacy had finished pumping her gas. She grabbed her receipt and got into her car. *Oh, shoot, why did I do that?*

Stephanie said goodbye to Jay and climbed back in the car. "You didn't tell me how gorgeous he is. His midnight black hair and his dark blue eyes are mesmerizing, and his smile makes your—"

"Makes your hands sweat and your heart skip a beat, I know. But he's overbearing, pushy, and infuriating, not to mention that he thinks he should always get his way. What was I thinking when I told him I'd meet him for dinner? Maybe I should have my head examined, because I'm not thinking straight. It has to be because of the football."

"You're not thinking about backing out, are you? Because if you are, maybe you *should* have your head examined."

"What will Spence say? He's already mad at me."

"I don't know what he'll say, but I know what he already told you today. He's out with the nut and plans to be tied up all night while you sit home waiting on him to give you the time of day. If you decide not to go, please call me and I'll gladly take your place," begged Stephanie.

"What about Andrew? I thought you wanted to get to know him better."

"I still do, but I'm not taken yet, and I don't want to miss any opportunities that may come my way, especially one that looks that good."

"Stop it! You're making me feel jealous with the way you're talking about him. Okay, I'll have dinner with him, and I'll try really hard to enjoy myself," Lacy replied, as if having dinner with Jay was going to be really hard.

"Oh, Lacy Rose, are you trying to convince me or convince yourself? Trust me, you'll have a great time," Stephanie said enviously.

Lacy dropped Stephanie off, and when she got home her dad was there with the kennel. He helped her set it up, which didn't take long, and then she sent him home with some peanut butter fudge she had made earlier that morning. The kennel was going to work out great. All she needed now was a doghouse to go inside the kennel and a fence around the yard between the back door and the garage. That would make it easier for her to let him out by himself and not worry about him getting out of the yard. He would have to be on a leash for the rest of the yard. Tomorrow she would find a good vet to give Sammy his shots and maybe find out how old the dog was.

The closer the time came for her to meet Jay, the more nervous she became, and the headache she had was getting worse. She didn't know what'd made her agree to meet him for dinner. Could it have been because she was jealous of the woman she saw with Spence or the way Stephanie was making over Jay or both? But in her book, two wrongs never made a right, and this was something she felt was wrong. It was too late now—at least she'd been smart enough to have him meet her at the restaurant and not come to her house.

The time finally arrived. She'd taken a bath and dressed in something casual, because she didn't want him to think this was a real date. But she made sure that what she wore looked good on her just the same. Her hands shook as she parked the car and entered the restaurant. At first she didn't see Jay, but then she looked to her right and saw him get up from his table and walk toward her. He was still wearing the dress shirt and blue jeans he'd had on earlier, which made her realize just how incredibly sexy he looked, which just made her feel even more nervous and a whole lot more excited, but she was glad he hadn't dressed for this dinner either.

"Hello, Lacy. You look as beautiful as ever, and I'm glad you came." *And glad you didn't stand me up.*

"Hi. Thank you, Jay. This is just dinner and not a real date. Oh, and you look good too." *You* do *know my first name.*

"Let's sit down and order dinner. I missed lunch, and I'm starving," Jay said.

The waitress took their orders and had brought their drinks before she could think of anything to talk about. Jay just sat there smiling at her. She asked him why he was in town and how the repairs were coming on her car. He told her he had business in town and that the repairs were on schedule. He also said he'd very much been looking forward to having dinner with her tonight. He didn't tell her that he'd gone to her house looking for her to ask her to have dinner with him. Luck had been on his side when he'd run into her at the gas station. He believed it was a sign that they should be together tonight and maybe many other nights to come.

"May I ask you a question?" He paused before going on. "What was your friend talking about when she asked you if you remembered the squirrel with the nut?"

Lacy couldn't stop herself from laughing. How was she going to explain this one to him? But she knew she had to say something, because he was looking at her with a puzzled expression on his face, waiting for an answer.

"Well, earlier we were out walking the dog in the park when we saw a friend—a guy—meeting a woman that isn't his girlfriend, and we were wondering what his girlfriend would say when she heard about it. We also saw a squirrel running up a tree with a nut in his mouth at the same time we saw this friend with this woman. So Stephanie associates the incident as 'the squirrel with the nut.'" Jay was still looking at her, even more confused. "She doesn't always make a lot of sense, bless her heart, but she always mean well." *Sorry, Stephanie, for throwing you under the bus, but I don't want him to think I'm the crazy one.*

"Does that mean you two are going to tell the girlfriend what you saw?"

"Oh, no, of course not, but she'll find out sooner or later. Things like that don't stay secret very long. The truth will come out, and he'll be caught. And she'll make him pay for it."

"This other girl must be a very good friend to you for you to get so upset about it."

"You could say that. I do feel sorry for her." That's why I'm having dinner with you right now. Oh, shoot, I hope Spence doesn't find out.

"Well, I hope everything works out for that couple."

The waitress brought their dinners, and, for the next fifteen minutes, they enjoyed their meal. She was glad he didn't continue asking her questions, because she'd become a little emotional talking about the "nut" incident. It was just starting to sink in that Spence had lied to her and chose to spend the day with another woman, and maybe the evening also. But, she was here with Jay, and she was actually beginning to enjoy being here with him.

Jay noticed several times during dinner that Lacy rubbed her forehead, and when they made eye contact, he thought her eyes looked a little weak. He wanted to ask her if she was feeling okay, but thought maybe she was still tired from the party she'd given the day before.

The conversation was moving along smoothly, and Lacy finally relaxed enough to enjoy listening to him tell her about the horses he had bought two years ago. He kept them on his dad's farm here in Pebblestone. He said he bought the horses' feed from her grandpa's mill and had been there a few times, but usually he ordered it on the phone or from the mill's website and had it delivered. Lacy was so surprised to learn that he'd been a customer when she worked there and didn't remember ever seeing him. It took a fender bender to bring them together.

When dinner was over, Lacy picked up the bill, but Jay took it from her hand. When she started to protest, he gently covered her mouth with his fingers and, with his other hand, motioned to the waitress that he was ready to settle the bill. His fingers only touched her lips for a couple of seconds, but she felt a small shock wave move through her body—was that butterflies she was feeling in her stomach? She didn't want to believe his touch had caused such sensations and decided it was due to the pain in her head, which had been bothering her since being struck by the football and knocked down.

Jay didn't want the evening to end and was trying to figure out a way to get her to spend more time with him. He knew he'd done most of the talking, and she seemed to have enjoyed listening to him, but he'd have liked for her to tell him more about herself. Although it seemed like something was bothering her, he didn't want to pry.

"How'd you like to go see a movie? When I drove past the theater today, I noticed several good movies are showing tonight. Could I persuade you to see one of them with me tonight? And don't tell me you have other plans." Before she could say no, he said, "Remember the squirrel with the nut?" Jay remembered that Stephanie had said that earlier, just as Lacy was about to turn him down, and it seemed to have changed her mind.

"I . . . I'll have to go home first, because I have a pet now."

"No problem. I'll follow you to your house, and we can ride together in my car."

As they got up to leave, Jay leaned over and kissed her on her cheek and told her he'd really enjoyed having dinner with her. She was so shocked to feel a fire slowly starting to burn inside her. Jay walked her to her car and, after she climbed inside, he closed the car door for her. She started the car and, as she drove she tried hard not to think about all of these feelings, but she could see his car in the mirror following her home. Her head was really starting to bother her now, but she wasn't going to let a little thing like a headache keep her from doing what she wanted to do. All she had to do now was decide if she really wanted to go see a movie with Jay.

Lacy parked the car inside the garage, went in the house to let Sammy out, and then climbed into Jay's car. They were on their way. She let him do most of the talking in the car and let him pick out the movie. He bought her a cold drink, which she accepted, but she refused the popcorn. The movie was full of action, although she kept closing her eyes, which didn't go unnoticed by Jay. At one point she lay her head on his shoulder, and Jay knew she wasn't doing that to get close to him. He now knew something was wrong with her.

"Lacy, are you okay?" he asked, gently laying his hand against her face.

She opened her eyes and was embarrassed to find her head on his shoulder. "What? I'm sorry. My head hurts. It's been hurting ever since the football in the park."

"What football?" Jay asked.

"While I was in the park, I got knocked down by a football. It almost took my head off."

"Are you okay? Maybe I should take you home." Jay could see that she wasn't feeling well.

"Okay, thank you. You are so sweet." Oh, boy, Lacy, just stop talking. Please.

Chapter 5

Two hours and a trip to the hospital later, Jay was helping Lacy out of his car and into her house. Earlier, when they'd returned to her house after the movie, she'd climbed out of his car and thrown up. Jay immediately put her back in the car and drove her to the hospital. The emergency room doctor told her she had sustained a slight concussion from the blow of the football and he sent her home with pain medication that Jay filled at the hospital pharmacy before taking her home again. Lacy hadn't protested when Jay put his arm around her and helped her inside. In fact, it made her feel a little better, although her head was still hurting, and she was weak. She heard Sammy whimpering as they neared her bedroom.

"Oh, Sammy, I'm sorry. I'll let you out," she said weakly.

"No, I'll let him out while you get your nightgown on and get into bed. Be right back," Jay told her.

"How'd he know I wore a nightgown?" she asked herself after he left the room with the puppy on his heels. Lacy was just pulling up the covers when they came back. Jay lifted the puppy onto the bed so he could lick Lacy's face, and then he put him on the floor.

"What can I do for you?" Jay asked softly.

"Tell me how the movie ended. No, really, thank you for all you've done for me already," she replied.

Jay handed her one of the pain pills and a bottle of water. After she had swallowed it, Jay took the bottle and set it on the night stand beside her bed. She closed her eyes when he bent down to kiss her before turning off the light.

Lacy woke up the next morning and, realizing that Sammy wasn't in her bed, started to panic. As she sat up to go find him, she felt dizzy and a little light-headed. She slowly walked into the living room, but he wasn't there either. Before she could call his name, she smelled bacon. She thought her mom must've come by to check on her and was fixing breakfast. She shuffled into the kitchen and—Jay! Jay was standing over the stove, turning sizzling bacon in the hot skillet, the puppy sitting next to his feet, hoping to get a bite.

"Oh sh— Sugar! What are you doing here?" Lacy demanded, just barely avoiding saying a bad word.

"Good morning, my sweet Rose Petal. How're you feeling this morning?"

"I'm not your sweet anything, and you didn't answer my question."

"I spent the night so I could watch over you, and your mom was so grateful that I did."

"My mom! When did she call?"

"She didn't call. I called her this morning. I found your address book with your phone numbers, and I called her. Oh, and by the way, you looked so sweet before you fell asleep after I kissed you good night."

Her hands began to sweat, so she rubbed them down the sexy red nightgown she had on. When she realized she'd forgotten to put on her robe, she turned and ran—more like stumbled—out of the kitchen. She put on the matching robe and grabbed her cell phone and turned it on—she'd turned it off while they were at the movies. Before she could call her mom, it rang.

"Lacy, why aren't you at work? You okay? I've been dying to ask you how your date went with sexy Jay last night," Stephanie asked in a very excited voice.

"I had to stay home today. The doctor told me I had to after Jay made me go to the hospital," she explained.

"What? Why? What'd he do to you? You were fine when I left you."

"I had a headache all day after that football hit me, and it got worse during dinner. We went to the movies after dinner, and I may have thrown up on his shoes when I got out of his car after he brought me home."

"He took you to see a movie too?"

"Yes, but we didn't stay to see the end, because my headache got worse, so he made me go to the hospital. I have a slight concussion, and the doctor said I need to stay home until my headaches go away, and then maybe Jay will go away too."

"What do you mean maybe Jay will go away too? Did Jay spend the night with you?"

"No. I mean yes, he stayed here, but not with me. I didn't know he was here until I went into the kitchen to find out who was frying bacon. It was Jay, and I was wearing that sexy red nightgown you got me for my birthday, and I wasn't wearing my robe."

"Oh really? What'd he say about that?"

"He called me his sweet Rose Petal. Then I ran out of the kitchen to get my robe. Then you called me."

"How long is he staying? And he can cook too?"

"Mom is coming over soon, and I'm getting ready to tell him he can leave now. I need to go, because I have to take care of the pain in my life . . . I mean in my head. Talk to you later, Steph. Bye," she said, and she hung up.

Jay came to her bedroom door and told her breakfast was ready. She went to the kitchen and sat down to eat. Jay told her that he'd taken Sammy out once during the night and once more this morning, and he'd filled his bowl with puppy food. She thanked him for all that he'd done for her, and they sat down at the table and ate their breakfast together.

"I've got to go out of town for a few days on business, but I'll make sure you get your car back when I return. I'll call to check on you." Jay didn't want to leave her, but he had no choice.

"You don't have to worry about me."

"But I will. You take it easy and get better, okay?"

"Are those your orders?"

"Yes. Mine and the doctor's. Goodbye, Lacy Rose Gardenia." He kissed her on top of her head and was gone.

She sat at the table shaking her head and wondering just what she had done, and how she was going to explain this to Spence. Or maybe she'd take Stephanie's advice and not mention it—ever. Her mom came into the kitchen just as she was getting up to do the dishes. She hugged her, checked her for bruises, kissed her on the cheek, and then sent her to bed. On the way to her bedroom, she stopped to see if there were any missed calls on her answering machine and realized that the phone jack was unplugged. At first she thought maybe Jay had unplugged it, but she saw Sammy's teddy bear stuck behind the table and knew he must've pulled it loose trying to get it out. She grabbed the teddy bear and plugged the phone in, then went and climbed back into bed. Jay had left her pain pills on the table next to bed with the bottle of water. She took one before lying down, then pulled up her covers and fell asleep with Sammy curled up next to her.

The ringing of her cell phone woke her up a couple of hours later. It was Spence, and he had a lot of questions he wanted answered. "Where have you been all night, and why haven't you answered your cell phone? I've even tried your home phone, but the answering machine didn't come on."

"I went to see a movie last night and had to turn off my cell phone and forgot to turn it back on, and Sammy must've accidently unplugged my home phone when his teddy bear got stuck behind the table. What'd you want? You told me you were going to be tied up all night."

"I felt guilty for not being able to take you to dinner," Spence explained.

"I bet you did, but that's okay, because I ran into Jay at the gas station, and he mentioned he wasn't tied up for the evening, so I met him at the restaurant for dinner." *So much for not mentioning it— ever!*

"I thought you just said you went to see a movie," Spence shot back.

"Oh, that too. You and I haven't been to one in ages, have we?"

"What's going on with you and Jay?" Spence asked, starting to get anxious.

"What do you mean? He's taking care of my car." *What about you and the nut?*

"I think it's more than that. I saw the way he looked at you the other day."

"How? I don't know, Spence. The man irritates me to death one minute and makes me laugh the next. He kind of grows on you."

"Like a parasite, if you ask me," said Spence, sounding a little jealous.

"Yes, you really do know how I feel. Sometimes I feel like I want to hit him, and then I kind of like him. He can be rude and funny." *And he can be a sweetheart.*

"You aren't planning to see him again, are you?"

"No plans. I told him I'd pick my car up when it's repaired."

"Good. I don't like the way he's pushing himself at you. And one more question: were you really just about ready to ask him to the party?"

"Oh, Spence, you know I wasn't. I'd already told you I wasn't. That was Jay pushing himself on me, and you fell for it. Oh, and by the way, Stephanie and I were at the park Sunday afternoon having our lunch and walking the puppy. Did you happen to see us there? Or maybe you were too busy with the nut—I mean the woman."

"With the nut? What nut? You don't always make a lot of sense to me."

"Okay, then. I have to go now, doctor's orders. I have to take it easy for the rest of the week, and I won't be at work, so don't call my office." *Or my cell phone or my home phone.*

"Why, what's wrong, Lacy?" he asked, sounding worried.

"A slight concussion from a football hitting my head really hard in the park, but don't ask me anything else, because I'm not making very good sense right now. Talk to you later. Bye, Spence."

Lacy hung up and wanted to scream, but she knew it'd make her head hurt much more, so she went into the living room and turned on the TV instead. Her mom had left a note saying she'd gone, but that she'd be back at lunch time, which would be soon since she'd slept so long. "What am I going to do for the rest of the week?" she said to Sammy. "I'm not good at lying around and doing nothing."

She remembered an advertising job that her boss wanted her to take on to see want she could do with it. The job involved helping a Pebblestone animal shelter come up with ways to find "forever homes" for their homeless animals or, as they said, "find friends to adopt them." She could start working on it today after lunch. As it turned out, however, her mom didn't want her to be alone and wanted to stay with her for the rest of the day. They came up with a solution that they both liked: Lacy packed her bags, and she and Sammy went to her grandparents' farm. They were very pleased when she called to ask if she and Sammy could stay with them. She said she was looking forward to being in her old room in the barn and sharing meals with them. And this way, if she needed help, they'd be there for her.

Sammy got excited when she pulled into the driveway at her grandparents' farm. He jumped out of the car as soon as she opened the door and ran to meet Lily Rose, his tail wagging like a fast metronome. Lacy knew they would have a great week on the farm. She wouldn't have to bother answering her home phone, and using her cell phone would be more like walking around asking "Can you hear me now?" She could decide who she wanted to talk to, and her mom could call her with their home phone if she needed to speak with her. Now she knew the reason for being hit by the football: she got paid leave, got to stay in her old room, and got to visit with her grandparents.

Lacy felt a little shaky when she got to the farm. She knew she wasn't supposed to drive, but she was there now and planned to take it easy for the rest of the day. After calling her mom to let her know she'd made it safely, she grabbed a light blanket, a pillow, and her notebook and pen, and headed to the large hammock that hung between two big shade trees in the side yard. It was spring and the bright sunshine made it feel warm, but there was a cool breeze blowing—a coat would've been too much to wear, but the blanket would be just right. She settled her head on the pillow and pulled up the cover after Sammy curled up beside her. And that's where they were found later when her grandpa came to tell her it was time for dinner.

Lily Rose wouldn't let Lacy help clean up the kitchen after dinner, so she decided to call Stephanie. Grandpa Robert took Sammy out with him on the tractor to go check on some of the cattle grazing in the fields.

"Hi, Steph. How was your day?"

"Busy. Where are you?" she asked, sounding concerned. "I called and called, but no one answered on either phone."

"If you promise not to tell anyone—and by that I mean no one—I'll tell you," she replied, hoping Stephanie knew she meant Spence too.

"I'm not sure I can promise that, but I'll try real hard," she answered with a little snicker.

"You're hopeless. Why do I hang out with you? I must need my head examined. Oh, wait, I've already done that."

"You know I'm the only one who'll hang out with you, Lacy. So, did the doctor tell you what I've been saying all these years? That you've lost your mind?"

"Cute. I'm staying on the farm because Mom doesn't want me to be alone, and she has a lot going on right now."

"Well, that's sounds like a good idea, but she could've stayed with you during the day, and Spence and I could've been there in the evening."

"I don't want Spence . . . I mean, he . . . I don't want to talk to him right now." *I don't want to see him either.*

"Oh, boy, did he find out about you and Jay? Maybe you shouldn't have had dinner with him."

"What do you mean? You're the one who encouraged me to go, remember?"

"And you listened? You should know better than to listen to me, 'cause what do I know about men? Who told him?" *I'm glad I'm not wearing her shoes.*

"I did. He tried to call me last night because he felt guilty about being all tied up, but my cell phone was off and Sammy had unplugged the other phone so the answering machine was off. He called this morning and asked me where I'd been. I told him, and I also told him that we saw him with the woman in the park, but I slipped and said 'nut' first. He focused on the nut part but said nothing about the woman. He also said that I didn't always make sense to him. So I told him not to call my office because I had to stay home for a while, gave a few explanations as to why, and then hung up."

"Sorry, Lacy. You don't need all this right now. I'll come over, and we can hang out if you want."

"No, actually, I'm lying around enjoying myself and being waited on. I'm fine, and I have a project to work on while I'm here. But if you want to come out and have dinner with us you can anytime. If you need to get in touch with me, call Grandma's phone, okay? Thanks, Stephanie."

"Okay. Call if you need me. Bye."

Lacy spent the rest of the evening with her grandparents before turning in early. She carried Sammy upstairs to her old apartment. Lily Rose had spent some time getting it ready for her earlier. She took a pain pill, because her head still gave her pain occasionally, and then she lifted Sammy onto the bed and climbed in. Her grandma had made sure to keep Sammy away from water during the evening to see if he'd make it through the night and not get Lacy up. And it worked, although he got her up early.

The next morning they were just finishing breakfast when the phone rang, and her grandmother asked if she would answer it.

"Hello, Gardenia residence," Lacy said.

"Well, good morning, Lacy. I'm so glad you answered. I tried calling your home, but got no answer, and I got worried. So I called your mom, and she told me where you were. I think that was a good move. Are you feeling better this morning?"

"Jay, where are you?" she asked, wishing she could look out the living room window to see if he was in the driveway.

"I'm still out of town, but I'll be back soon. Are you taking it easy?"

"Yes, I'm getting a lot of rest and also enjoying being back on the farm with my grandparents."

"Who's calling Lacy?" her grandpa asked, walking into the room.

"It's Jay. He just called to tell me about my car," she said to her grandpa and, into the phone said, "Isn't that right, Jay?"

"Tell Robert I said hello. It sounds like you're in good hands, so I'll leave you for now, but I'll call again soon. Bye, Lily of the Valley." He hung up before she could tell him no.

What was she going to do? The one man she wanted to be with was mad at her, and the one man she stayed mad at wanted to be with her. Oh, well, there was no use making her head hurt worse by trying to figure it out. She'd thought up some ideas for her assignment, anxious to get started on it. She grabbed her briefcase and laptop and headed outside, Sammy following on her heals. Oscar was outside, and Sammy ran over to try to take his ball away from him. Lacy sat down on the covered, wooden swing to get started.

***

She enjoyed her week on the farm and wished she could have stayed longer. Her headaches had almost gone away, and the bruise on her temple was finally fading. She'd called her boss to discuss her progress on her project. Stephanie had come out a couple of times to see her and have dinner. Jay called her every morning after breakfast to check on her, which she began to expect and enjoy. Spence finally figured out where to find her toward the end of the week and called her, but she was up in the barn. When she came down later, her grandmother told her he'd called. She tried to call him back, but got no answer and left a short message.

On Friday afternoon, she went back to see the doctor to get the okay to go back to work. Jay would be back on Monday also. He'd told her she'd get her car back when she got to work on Monday. He would meet her there to get the rental and take it back to get his own car. She stopped to check on her house before going back to the farm where she'd left Sammy, who was becoming quite a good little farm dog, as well as getting the hang of potty training.

Lacy stayed at her grandparents' farm through the weekend, and her mom and dad came out on Saturday to spend the day. She left Sunday morning to take Sammy home and to attend church. Stephanie was there, but Spence was a no-show.

Monday arrived, and, after dropping Sammy off at the farm, she headed to work. Lacy didn't know if she should feel bad about being excited to see Jay this morning, but she was, and tried to tell herself it was because she was getting her own car back. But she was disappointed when she got there and Jay hadn't shown up. She entered her office and before she'd had time to sit down the phone rang. It was Jay calling to tell her that he'd had an early meeting and he'd bring the car to her house that evening. She felt a little disappointed, but there was a lot of work to get caught up on, and she couldn't just sit there and pout.

She tried hard to concentrate on what she was doing, but her mind kept drifting back over all the crazy things that'd happened to her, beginning with the best thing: finding Sammy. He was the greatest little puppy ever, and she loved him dearly. She didn't know if she could say that about the two men in her life right now. When she'd finally got home yesterday, she'd listened to all her missed calls. Jay had called twice, sounding very concerned, but it didn't take him long to figure out where to find her. When Spence called, his message was for her to call him back. She felt bad that she hadn't told him where she was going, but she needed time to be by herself.

She was so deep in thought she didn't hear Spence when he came into her office, and it wasn't until he softly spoke her name that she realized he was there.

"Sorry, Spence, I'm trying to get caught up on some things," she explained.

He walked over to her and lifted her face with his hands so he could see the fading bruise on her temple. He bent down and kissed her temple gently. "I feel badly that you were hurt, and I wasn't there for you. Why didn't you call me so I could've been there to help you?" he asked sadly.

"I didn't know I was hurt until later that evening, and it was only a slight concussion. I've had headaches and felt weak and dizzy, but I'm better now. I could've taken care of myself, but Mom wanted me to have someone around, so I stayed on the farm with my grandparents. And I really liked being there. I got a lot of rest and tender loving care. I also got some great ideas for the project I'm working on."

"I was worried when you didn't answer my phone calls. Now I realize you weren't home to answer your phone."

"Cell phones are useless on the farm unless you like to walk and talk. I stayed up in the barn in my old room and really enjoyed being there. It was good for me to be there."

"I'm so grateful you're feeling better. Well, I'd better go and let you get some work done. I've been very busy at work lately, but let's go out for dinner soon, okay?" he asked her hopefully.

"Thank you. That would be nice. Don't work too hard, Spence." She wanted to say sweetheart, but wasn't sure she should. Although he didn't apologize or explain the woman, his actions proved he still cared for her.

She was able to get some work done after Spence left. She met Stephanie for lunch and told her about Spence stopping by her office that morning and all they had said. Then Stephanie told her about Andrew, the salesman from Lowe's.

"You have it bad for him, don't you? I've never heard you sound this excited about any other man before."

"I've never met anyone like him before. He's perfect, and I don't know if I can live up to his expectations. He's perfect, kind, sexy, handsome, and just perfect."

"Okay, I believe you, so quit trying to make me feel jealous." *I already have enough on my plate.*

"Hands off! You already have two men fighting over you, right?"

"No, I don't! Do I? I don't know what I'm doing anymore. You're right, I've lost my mind."

"I told you so!" She finally agrees that I'm right.

Chapter 6

Lacy was so glad to be home. She'd worked hard all day and was so tired—she didn't know being off work for a week could do that to her. Everyone had been glad to see that she was back and feeling better. She climbed into a tub filled with hot water and lots of bubbles and lay back and relaxed while Sammy lay close to the tub chewing on a doggie treat. "Oh, Sammy, this feels so good."

After a nice long soak, she climbed out of the tub and got dressed. Her phone rang, and she wondered if she should look outside before answering it.

"Hello, it's Mom. I just wanted to know how your first day back to work went."

"It was good. I got a lot of work done, but it made me really tired. I took a bath, and now I'm looking for something to eat for dinner." Her doorbell rang. "Mom, someone's at the front door, so I'll talk to you later." *I bet it's Jay with my car.*

She opened the door to Jay and Spence. Holy cow! Maybe I should just close the door and walk away.

"Hi, Lacy," Jay said. "I brought back your car. They went over it and made sure everything was fixed. I had them change the oil too."

"Thank you so much, Jay. Hi, Spence. Come on in. I'll get the keys for the rental car." She turned around and walked away, leaving the two men standing by the door.

When she came back into the room, they were still standing there waiting for her. She was so surprised when Spence said, "Jay and I would like to take you out to dinner. You probably don't have any food here since you've been gone all week."

She was so shocked that she didn't know what to say, so she said yes. She took Sammy out first and fed him, and then grabbed her purse. Jay suggested they take the rental, so she climbed into the back seat and let Spence sit in front with Jay. *Breathe, Lacy. Just breathe.*

She calmed herself down, and realized Jay and Spence were having a conversation in the front— a *friendly* conversation! They were speaking to each other as if they'd been friends for a long time.

Maybe she would survive the evening after all; she might even enjoy it. *That might be expecting too much*, she thought to herself.

When they got to the restaurant, Lacy excused herself and went to women's room. She hadn't had time to put on any make-up when they'd showed up at her door. *Oh, well, they will just have to live with it.* She pulled her phone out and called Stephanie and told her what'd happened and where they were having dinner.

"Oh, my. You like to live on the edge, don't you? I'm with Andrew right now, trying to decide where to eat. How about we come there and watch—I mean, eat dinner. Be right there. Oh, yeah. We'll have a good dinner and a show." She hung up before Lacy could decide if this was a good idea.

The two men were sitting at a table when she entered the dining room and walked over to them. Spence asked if she was okay, and Jay handed her a menu. She told them she was fine and turned her attention to the menu to choose what she wanted to eat. She began to smile when she wondered which one was going to pay for her dinner, because she sure wasn't going to pay for it. The waitress took their orders just as Stephanie and Andrew came up to them. Stephanie introduced Andrew to everyone, and Spence asked the two to join them. They pushed a table next to theirs with an extra chair. Stephanie had claimed the chair next to Lacy.

Lacy spent most of the time listening to Stephanie and Andrew, and she noticed that Jay and Spence were getting along very well—almost too well—and she figured she'd be waking up soon, because she had to be dreaming.

They all were enjoying their meal, including Lacy, but when she began yawning, Spence told her it was time to go, because he could tell that she was getting tired. Jay picked up the bill and left to take care of it while Lacy said goodbye to her friends. Spence walked her to the car. When they arrived at her house, everyone got out of the car. Jay came around, told her goodbye, kissed her check, and said he'd call her. She looked at Spence to see if he was mad, but he took her by the arm and walked her to the door, told her goodbye, kissed her, and said he would call her later. Feeling confused, she sat down on her couch and laid her head against the back and closed her eyes.

***

Lacy slowly opened her eyes and was shocked to discover that she was still in the bathtub and the water was cool. Now it all made sense—she had been dreaming. She climbed out and quickly, wrapped a towel around her, ran into her bedroom, and got dressed. As she was heading toward the kitchen, her phone rang.

"Hi, honey. It's Mom. Just wanted to know how your first day went."

"It was fine. I had lots of work to catch up on, and I'm very tired and hungry. I was on my way to the kitchen to see if I could find anything for dinner," she explained. She heard another call beeping in, so she told her mom she'd call her back later. *This is feeling a little weird.*

"Hello," she said after switching the call.

"Hi, it's Jay. How was your day?"

She ran to the door and looked out in the driveway and then looked up and down the road, half expecting to see both Jay and Spence coming down the street.

"Where are you?" she asked.

"About a block down the street. I tried calling twice, but you didn't answer."

"I'm sorry. I was soaking in the tub." She could see her car coming, so she hung up. He parked her car in the driveway, since the rental was parked on the street. He got out and handed her the keys.

"Thank you for fixing my car. I'm so sorry for stopping in front of you that day."

"So you agree it was your fault?" he asked, laughing.

"No, I do *not* agree. It was your fault for not being a more defensive driver," she answered, giggling. "Let's just say it happened for a good reason."

"You found a puppy, and I found a beautiful rose," he returned.

Before she could think of a reply, Spence pulled up. *I am still dreaming.* She briefly closed her eyes and pinched herself, but both men were still there.

"Hi, Lacy," Spence said, as he climbed out of his car. "I tried calling you earlier, but you didn't answer and I got worried. Hello, Jay. I see you brought back her car."

"Hello, Spence. Yes, I brought it back. I was just about to take Lacy out to get a bite to eat, since she hasn't been home all week and her kitchen is bare. Care to join us?"

"I'm, sorry, Spence," Lacy interrupted. "I was taking a bath and didn't hear my phone." Then she whispered for his ears only, "There may be a little pushing going on." *Just say no.*

"How about if we go get a pizza? There's a pizza place not too far away from here," answered Spence. "And we can celebrate Lacy getting her car back." *And put an end to this crazy mess.*

"I've got to go take care of Sammy," she said, and she went back into the house. She thought maybe she should sit down and close her eyes again just to be sure this was happening, but Sammy was at the back door waiting for her to let him out. She filled up his dish with food and put him in the kennel. When she came back out the front door, with purse and keys in her hands, both men were still waiting for her. *If I weren't so hungry, I'd go back inside, lock the door, and just go to bed.*

"I'm going to drive my car. I'll see you two there, if I don't wake up first," she said, heading toward her car. When she got in, she locked the doors, and then waited for Spence to back his car out. Jay got into the rental, and they all drove separately to the pizza place.

She was happy to find a round table, because she didn't want to sit in a booth and have to make a choice of which man to sit next to. She was so tired that she didn't participate in the conversation, nor did she pay that much attention to what was being said, but there wasn't much talking going on. When she'd eaten enough to satisfy her hunger, she told them both that she was very tired and was going home. She shook Jay's hand, told him thanks, and gave Spence a quick hug and left. She decided to let them deal with the bill.

An hour later, Lacy was in bed, with Sammy curled up next to her. "Sammy, I hope when I wake up this time, I won't find myself soaking in the tub." It had taken her skin a long time to quit looking like a prune.

This time she didn't wake up until her phone alarm—the one she finally learned how to set—went off. She got up and prepared to get ready for work. While she was getting ready, and thoughts were floating throughout her mind, she began to believe she'd dreamed the whole sequence of events last night, until she saw her own car parked in the garage.

"Sammy, we're going to have to move to another state," she said to the puppy, and he cocked his head to the side, which made her laugh.

She decided to tackle all the projects on her desk without thinking about anything else. There was no way she was going to explain or apologize to either one for what happened last night, because in her mind, all that had happened was three people getting together and going out to eat pizza. Plus, she got her car back. Although she'd told Spence she was going to pick up the car herself, that didn't happen, because Jay was being pushy—and thoughtful. And now she was doing exactly what she wasn't going to do: think about it.

Ten minutes later her phone rang, and she answered it. "Hi, Lacy. I hope you were pleased with your car?" It was Jay calling, just like he'd been calling every morning since the accident.

"Yes, as pleased as punch, thank you. It drives like a different car, but better," she explained.

"Good! It should, because I had them put on new tires, new shocks, and new brakes. I wanted to be sure you'd be safe driving it."

"You didn't have to do that, but thank you so much." *He can be so sweet.*

"Well, I'll let you go now. I know you're busy. Goodbye, Sweet Pea," he said, and then he hung up.

After giving up on trying not to think about him, she figured this was just what he wanted her to do: think about him. She'd managed to get caught up on some things at work before calling Stephanie to see if she could meet her for lunch.

They met at the park and sat on a bench to eat as Lacy began telling Stephanie all about the evening she'd had.

"The dream seemed so real, and I was so nervous. They were getting along like they'd been friends for a long time. Don't you agree?" she asked.

"I don't know, since I wasn't there. Remember?" Stephanie shot back.

"Oh, that's right. Then I woke up, and it started all over again, except we ate pizza."

"You really do like to live on the edge, don't you?"

"You've said that to me before." Stephanie was shaking her head no. "I'm so confused now," Lacy said. "I really don't know what did or did not happen, and I'm afraid to ask either one. I talked to Jay this morning, but I haven't talked to Spence yet."

"You talked to Jay?"

"He called to ask if my car was okay, and I told him it was. Do you know that Jay paid to have new tires, shocks, and brakes put on my car? I think that's what he said."

"Maybe you should have your head examined again. I was hoping the football knocked some sense into you, but it sounds like it made you worse," Stephanie said, laughing.

"Really? You might be right," Lacy said, agreeing with her.

She gave Stephanie a hug, and when she let go, she saw the shocked look on her friend's face. Lacy looked toward where Stephanie was looking and understood why. There was Spence walking with that woman again, and they were heading toward them.

"Wicked witch!" Lacy exploded as she stood up, facing toward them.

"What are you going to do, Lacy?"

"I'm going to go meet the nut this time. Are you coming? I might need some help dealing with the squirrel."

"Okay, lead the way. I'm right behind you." *Look out, nut, here she comes!*

She and Stephanie started walking toward Spence and the woman, but he didn't see Lacy until she was almost in front of him because his head was turned toward the woman, listening to what she was saying.

"Hi, honey," Lacy said, putting her arms around him and giving him a kiss. "The park is a great place to meet for lunch, isn't it?" *You better have a good explanation ... please.*

Spence was very surprised to see her, and it showed on his face. "Oh, hi, Lacy. It's nice to see you and Stephanie."

"Hi, Spence, it's nice to see you too. And just who are you—" Stephanie began, but Lacy interrupted her before she could finish.

She turned to the girl and said, "It's a nice park, and you never know who you'll run into here. Do you come here often? It's one of our favorite places, right, babe?" she said, looking into Spence's eyes when she said it.

"I'm sorry, we didn't catch your name," Stephanie continued, addressing the woman.

"I'm Lori. Um, I've got to go back to work now, so please excuse me. It was nice to meet you," she answered, a frown showing on her face. Then she turned to Spence, told him goodbye, and walked back the way they had come.

Feeling very awkward and very frustrated, Lacy kissed Spence again and told him she'd see him later. She then turned and, almost running, headed back, leaving her friend behind with a very surprised look on her face. Stephanie had to jog to catch up with her.

"Really? That's all you're going to say?" Stephanie asked, taking Lacy by the arms and forcing her to look her into her eyes.

"What would you say? It was apparent he was surprised to see me, and he sure wasn't in any hurry to explain who she was or why he was with her. He didn't even introduce me to her."

"Don't know, but we'd better get back to work and figure this out later, okay? I'm sorry, Lacy."

"Okay, but answer one question for me. Was I wrong for the way I acted? That's how I always greet him when we run into each other unexpectedly."

"No, it wasn't wrong. I'm glad you acted that way, because if you hadn't, I might have myself. She didn't seem to like it, did she?"

"It seemed that way to me too." He'd better have a good explanation for this.

Lacy made it through the rest of the day without calling Spence, but just barely. What was happening to them? She'd never hesitated about calling him before, except when she knew he was busy. And he called her every day, or came over to her house, and they spent their evenings together. But since she'd been rear-ended by Jay, it seemed everything had changed between them. She didn't like it, and she was beginning to dislike the nut he was hanging out with in the park. Spence was *her* squirrel, and that nut had better find herself another one to hang out with.

When she could no longer stand it, she picked up the phone and called Spence. "Hi, honey. I was surprised to see you at the park today, but it was very nice," she said sweetly.

"Hi, honey. Are you feeling better? I noticed you were a little quiet last night," he replied.

"Yes, I was really tired out from my first day back to work. I wanted to stay home with you, but since there was nothing there to eat, it turned out fine. And I got my car back. Are you coming over tonight? I can stop by the store on my way home from the farm and get some groceries."

"No, I'm going to be tied up tonight. I'm working on a big story, and I have some inquiries to make. But you have a good night and get some rest, okay?"

"Okay, but we need to get together soon and spend some time together," she said sadly. *I have some inquiries to make myself, and I will find out who she really is.*

She told her boss she had to leave early. She picked up some groceries and Sammy before going home. After taking care of things there, she called to see if Spence was still at work and was told he had left early. She thought as much, so she called his home phone and got the answering machine. He wasn't at home either, so she decided to call his friend Mitch.

"Hi, it's Lacy. Heard you enjoyed the ballgame. How's it going?"

"Yeah, we had a blast. I meant to call and tell you thanks for letting me have your ticket. How are you? Spence told me about your rear-ending and your knock down. Hope you've learned how to avoid other cars and how to dodge footballs," he said, giggling.

"Yes, I've learned some good lessons. Have you talked to Spence today?"

"Yes, about an hour ago. He said he was going to have dinner at the Grilling Steak House tonight, but I guess you know that already. You guys enjoy your dinner. It was good talking to you."

"You have a great evening too." Lacy was surprised to get the information without even prying.

She called the restaurant to see if he'd made a reservation, pretending she'd forgot the time, and was told it was at five o'clock. She also told them that there might be more than two at the table. She had just enough time to get there and see what was going on. She called Stephanie to see if she could go with her, but she already had plans.

As Lacy got closer to the restaurant, she realized a car seemed to be following her. *Oh Lacy, your mind is working overtime.* But when she turned into the parking lot, the car turned in too. She found a parking spot and watched as the other car pulled into the one next to her. Her mouth dropped as Jay got out and walked over to her car.

"Fuzzy frogs!" *Where'd he come from?* She rolled down her window and looked up at Jay.

"Hi. Are you meeting someone for dinner?" he asked before she could think of what to say.

"I might . . . uh . . . maybe," she mumbled. "Were you following me?"

"No, I wouldn't do that. The last time I did you pulled a brake job on me." *I'm so glad you did.*

"Just remember that, buddy. Are you meeting someone for dinner?"

"I was hoping I could join you. Would that be all right?"

"I . . . guess that'd be okay." *Oh, shoot, what am I going to do now?* she thought to herself.

"Great. I'm glad I decided to take this street, or I would've missed seeing your car turn in here."

"Great," she returned.

As soon as they entered the restaurant, she started looking around at the tables to see if Spence was here with that woman, and she saw them sitting at a table holding menus. The hostess took Jay and Lacy to a table that was close to the other couple, but situated behind Spence's back. Lacy could see Lori's face though, and she didn't look very happy about something.

Lacy tried to pay attention to what was Jay was saying during dinner, and even tried to add to the conversation, but her eyes kept glancing at the other couple, and Jay noticed it.

"Am I boring you?" he asked.

"No. You're not. You know when you see someone that looks familiar and you think you know them but you can't think of their name or where you met them? Well, that's happening now. I'm sorry. I'll try to let it go," she explained.

"No, that's okay. Who are you talking about? Maybe I'll know who it is," he returned.

Her glance automatically went to their table, and he turned to see who she was looking at.

"That's Lori! How do you know her? Oh, your friend Spence is with her. Do you want to go say hello?" he asked. "From the look on your face I'd say the answer is no."

"Do you want to?" Why did I say that?

"No, I'd rather enjoy your company and let them enjoy their dinner."

"I remember now where I met her. I ran into her in the park when Steph and I went there for lunch. But I don't know anything more about her except her name is Lori. Does she live in Stoneybrooke?"

"Yes, she moved back here a couple of months ago, after her divorce. She was born and raised here, but left two years ago when she met and married her husband, who was older and, I heard, had money. But it didn't work out, and she's back in town. The rumor is she didn't get a good settlement."

"Do you know her well?"

"Went to school with her, but I never ran with her crowd, and she's not my type. Heard she always had a crush on somebody. Her dad is a farmer, but she never wanted to stay on that farm. She's an only child and was spoiled. Although her family wasn't rich, they made a good living and gave her everything they could afford. She finished her first two years of college before she decided to give that up for a rich husband. But I guess that didn't work for her. He was a lawyer before he got into politics. He made sure she couldn't get her hands on his fortune. She got a small settlement and moved back to the farm about a month ago. I'm sorry, I didn't mean to ramble."

"No, I asked. Does she have a job, or is she looking for another rich husband?" she asked disapprovingly.

"I don't know, but she seems to have found her next victim."

"Oh, no, she hasn't!" With that, she got up and walked over to their table without thinking about what she was doing or what she was going to say.

"Hi, Spence," she said. Turning to the woman, she said, "Hello . . . what did you say your name was? I'm glad you decided to eat here, Spence. I know you said you were going to be busy tonight, but I'm happy you decided to take time to eat dinner. I thought I'd see if I could catch you and spend a little time with you, since you've been working so much, and I miss you."

Jay walked up behind her. "Look who's here. Jay saw me pull into the lot and decided to come in and eat dinner too. Mind if we join you?" She turned and winked at Jay before sitting down next to Spence. Jay decided to sit down and play along. He didn't know Spence very well, but he knew Lacy did, and he didn't want Lori to cause them any trouble, so he sat down in the empty seat.

"How'd you know I was here?"

"Oh, I called your office and was told you had left already, so I decided to come here, and here you are. I know you like a book." *Yeah, one I don't like right now.*

"Hi, Lori. Long time no see. I'm sorry to hear about your divorce. Have you made any plans about moving on?" Jay asked, turning to wink at Lacy.

"I . . . uh . . . haven't yet. Um, no . . . not at the moment. Could you please excuse me? I'm going to the ladies' room," she muttered. Then she got up and left the restaurant.

"Hello, Jay. So you saw her turning into the restaurant and decided to pull in also."

"Yes, I did, since I had no plans for dinner. This is a great place to eat, and it turned out to be a good idea. How'd you meet Lori, by the way?"

"I . . . uh . . . I was told she had a good story and to investigate it and write an article about it."

"Well, if you need a little background on her let me know, because I've known her for a long time, ever since we were classmates, actually. She didn't finish college, though, because she met and married a rich man, older than she, and it ended badly, poor little thing. I don't think she's coming back, is she?"

"I think I saw her go out the front door. She leaves every time she sees me. Is it my perfume?" Lacy moved closer to give them a sniff. "Oh, shoot, I forgot to put it on today," she added innocently.

When she looked at Spence, he didn't seem to be as amused as Jay. "I'm sorry, Spence. I didn't mean to interrupt your dinner with her. Jay and I will leave now and you can finish doing your job." She got up and left, with Jay following her out the door. Spence didn't say anything to stop her.

"Well, that went well, don't you think?" The look on her face made him feel badly. "What're you going to do now?" Jay asked.

"Let's take a walk in the park. I'll go pick up Sammy, and we can go to the park close to my home. You're invited to join us."

"I'd love to."

Chapter 7

On her way to work the next day, Lacy decided to find out just what Lori was up to and confront Spence and make him explain why he acting the way he was. Something was changing between the two of them. They always spent all their time together when they weren't working—and enjoyed it!—but since the party for her parents, they hadn't spent any time with each other. And she wasn't going to let anyone come between them, especially Lori. Stephanie had promised to search the Internet for anything she could find on the woman, since she was an expert at it. Lacy would have to ask Jay for the Lori's last name, since Spence didn't seem to want her to know it.

Lacy was surprised at how easy it had been to find Spence last night, although she hadn't expected to see him having dinner with that woman. She thought he might be with a client. Did making inquiries and being tied up mean having dinner too? He hadn't called her last night, and she didn't call him either. But he was going to hear from her today. "Watch out, honey, because here I come!"

Jay had called earlier to thank her for the walk in the park and told her he couldn't believe how fast Sammy was growing. She'd really enjoyed their evening stroll, although she was quiet for most of it, but Jay knew she needed some quiet time and was just happy she'd let him share it with her.

Lacy had an appointment that morning with Stacy Littlebook, the woman who ran the local animal shelter. She was going to share her ideas for the events she'd been working on to find good homes for the animals and for the donations that were much needed for their care. The week off work had given her a lot of time to work on it, and now she was anxious to get started. The shelter was becoming very crowded and running out of room and supplies.

Lacy told them that she planned to run ads encouraging individuals and businesses to sponsor an animal and to let folks know how to go about adopting. She also said she was working with the Pebble County Fair to put on a festival and perhaps they would have a parade. The meeting went very well, but she had to leave as soon as it was over to check on Sammy.

Her next stop was the newspaper office to see Spence. She'd only been to his office a couple of times before and only when he'd invited her to meet him there before going out to grab a bite to eat. He was sitting at his desk when she walked in. She felt like crying when he looked up at her. "Hello, Spence. Are you free for lunch?"

"Hi, Lacy. Sure, I can have lunch with you. Where do you want to eat?" Spence replied, turning his computer off.

"Your choice, okay? I'm just glad you have some free time for me."

They went to a nearby café. Spence paid for their food while she found a place for them to sit. After they had finished eating, Lacy decided it was time to have a serious talk with him.

"What's going on with you, Spence? Are you mad at me about something? And I see you twice—once in the park and once at dinner—with a woman you've never introduced me to. And she seems to get angry every time she sees me. Is she the good story you're working on, or is the story about how she's working on you?"

"I'm sorry, Lacy. I shouldn't blame you because Jay has a thing for you. But it seems every time I see you, Jay is with you," he returned.

"Seriously? He was trying to take care of my car. I know I shouldn't have accepted his dinner invitation, but I saw you walking with her. I also saw you answer your phone when I called you. You told me you couldn't have dinner with me because you were going to be tied up for the night. I admit I got jealous, but Stephanie kind of encouraged me, because she saw you too. I was ill and not thinking straight. Everything that happened the rest of that night was out of my control. I couldn't call you for help because you'd made it clear you didn't have time for me that night. The night Jay dropped off my car, I was hoping to spend that evening with you, but you decided to go have pizza with him. Last night I was trying to find you to spend time with you again, and you were with her. Jay was telling the truth when he said he saw my car and followed me into the parking lot. He's been truthful with me, while you seem to be having trouble explaining to me what's going on with you and that woman. If she's the subject of your next article, why is it so hard for you to tell me? I'm not trying to keep you from doing your job, but you've never let your job keep us apart before."

Spence looked upset at what she'd said. "I'm sorry, Lacy. I've been interviewing Lori Brooks for an article. She was married to Donald Williams, who is a very important man. I've been neglecting our relationship, and I let you down when you needed me. I've been a little jealous myself lately, and I'm sorry."

"I love when you're right," she said with a smile. "Oh, boy. Look at the time. I've to get back to work. I'm glad we had lunch together. Talk to you later." She then kissed him goodbye and left.

Well, she thought to herself on the way back to work, *that was a good start, but I still plan to do some investigating on my own.* She knew something was going on, and she was going to find out what it was.

When she got to the door of her office building, her shoe slipped on something, causing her to hesitate a moment before she reached for the door handle. For the third time, she was hit from behind. "Okay, Jay, this has got to stop."

She turned around, and there stood a man she'd seen many times before. He worked on the first floor, but she didn't know his name.

"Oh, I'm so sorry. Are you okay?" he asked.

"Yes, I'm fine. My shoe slipped," she tried to explain while her face turned red.

She opened the door and moved away quickly. She was glad when she reached her office. "I'm going to have to get my taillights checked."

Lacy worked with her boss for the rest of the day. Jason was pleased with what she had planned already, and Stacy had called earlier to tell him she was going to enjoy working with Lacy.

On the way home Lacy wondered if she should call Spence to see if he was coming over tonight to spend the evening with her. She'd picked up everything to grill out, hoping he'd just show up like he always did before her accident. Sammy was so excited to see her that she decided to stay in the backyard for a short time and play with him before going back inside. She heard the doorbell ring as they came through the back door.

"Oh, Sammy, do you want to make a bet on who that might be?

Maybe I shouldn't answer the door." But she'd left her car in the driveway so she had to go see who it was. Before she could reach the door, Stephanie walked in.

"Hello, stranger. Where's your boy toy?" Lacy asked.

"Andrew is working tonight. Where're your pair of love-sick dudes?" Stephanie shot back.

"Who knows? Frankly, my dear friend, I don't give a hoot."

"Are you trying to convince me or yourself?"

"Honestly, I was hoping Spence would stop by like he used to, but I don't feel like holding my breath. It makes my head hurt."

"Aw, does your head still hurt?"

"A little, especially when I overthink. Are you staying for a free meal? I have everything for grilling out except a companion."

"Yes, of course. I'd love to stay."

Lacy forgot all about calling Spence as the two worked together to fix their meal. Since they were grilling out they decided to eat outside. As they were sitting down at the picnic table, Spence came walking out the back door. Lacy was glad she'd put on an extra steak.

"Hello, Spence," Stephanie said with a big smile on her face.

"Am I still in the tub?" Lacy said softly.

"What?" Stephanie asked.

"Oh, nothing. Hi, honey. Grab yourself a plate cause there's plenty to eat. I'm glad you could join us." Lacy was surprised but very glad to see him.

"Thanks, sweetheart. I'm starving, and I can't think of a better place to eat dinner, except here with two beautiful young ladies."

"He always was a charmer, wasn't he Lacy?"

"Yes, he always was." Hope he hasn't used his charm on that woman.

The three sat together enjoying their meal and discussing all the funny things that'd happened while they were in school together, and Sammy begged bites from their plates. Stephanie finally said she had to go home, but stayed to help clear up the mess first. Spence helped Lacy wash the dishes, and then played with Sammy for a while in the backyard. Lacy watched as they played together and was happy just having him here. When they went back inside, he told her he was going home and that he'd enjoyed the evening with her. He put his arms around her, gave her a big hug, and kissed her good night before he left. She was left standing by the front door wondering if she'd been dreaming or if he'd really been there. Although he'd seemed happy to be there with her, she could tell that something was still not completely right with him. But at least he'd come by without her calling and begging him.

Lacy decided to get ready for bed early so she could take her laptop with her and work on her extra assignment. She had plans for many events to help raise money for the shelter. She needed lots of advertising from the newspaper and was hoping to ask Spence to help her. Lori wasn't the only one in town who had a good story—if she really had a story. So far there was nothing in the newspaper which made Lacy think the woman had other intentions. "Not on my watch," Lacy said to herself.

***

Lacy forgot to put her car in the garage that night, and when she realized that it was still sitting in the driveway, she raised the hood and checked for Tom before starting the engine. "All clear, thank goodness." Before she could close the hood, Tom jumped up on the engine and meowed.

"Jumping jellybeans, what are you doing? Get down from there and go back home, you silly cat." Tom jumped down and ran next door. *What am I going to do with that cat?*

Today Lacy had an appointment at the newspaper office, which Jason, her boss, had set up for her and Stacy Littlebook, the woman from the shelter. They were going to meet with the editor and discuss plans for placing ads for their fund-raising events, which they hoped would generate enough money to help the shelter find permanent homes for their animals, as well as help run the shelter. The meeting went very well. Before they left the editor's office, Stacy asked if they could work with Spence. She told him that she was friends with his parents and knew he'd be perfect for the job. Lacy was surprised, but pleased, because she was wondering how she was going to ask to have Spence help them.

***

Before Lacy reached the front door of her office building, she stopped and looked behind her. There was no one there. *I'm starting to become paranoid*, she thought. She took the last three steps to the front door when she heard, "Hello, Miss Rose Petal."

When she turned around there was Jay. "Where did you come from?"

"From across the street. I jay-walked, but don't tell anyone. I am running late for a meeting. Where did you come from?" Jay returned.

"I had an appointment at the newspaper office for a project I'm working on for the shelter. We need homes for the animals and donations. Would you like to adopt a dog or a cat? Or maybe give them some money for supplies?" Lacy said with a big smile on her face.

"Yeah, I'll take three of each, and how much do I make the check out for?" Jay smiled back at her.

"How about a thousand? And when can you pick up your pets?"

"I'm running very late now, but who do I write the check out to?" he said over his shoulder as he was going through the door.

Knowing that he was joking with her, she said, "Just put my name on it, and I'll see that they get it, okay?"

Holding the door for her he said, "Okay, see you later." Then he took off for the elevator, leaving her standing there.

"Jay always seems to be in a good mood," she said to herself. If she didn't have Spence she might . . . what? Fall for him? *Oh, Lacy, get serious and get back to work, you silly girl.*

Lacy managed to get a lot of work done before leaving work that day, but her mind was on what she was going to fix for dinner, hoping Spence would come over. She was excited about working with him on her project. She had so many things planned and was excited about putting everything in motion. She was hoping to get the whole town involved in finding forever homes for all the animals and raking in lots of money and supplies for the shelter. She had worked past her bed time last night and realized on her way home how tired she was.

When she got home, she took care of Sammy first. Then she decided a nice warm bubble bath might be just what she needed. If

Spence stopped by while she was in the tub, he could start dinner like he used to.

After some time had passed, she decided to get out of the tub, because she'd started to wrinkle and get cold. Spence hadn't stopped by, but she didn't feel like cooking a meal or going out. "Sammy, tonight we shall have pizza. Yay!" Sammy got all excited, and she wondered if he really knew what she was talking about, or if it was because of the way she'd said it. It was still early, but she decided to go to bed as soon as she ate her pizza. "It's just you and me, boy," she said to Sammy as they waited for the pizza to be delivered.

She decided to put on her sexy red nightgown with the matching robe, and then waited for the pizza to arrive. After she paid the delivery boy and gave him a five dollar tip, she carried the pizza to the kitchen. She hung her robe on the kitchen chair before getting a root beer out of the fridge and a plate out of the cupboard. Before she could get a slice of pizza, Sammy began to bark, and the doorbell rang.

"Oh, perfect timing! Spence decided to join us, Sammy." Without thinking, Lacy raced to the front door and opened it. "Hi Sp— Jay?"

"Hello beautiful, sexy Lacy. What a nice surprise," Jay replied, looking excited.

"Oh shoot," she shot back, and she raced to get her robe. "What are you doing here?" she shot over her shoulder

"I told you earlier today that I'd see you later," he said, following her into the kitchen, "so I didn't think I needed to call first. Is that pizza I smell?" asked Jay.

"Yes it is. Haven't you had dinner yet?" As soon as she'd said it, Lacy wished she hadn't asked him that.

"No, I haven't, but pizza sounds good, thank you."

She hadn't invited him in to eat pizza with her, but he'd managed again to invite himself. She got out another plate and reached for another root beer without first asking him if he wanted one. They both sat down and ate the pizza.

After a short while she asked again, "What did you say you came by for?" *I know it wasn't for the pizza, although it was really good.*

"Oh, yes, I brought the check you asked for this morning. I wrote your name on it just like you said. Hope it helps your cause."

"The check I asked for? What check? Wait, are you talking about what I said this morning? I thought you knew I was just joking." As she said this, he handed over a check written for a thousand dollars.

"One thousand dollars? Oh, no, Jay!" Lacy yelled.

"Isn't that what you said? I can make it bigger if you want me to," Jay answered.

"No! I was joking with you this morning, but this money will really help."

"Good. I'm glad I can help you out, and if you need any more money, or if there is anything else I can do to help, just let me know. I can't take on a pet right now, but maybe later." *Sammy is starting to grow on me.*

"Okay, then. And thank you for the check. Stacy is going to be very pleased. She doesn't like to turn away any animals, but she's running out of funds. Jay, I'm glad you stopped by, but I was going to turn in early tonight. I was up late last night, and I'm feeling a little tired right now."

"I'm sorry. You're not sick are you?" he asked, starting to worry.

"I'm okay, just a little tired. So I think I'll say good night and thank you for your donation and your offer to help us," she said, walking to the front door with Jay following after her.

"Well, thank you for the pizza and for wearing that sexy red number for me again," Jay said. "And you really wear it well."

Before she could react or comment on what he'd just said, he pulled her into his arms and kissed her with passion, said good night, turned, and was gone. Lacy slowly closed the door and leaned her back against it. "What the heck is going on with that man?" Lacy asked out loud. After she shook her head to try and clear it, she decided to go clean the kitchen before tending to Sammy's needs and then going to her bedroom. She'd just settled down and pulled up the blankets when the phone rang.

"Darn ding-a-ling! Who can that be now? Hello?" she said into the phone.

"Hi, girlfriend. What'd you do this evening? Before you ask, my guy had to work, but we spent his lunch break together," Stephanie said with excitement.

"Hi, Steph. I ordered a pizza when Spence didn't come by, and ate it with Jay."

"That'll teach Spence, darn him. What happened with Jay?"

"What do you mean? Nothing happened with Jay!"

"Oh, I think you're hiding something. Give me details. Did you kiss him?"

"Yes . . . I mean . . . no, I didn't, but he sort of kissed me," said Lacy, sounding confused.

"One question. Did you sort of like it?" Stephanie asked.

"Can I answer that later when I've had more time to think about it? To answer your next question, I didn't know he was coming by."

"Did you ask him why he came by?"

"Yes. He said he'd told me he'd see me later when I ran into him earlier, but I thought he was just saying that at the time. I thought it was Spence when I opened the door, and he saw me wearing that sexy red nightgown you gave me."

"I'm glad you're getting some action out of it. What else happened?" She wished she'd been a fly on the wall.

"He gave me a check for one thousand dollars." *Shoot, I wish I hadn't said that.*

"Oh really? That much? Just what did you do for that amount of cash?" *Lacy, I thought I knew everything about you.*

"Nothing. It's written in my name, but it's a donation for the shelter. The project I'm working on, remember?"

"Oh, I'm sorry, okay? When did he kiss you?"

"After we ate the pizza and he was leaving. He thanked me for the pizza, for wearing the sexy red nightgown again, and told me I wore it well. Then he kissed me and said good night. Why does he think he can just kiss me whenever he feels like it? He knows Spence is my boyfriend."

"Oh no he doesn't know, because you introduced Spence as a friend, remember? Have you told him anything different?"

"Oh, shoot, no wonder he keeps coming back!" Lacy forgot about the friend thing and wished Spence would forget it too. "No, I haven't because it's never come up, and I never thought I had to before now."

"Wait, what do you mean keeps coming back?" Stephanie was really confused now.

"I meant . . . I don't know why I said that. Listen, Steph, I'm glad you called, but I was going to bed early, because I've been tired all day. I'm not sick, just tired, so I'll see you tomorrow. Okay? Good night, girlfriend." Lacy hung up as Stephanie was saying good night.

Chapter 8

On her way to work, Lacy had trouble keeping her mind on her driving because she kept reliving the kiss Jay laid on her last night. Every time she thought about it, she felt butterflies in her stomach. She turned on the radio to get her mind off the kiss and began singing along with the radio as she traveled through a small town where the speed limit was thirty-five miles per hour for a short distance. She didn't realize that, as she sang along, her foot was applying pressure to the gas pedal, causing the car's speed to exceed the speed limit. Before she reached the area where the speed limit returned to fifty-five miles per hour, she saw a patrol car sitting to the side of the road. She glanced at her speedometer and realized she was speeding. She put her foot on the brake to slow down but it was too late—she saw the red lights go on.

Lacy pulled over and rolled down her window, waiting for the officer to approach her car. She took her driver's license out of her purse and reached over to her glove compartment to find her insurance card when she heard, "May I see your driver's license and proof of insurance, please?"

"Yes, here you are, sir," she replied, handing him her driver's license and insurance card.

"Your insurance has expired," the officer said, handing back her insurance card.

"Oh, I'm sorry. Wait a minute," she said, reaching back in to grab another card.

"This one has expired also."

"Shoot." Lacy leaned over so she could see what was in her glove compartment and pulled out a small stack of cards. "I'm sure one of these is good," she said, noticing that he was trying not to laugh at her. "Well, you can see that I keep insurance on my car. All I need to do now is learn how to throw away the old cards, don't I?"

She handed him the cards and waited while he found the new one. "Here it is, but it's going to expire in a couple of months. Do you still live at this address in Pebblestone?"

"Yes, I do, but I work in Stoneybrooke."

"So you drive this road every day?"

"Yes, sir."

"Are you aware that the speed limit is thirty-five through here?"

"It is?" Lacy said, with her sweetest smile.

"And it doesn't go back to fifty-five until you pass that sign," he said, pointing toward the sign.

She looked where he was pointing and saw a sign about twenty yards away that read 55 MPH. "Oh, I'm sorry. I wasn't aware," she replied again with another sweet smile.

"You passed several signs pointing out the upcoming speed limit. You have to drive this way back home, don't you?"

"Yes, sir."

"I clocked you going fifty-two in a thirty-five zone. Usually we give a break for seven or eight miles over the speed limit, but you were going seventeen over," he explained.

"I'm so sorry," Lacy said sweetly, looking up at him.

"You don't want me to give you a ticket, do you?"

"No, sir, please don't do that."

"Will you be careful from now on?"

"Yes, sir, I promise to be careful from now on."

"Okay then. Drive carefully and have a good day," he said with a smile.

"Oh, thank you. Thank you so much," she said, shaking his hand.

As she drove away she thought, *What a nice man he is to do that for me. I guess I'd better keep my mind on my driving from now on.* She really felt lucky this morning and thought maybe she ought to buy a lottery ticket, since the amount of the payout had grown quite large.

Lacy was sitting at her desk when Stephanie walked in.

"Okay, girl, I gave you plenty of time to think about Jay's kiss. Tell me, how did it make you feel?"

"I got butterflies in my stomach, and I almost got a ticket this morning for speeding, because I couldn't stop thinking about it, so I listened to the radio and sang to get my mind off it. I must not have been paying attention, because my foot pressed too hard on the accelerator, making me speed up," said Lacy, out of breath.

"Slow down, and take a deep breath. It was that good, huh?"

"Yes, it was pretty amazing, but it's got to stop, and soon," Lacy said with a sigh. "And that was said for your ears only, Stephanie. Remember our promise to each other? Any remarks we make about a man are never repeated to that man, or to any other man. Or anyone else."

"I remember, don't worry. Spence will never hear from me that you almost got a speeding ticket this morning."

"Stephanie Louise!" Lacy scolded.

"Or tell him that Jay's kisses give you butterflies," she returned.

Jay walked through the door and said, "Why does she need butterflies?"

Stephanie started laughing and winked at Lacy as she left and went back to her own office. Lacy didn't have an answer for Jay, so she smiled and waited for him to tell her why he had come to her office.

"On my way to a meeting, and thought I'd stop and tell you how much I enjoyed our evening last night. You have a good day, Miss Daisy."

"Okay, Jay. You do the same," said Lacy, laughing as he left her office. How was she going to get any work done with these two clowns showing up?

Lacy had a meeting with Spence that morning to work on her ideas for a series of articles he had been assigned to write on the shelter project. She also would give him the dates and times for all the activities she had planned for an upcoming, fun-filled weekend to take place in a couple of weeks. She gave him a flyer with the information on it that he could post for anyone who wanted to sign up to help or participate in the events. She had sent mailers to businesses in Stoneybrooke and Pebblestone as well as the small towns in between. One event was to choose a shelter animal that needed a home and post its picture, including information about it, in stores, offices, or churches, letting people know that it was available for adoption. If they couldn't adopt, they could donate money for the shelter or supplies the shelter needed. The article also invited all of the surrounding shelters to join in the activities so they could receive help with their shelters as well. The big weekend event would be held at the Pebblestone County Fair Grounds. Lacy was hoping to get some local bands to play music and some of the grocery stores to donate food and host the stands to feed the crowd—the possibilities were endless. First, though, Spence had to help her get the word out to get the help she needed to organize the whole thing.

The meeting only lasted an hour, after which they decided to grab a bite to eat. While they were eating lunch, Lacy told Spence more about what she'd planned and what she hoped the outcome would be.

"Honey, you've done a great job putting this together. Editing these articles is going to be easy for me, because they don't need a lot of work. You're a great writer. Maybe you should think about working here at the newspaper."

"Thanks, sweetie, but my degree is in advertising, although I did have to learn how to write articles. This account is one of my own that I chose, but my boss is excited about it and is giving a lot of his time to help me. I missed you last night," Lacy added.

"I missed you too. I had a meeting to go to, so I picked up a pizza and ate it at home," he told her.

"I had pizza too. We still think alike. Let me know next time you do that so we can eat our pizzas together. But right now, I need to get back to the office."

"Okay. I'll let you see the articles after I've edited them. Bye, Lacy." He hugged her and gave her a kiss before he left.

"Okay? Okay what? 'Okay I'll call you to eat pizza together' or 'okay I'll call you when I get your articles edited'? What's wrong with you, Spence?" Lacy said to herself after he was a block down the street. She was going to have to call him more often and not just wait and see if he was going to show up.

Lacy walked back to her building and opened the door without caring if she got rear-ended again. Although, with the mood she was in right now, she might enjoy it. She enjoyed the hugs and kisses she got from Spence, but she missed their nights together curled up on the couch watching television or listening to music and eating dinner together or going out with their friends. What did she have to do to get all that back? She decided to pay a visit to Stephanie at her office to see if she'd found any information on Lori.

Stephanie was at her desk when Lacy got there. "Steph, what did you find out about Lori?"

"Hello, Lacy. I'm fine, thank you, and how are you today?" Stephanie said sweetly. "Sit down and let me tell you what I dug up on the *nut*. She's from a family of farmers in Pebblestone. She went to school there and graduated the same year as Jay, a year ahead of us. Married an older man named Donald Williams and moved to Iowa, where he lived. He's a congressman and has more money than he needs, and that was what Lori was looking for since she couldn't get the rich boys in her class interested in her. Rumor has it that she was always trying to get Jay's attention, but he wouldn't bite. Seems she went to Iowa with friends after graduation and met Donald, who became smitten with her, and a couple of months later they eloped. A little over two years later they divorced, and she came back home. She got a small settlement, because, as she claims, she was tricked into signing papers he'd had drawn up and asked her to sign without having a lawyer explain what she was signing. She claims to have some interesting stories to tell the newspaper about Donald. Sounds like payback to me. And we know who she picked to write the stories, although I haven't seen anything in the paper yet, have you?"

"No, not yet, but I think she's up to more than a newspaper article about her ex. I think she has a thing for Spence. And I think he's confused and doesn't know what's happening. Or he does and feels guilty," Lacy said, feeling sad.

"Oh, and listen to this: a co-worker who knew her growing up told me she tried to get in touch with Jay, but without success, and that she's been asking questions about you. Now what have you done to make her curious?'

"Me! What does she want to know about me? Do you think she's trying to take Spence away from me?"

"No, that won't happen. Will it?" Stephanie shot back.

"Not while I'm still breathing! I think I'm going to have to pay a visit to her soon," Lacy said.

"Not without me, okay? Promise me, Lacy. I want to be there."

"Yeah, okay, you can be there, because you may have to drag me off of her. All right, I've got to get back to my office to get some more work done. Thanks, best girlfriend."

"When are you going to tell me what you did to get out of that ticket you so well deserved?"

"I have a very sweet smile."

It took her a while to get her mind off of Lori and back on the task at hand. She decided to call Spence and invite him out for dinner. When she called his office, he answered the phone on the first ring. She told him they were going out to eat after work and that she expected him to pick her up at her house. He asked her what time, and they set a time that would work for both of them. She also told him he could pick the restaurant.

Lacy was so excited the rest of the day, and she decided to leave a little early so she could go home and get ready for her evening with her man. "That's right, he's my man, and I'm going to make sure Lori knows that. And that Spence knows it too."

When she got home, Sammy could tell something was going on with Lacy, and he got caught up with all the excitement—he was so excited, in fact, that he ran into the bathroom and leaped into the tub with her. Lacy tried to scold him for it, but all she could do was laugh at him, because his face was covered in bubbles. She'd decided to have a nice warm bubble bath and, apparently, so did Sammy. She had to cut her bath short to towel Sammy off and put him outside to dry. She put on a new outfit that Spence hadn't seen yet. Stephanie had dared her in the store to try it on, because it was more daring than what she was used to wearing. It also was very sexy, and it looked really good on her. She liked the way it made her feel and she hoped Spence would feel the same.

The doorbell rang, and she went to answer it, saying a little prayer that it wasn't Jay. She opened the door.

"Wow! Lacy, you are so sexy, honey. I'll have to take you to a special place," Spence said, pulling Lacy into his arms and placing a big kiss on her lips.

"Are you talking about these old rags?" Lacy replied, turning around in a complete circle. "Thanks, sweetheart. Stephanie talked me into trying in it on, and I decided to buy it so I could wear it for you."

"Remind me to thank Steph."

"Okay, then, are we ready to go?" she asked, petting Sammy on the head and telling him bye.

Spence opened the car door for Lacy and waited for her to get in. Then he climbed behind the wheel and headed for the newest restaurant in town. Had Lacy known that all she had to do was call him and tell him what she wanted, she would've done it weeks ago. He seemed to be in a good mood and more like the Spence she'd grown up loving—her man.

When they arrived at the Bloom 'N' Steak House, Spence got out of the car and opened Lacy's door and they walked inside holding hands. This new restaurant had opened about six months ago and had become very popular, and the food was great. They were seated and given menus, and had ordered their drinks before Spence told Lacy that he had finished her articles and brought them for her to read over and give the okay for publication. Lacy thanked him for working on them. She didn't want to ruin the evening, but she needed answers about Lori.

"So does this mean that you finished what you've been working on for the last few weeks?" She didn't want to use Lori's name.

"Not really. I have to do some investigating about the information I was given before it can be released to the public," he answered, without looking at her.

"Do you think what she told you was lies?" *I hope so.*

"I'm just being cautious and the good reporter that you know I am," he returned, trying not to give away any confidential information.

"Okay, but I do have one more question and then I promise to say only good things about you for the rest of the night. Why is that girl asking questions about me?"

"Is she? I don't know, but I intend to find out, okay? Have you decided what you're going to order for dinner?"

The waitress came back, took their orders, and left. Spence was quiet for a while, and she hoped she hadn't ruined the night for them. The music playing was relaxing, and soon they were having a great time catching up on the time they had been apart. Lacy looked up and saw Stephanie and Andrew sitting at a nearby table, and a waitress was taking their orders.

"Look who's sitting over there with her new boy toy," Lacy said, pointing to Stephanie's table. Spence turned to see who she was talking about.

"Oh, it's Stephanie. Why don't you ask them if they want to join us? I want to thank her for your outfit, remember?" he said, winking at her.

"Okay, I think I will. Thank you, sweetie," she said, smiling very sweetly.

Lacy went over to Stephanie and Andrew and invited them to sit with her and Spence. They agreed and followed Lacy back to her table where Spence was waiting. Stephanie introduced Andrew to Spence before they sat down.

"Hey, Steph, Lacy said you were the one responsible for her new outfit. I want to thank you for your part. She looks amazing and sexy, don't you agree?" Spence said, looking at Lacy.

"Yes she does, and thank you. You call me again if you need me to repeat the good deed," Stephanie said, and she laughed at the look on Lacy's face. Lacy had wrinkled her nose at her.

Dinner arrived—the waitress had made sure that Stephanie and Andrew's dinner was delivered to Lacy and Spence's table. Lacy was enjoying her meal when she happened to look toward the back of the restaurant and saw Jay standing by the kitchen door, with Lori standing in front of him. Jay didn't look happy and Lori seemed upset about something. Then Lori turned around and came walking in the direction of their table. She stopped short when she saw Lacy sitting at the table and looked shocked when she saw Spence sitting next to her. Stephanie was hoping this would be the meeting Lacy had promised her she could be there for. Spence turned to see who Lacy was staring at, and he was shocked to see Lori standing there.

"So this is the reason you couldn't have dinner with me?" Lori said to Spence.

Before Spence could open his mouth to answer, Lacy stood up and said, "Oh, you didn't get the memo. His interviews with you are over, and now all he has to do is make sure what you have told him is the truth before he can put it out for the public to read. But don't leave town too soon, because if he finds something wrong, he may have to inform you that it has to be pulled. And by the way, Spence and I want to know why you've been asking questions about me. What reason could airing your dirty laundry about your past have anything to do with me? And just to set the record straight, Spence is my man, right, honey?"

When she turned to look at Spence, she saw that his face had turned red. "Oh, I'm sorry, Spence, you wanted to tell her that yourself, right?"

Spence looked up at Lori and back at Lacy, but kept quiet.

"So, do I get an answer for why you are asking questions about me?" Lacy looked at Lori for an answer.

Before Lori could say anything, Jay walked up behind her and said, "I thought you were leaving."

Lori turned and looked at Jay and said, "You'll regret this." Then she walked out of the restaurant.

"Thanks, Lacy. You kept your promise, but I was hoping for a little more from Lori," Stephanie said, laughing and hoping to ease the tension at the table.

"Jay, what are you doing here? No, you don't have to answer that, I'm sorry. It's a public restaurant, and you never know who you might run into," Lacy said.

"I came to have a meeting with my dad, and Lori tried to intervene, so I asked her to leave. She's gone now, and I hope you and you friends enjoy your dinner." And, for her ears only, he whispered that he would see her later.

Lacy sat back down and wished she could just disappear. She'd said most of what she'd wanted to say, but she hadn't planned on saying all of that in front of Spence. At least he knew how she felt now.

She finished her dinner while Stephanie told jokes and had the others laughing. She laughed too, but her heart wasn't in it. She was putting on a good show and wondering if Spence was doing the same. Then her mind was wondering if Jay meant he'd see her tonight or some other time. What if Spence wanted to come inside when they got back to her house? What if Jay dropped by? Why was all this happening? *What did Spence just ask me?* Oh, he asked if she was ready to go. She told him she was, and they said goodbye to the other couple, and Spence drove her home.

When they reached her house Spence turned to her and said, "I'm sorry that you got upset. I didn't know Lori and Jay would be there. And you're right about it being a public place and anyone can be there. But I still enjoyed dinner with our friends and being there with you. I really like Andrew and hope Stephanie has finally found Mr. Right."

"Are you trying to cheer me up?" Lacy asked, starting to relax.

"Is it working?" he asked.

"Yes. You always know how to make me feel all better. And you always could." *That's why you're my man, and don't you ever forget that.* "Are you coming in?" Lacy asked, holding her breath.

"No, I have to go see Mitch before I go home, but I'll see you later, my sexy Lacy." Then he pulled her into his arms and kissed her very tenderly and told her good night. He waited until she had gone into the house and closed the door before pulling out of her driveway.

As she was letting Sammy out the back door, she heard the doorbell ring. So Jay did come by. She opened the door and said, "So you couldn't stay away." There stood Spence.

"Well, as much as I love your sexy outfit and the way you look in it, I still have to go to see Mitch. Here, I forgot to give you the proofs. Love you lots." He handed her a big folder and gave her another kiss and left.

She let Sammy back in and headed to the kitchen. It was too early to go to bed, so she thought she'd make herself a cup of tea. The doorbell rang again. What did he forget now? She opened the door and said, "You back for another kiss?"

Jay reached out and pulled her into his arms and kissed her, making her heart race. The butterflies were tickling the inside of her tummy as her arms went up and around his neck, and they weren't there to help hold her up, although it did help, since her knees went weak. To say she wasn't enjoying this would be lying, but should she be enjoying it this much? That was the real question. *Oh, well, just enjoy it until it ends,* she thought, and that's just what she did.

Finally coming up for air, Jay said, "I'm so glad you were waiting for me to kiss you again. It's all I've been thinking about since I saw you this evening with your friends. Sorry Lori tried to ruin your dinner. But I can't stay, my sweet Rose. I've been on the go all day and need to go home. Thank you for the kiss. I can't wait for the next one. Sweetheart, if you play your cards right, you may get your bloom. Good night, honey." And she watched as he walked to his car and drove away.

Chapter 9

Lacy was sitting at her desk trying to finish an assignment that she had been given that morning but she was having trouble keeping her mind on what she was doing. She'd been very confused and very excited at the same time after Jay left. She had put on her nightgown, curled up on her bed with Sammy next to her and the papers Spence had given her to look over, and read through them. He'd done a great job on them. They were ready to be published. Then came the hard part for her: trying to sleep without thinking about Jay.

***

He'd already called her this morning to say he'd enjoyed the kiss last night and wished her a great day. She finally realized that, in his mind, he was having a romantic relationship with her, and she was shocked at herself for letting it get this far before realizing it. Or maybe she did realize it, but she was enjoying his attention so much that she was letting it go on—and on and on. She missed Spence so much and all the attention she had been used to getting from him. Then Jay came crashing into her life, giving her all his attention every day. And not one day had passed that he hadn't called her or came by to see her. "Steph was right when she implied that I have two boy toys!" Lacy said out loud. "Lucky me. But what am I going to do about it?"

Lacy finished her assignment and picked up her phone. She called Spence to let him know that she was pleased with his work and to send it to the printer. She also told him she enjoyed having dinner with him and that she loved him. Then she was back to work. Later that morning, she thought about their conversation and realized that he hadn't told her he loved her too. This was a first for Spence. This thought frightened her, and she knew she needed to talk to her best friend about it. She called Stephanie and asked her to go to the park with her on their lunch break. Stephanie knew right away that something wasn't right with Lacy.

"Okay, Lacy, what's bothering you today?" Stephanie asked after they sat down on a bench to eat their lunch.

"I think I'm having a relationship with Jay—at least *he* thinks so—and Spence didn't tell me he loved me this morning when I told him I loved him. He always tells me that," Lacy said with tears in her eyes.

"Maybe he was busy and had something else on his mind," Stephanie returned.

"Yeah, something like *Lori*?" Lacy shot back. "He was awfully quiet when I was letting her have it last night, and his face was a little red. Did I embarrass him?"

"I don't know, but I'm really proud of the way you let her know he was your man. Oh, maybe he did get embarrassed. But that should've made him happy. Did he say anything to you when you got home?"

"He said he was sorry Lori and Jay showed up, that I was right about the fact that anyone could be there, that he enjoyed you and Andrew having dinner with us, that he liked Andrew, and hoped that you had found your Mr. Right. Then he kissed me goodbye, said he loved me, and said he was going to go see Mitch."

"Aw, that was nice of him. So he left you at home alone?" she asked.

"But he came right back, because he forgot to give me the edited copy of the article for the project I'm working on. He's getting it published for me. Then he kissed me and left again. Then the doorbell rang again, and I opened the door and asked if he was back for another kiss."

"What did he say?"

"He didn't say anything because it wasn't him."

"Who was it?"

"Jay!"

"What did he say?"

"He didn't say anything. But I thought it was Spence again, and when I said 'You back for another kiss?' he grabbed me and kissed me until my toes curled, butterflies tickled my tummy, and I think my right foot lifted off the ground. Then he thanked me for the kiss, said he couldn't wait until the next one, and said something I didn't understand. Then he said he just wanted to see me, but that he couldn't stay. Then he left," Lacy explained.

"What did he say to you that you didn't understand?" Stephanie asked, getting excited.

"He said if I played my cards right I may get my bloom."

"What did that he mean by that?"

"I don't know, but don't you agree that he thinks we're having a relationship?" Lacy asked.

"Girlfriend, you are in a relationship with him, whether you believe it or not. And you're worried because Spence forgot to tell you he loves you? I think you have a much bigger problem to worry about. Did you tell Jay that Spence was your man?"

"No."

"Lacy Rose, why not?"

"I'm waiting for the right time. He comes and goes so fast I don't have a chance to say anything," Lacy said, trying to explain.

"You're starting to like Jay, aren't you? I know you like his kisses because of the look on your face when you describe the way he makes you feel when he's kissing you. Does Spence have competition?"

"I don't think so. I love Spence. He's my man and has been forever. I have a big problem, don't I? Help me, Stephanie."

"I'm here for you, but you have to decide who you really love and who you want to be with. And you'd better do it soon, because there's going to be a lot of hurt for someone by your decision," Stephanie explained. "There is one thing I wanted to ask you. Did Spence explain to you why Lori asked him if having dinner with you was the reason he couldn't have dinner with her? And why would she tell Jay that he'd regret what he did?"

"No, I forgot that she said all that. But I'll ask both of them the next time I talk to them. We better get back to work now," Lacy said, standing up.

When Lacy got back to her office, she decided to get one question answered right away. She picked up her phone and called Spence. He answered his phone, and she said, "Hi, Spence. I just called to say thanks for dinner last night. I really enjoyed being with you and our friends. I do have one question, though. What did Lori mean when she asked you if having dinner with me was the reason you couldn't have dinner with her?"

"She'd stopped by my office that morning to invite me to have dinner with her, and I told her I had other plans. Then you called and told me I was taking you to dinner. But the funny thing about that was I was reaching for my phone to call you to ask you out for dinner, but you beat me to it. You always could read my mind. I told her I had other plans, and thanks to you she found out that I wasn't telling a lie. I had a good time too. Oh, by the way, your article went to print and will be coming out in the morning paper. Sorry, honey, my boss just walked in and I need to go. See you later," Spence said.

"Okay, sweetheart. See you later." *Good answer, Spence.*

Now she had to wait for Jay to call or drop by, and she'd ask him what Lori meant when she told him he'd regret what he did. Lacy wondered why Lori hadn't told *her* that she was going to regret what *she'd* done. *I'm not afraid of her*, she thought.

Lacy finished her assignment quickly so she could spend time on the upcoming events she had planned. She'd received so many requests from people in all the surrounding towns to pick a pet from a shelter and to advertise to help find it a home. Some had even asked if they could keep the pets with them so everyone could see them in person. She gave the requests to Stacy, who was working with all the shelters to make sure all those interested could pick out the animal they wanted to help. She also made sure they knew how to care for the animal and that they knew the procedure that had to be followed for adopting that pet.

Lacy was lost in her work when she heard a knock on her door. She looked up in time to see Jay walk in. "Lacy, my sweet Rose, how are you today? Just dropped by to tell you I have to go out of town for a couple of days, and I'm going to miss you."

"And you're telling me this, because—"

"Because I'm really going to miss you," Jay said, interrupting Lacy before could finish what she was saying. "Are you going to miss me too?"

"Yes! Sure." *Like a thorn in my side.* "I have one question for you. What did Lori mean when she said you were going to regret what you'd done?" It was really none of her business, but she hoped he'd explain it to her anyway.

"Lori is a drama queen and a spoiled brat. All she ever wanted was to find a rich man to marry so she'd have lots of money to spend. In high school she always tried to get the boys from wealthy families to take her out. No one was interested, including me. The more I turned her down the more she tried. Then she ran off and got married. But she came back divorced with a small bank account. Now she's decided to take up where she left off, and I told her I hadn't been interested in her in the past and I'm still not interested. I think it made her angry, but she needed to be told."

"So now you're going to regret it. I think I made her list of people who are going to regret it. I kind of feel sorry for her, but not too much," Lacy said, shaking her head.

"Well, I've got to go now, but you'll hear from me." Jay kissed her quickly and left before Lacy had a chance to have the talk she needed to have with him. But maybe it was for the best, because she needed time to think about what she wanted to say to let him down easy . . . if there was an easy way.

When the phone rang, Lacy answered it. She was surprised to hear from WWSP, the local news station that covered all the surrounding counties. WWSP News had a segment every day called "Help Find Forever Homes," a program where shelter pets were brought to the station to be seen on air to help them get adopted. It also was good advertising for the shelters in the area.

WWSP News had heard about her shelter project and hoped the station could get involved. Lacy was so excited that she asked her boss to come to her office so he could be a part of the conversation. He was impressed with the way everything was coming together for the big event and was proud of Lacy for all the extra time she'd put in to bring it altogether. She'd managed to reach out to all the people in the surrounding communities and inform them about the problem of increasing numbers of homeless or abandoned dogs and cats, or other types of pets, and the problems that the shelters were facing to find funding to feed and care for all of the animals. Some shelters needed more space to house them, but most of all, they needed forever homes.

Lacy had worked hard all week and was glad it was Friday, which usually meant that she and Spence would go out and celebrate the fact that they'd made it to the weekend, but since he didn't say anything about it when she talked to him earlier, and he had quit coming by after work, she decided she wasn't going to wait for him to call her or drop by. When she got home she called Grandma Lily Rose and told her that Sammy and she were coming to stay for the weekend. Then she got their things together, packed up the car, and left.

Lily Rose was happy to see Lacy and Sammy, who'd grown so much. After all the hugs from her grandparents and a delicious home-cooked dinner, Lily sat down with Lacy to catch up on what had happened since her granddaughter's last visit. They'd kept in touch over the phone, but had short conversations because Lacy had been so busy. But now she wanted to have a heart-to-heart with her. She knew why Lacy looked tired, but Lily Rose could tell that something else was bothering her. "Okay, kid, tell your old grandma what's bothering you."

"Oh, Grandma, you always know when I'm sad or confused or . . . I don't know what I'm doing wrong," Lacy confessed.

"So hit me with it, and no holding back," Lily Rose returned.

Lacy started with the accident, the day Jay came crashing into her life. She told her about introducing Spence to Jay as her friend. "But, Grandma, he *is* a friend, a *boy*friend. He's never asked me to marry him, so he's not really my fiancé. But I should've said boyfriend. Jay got the wrong idea, and Spence got mad."

Then Lacy told her about seeing Spence and Lori in the park together after he'd said he was working on an article, which hadn't been published so far, and how she'd gotten mad at him so she had had dinner with Jay. Thirty minutes later, Lily Rose had heard everything and had kept quiet, not interrupting her, so Lacy could say what she needed to say. Lacy wanted to clear her head—and her heart—and had shed a few tears along the way. Her grandma always kept tissues close by and gave Lacy one when needed.

"I decided to take a break this weekend so I could figure out what I'm doing wrong and to get your advice. Jay's out of town for a few days, and when I spoke to Spence this morning, he didn't say anything about getting together tonight, and he's quit coming over in the evening after work unless I call and tell him he's coming over," Lacy said. "Oh, and Stephanie told me I have to pick one to love and break the other's heart."

"So she told you that you have to decide who you love and want to spend the rest of your life with and who can only be your friend, if his heart doesn't get broken," Lily Rose replied.

"Yeah, that's what she meant. How did I get into this mess? I love Spence and have forever and always will, but Jay wrecked my car and is trying to wreck my life. I don't know how to stop him, and I don't know if I want to stop him, Grandma. He's so cute and so sexy. His kisses make my heart skip a beat, and he just kisses me without permission and then leaves. He makes me laugh and calls me every day. He thinks we have a relationship, which Steph says we do, unless I tell him otherwise. But I never get the right moment to talk with him about it. And I get less time with Spence. Am I just making excuses?" Lacy asked.

"Well, I think you really love Spence, but you've spent over half of your life with him, and you've become comfortable with him. Like you said, he hasn't been in a hurry to ask you to marry him. Most men would break a leg to ask their girl to get married, especially if another man came crashing into her life. I think Spence loves you too, which is why he got mad at being introduced as your friend. But maybe that incident has made him do some thinking, and with Lori flirting with him to make Jay jealous, he has a reason to be confused as well.

"It seems like Lori is also trying to make you mad, because Jay made it clear that he wants to be with you. Jay's not doing anything wrong, because he doesn't know that you and Spence are a couple, and he *did* tell Lori he wasn't interested in her. So, it's up to you to decide what you want—or should I say *who* you want. You and Spence need to talk about what's been happening and how you both feel about it. And you need to be honest with each other. Then each of you can decide what you want and how to move forward. Jay has been courting you because he's developed feelings for you and even maybe loves you. You enjoy being with Jay, because a new relationship is always exciting, and he *is* quite a catch. So it's up to you to figure out what you want before Spence gives up and Jay does too. Does that help you at all?"

"Fancy footwork! How did you figure all that out so quickly?" asked Lacy.

"I went through a similar situation with Gramps."

"You did?"

"No, honey, I was just kidding. I watch a lot of romance movies and read books. You'd be surprised at what you can learn," Lily Rose said, laughing at the expression on her granddaughter's face.

"Did you ever think about being a couples' counsellor? All this time Lori has been trying to make me jealous with Spence? Poor Spence. Should I tell him that?"

"No to the first question, and no to the second question—didn't that ever cross your mind? And, for the third question, you need to tell him what Lori has been up to so he can decide what he wants to do about it."

"I'm so glad I came here this weekend and we had this talk. You have helped me so much, and I do feel better. I've been so busy with work and all this other stuff that I don't have time to think. It's like being in a love triangle, except it's a love square. Lori wants Jay, Jay wants me, I want Spence, and Spence is torn between Lori and me. Not to leave out that I'm a little confused about what I want from Jay. Who knew?" Lacy exclaimed.

"Sounds like a good romance novel to me," laughed Lacy Rose.

"You're right again, Grandma, but you already knew that. I hope you and Gramps don't mind if Sammy and I go to the barn. I'm very tired. Oh, and before I forget to tell you, WWSP News wants to get involved with the project I've been working on. You may see me on television soon," Lacy bragged.

"Oh, that's wonderful!" she said, giving Lacy a big hug. "You go ahead to the barn. We certainly don't mind, and we'll see you at breakfast in the morning. Good night, dear," she said, hugging Lacy and patting Sammy on the head.

Lacy was very tired, but she felt at peace with all the confusion she was going through. Lily Rose had summed up and explained everything very quickly for her. "Way to go, Lily Rose! Let's go, boy," she said to Sammy, who was wagging his tail, waiting to head up the stairs.

After enjoying a big breakfast with her grandparents the next morning, Lacy's phone rang as she stood in the yard watching the dogs play together. She hadn't told anyone she going to the farm for the weekend and was surprised her cell phone was working, since the farm wasn't close to any towers.

"Hello," Lacy said, answering her phone.

"Lacy, are you okay? I've been calling you for over an hour now. I also tried your home phone," Jay asked, sounding worried.

"Yes, Jay, I'm fine. I decided last night to stay with my grandparents for the weekend," she returned. "You're lucky my phone is working. I'll have to mark this spot in the yard so I'll know where to stand when I want to use it."

"Thank goodness. I'm relieved to hear you're all right. Yesterday Lori found out that I was going out of town. After she learned that I had left, she had someone watch you, and when you left last night and didn't come home, she thought you were with me. This morning she managed to find out where I was staying and called to tell me what she'd done. She was very upset. She asked if you were with me, and I told her no, but that it wasn't any of her business if you were, which made her more angry, and she hung up. I'm glad you're on the farm," Jay explained.

"Crazy critter! What's her problem? Wait till I see her again," Lacy said, outraged.

"No, Lacy. I want you to promise me you'll stay away from her. I'll take care of her, and when I'm done with her, she won't bother you or me again, and I think you need to warn Spence about her. I've got to go now. See you when I get home, Rose Petal." He hung up after Lacy promised to let him handle it.

Lily Rose overheard the conversation and knew Lacy was very angry with what Lori had done. She couldn't blame her, but she tried her best to calm Lacy down and made her promise to let Jay handle it. Lacy promised she would, and they both went to work in the garden. Sammy was already playing with Oscar.

The rest of the weekend flew by. It was delightfully relaxing and enjoyable, and Lacy hated to go back home and to the rat race she was running, but she didn't have any choice. She packed up and, after attending church with her grandparents, went back home.

Lacy couldn't help herself from glancing around the street when she got home. She spotted a man sitting in a car that she hadn't seen on her street before and began to feel angry again. The car was parked in the grass across the street two houses away, so she and Sammy walked down to it.

"Do you care to explain why you are sitting in your car looking at my house?" Lacy asked with irritation in her voice.

"Excuse me? I'm waiting to pick up my daughter who spent the night with her friend." He pointed to his daughter walking toward the car.

"I'm so sorry . . . I . . . someone's been watching me, but it's not you. Have a great day," she said, turning and running back to her house, with Sammy behind her. She could feel her face turning red. She could hear laughter as she ran, and was glad to know she hadn't made another enemy.

After Lacy let Sammy out the back, she listened to her messages. There were three from Jay, one from Stephanie, and one from Spence. Spence was calling to tell her that he'd be tied up for the weekend because he'd be out of town investigating an article he was working on. So she called Stephanie to see what she'd planned for the rest of the day, but she got her voicemail. She was hanging up when she heard the doorbell ring and in walked Stephanie.

"How were Lily Rose and Robert?" Stephanie asked before Lacy could say hello.

"How'd you know I was there?" Lacy asked her.

"Because when you don't answer your cell phone for two days, it means you're out on the farm or mad, and I couldn't remember saying anything to make you mad," she returned.

"You're right as always. I just needed to get away. I had a good talk with Grandma, and she helped me see what's going on with my life. She said Lori is going after Spence to make Jay jealous and to make me jealous because she thinks I'm after Jay. Did you know that?" Lacy explained.

"Yeah, I knew. Did you find out why Lori said what she said to Spence at dinner?"

"Yes. Spence said she'd called and asked him out to dinner, but he'd told her he had other plans for dinner. Then he said that he was just about to call me and ask me to dinner when I called him. Then I asked Jay what Lori meant when she told him that he was going to regret what he'd done, and he said he'd told her he hadn't been interested in her in the past and he isn't now," Lacy answered.

"Bet that made her mad."

"You got that right. Listen to this: Jay had to go out of town, and he called me this morning to make sure I was okay, because he had trouble trying to reach me. It seems Lori found out that he was going out of town, so she had someone watching me. When I didn't come home Friday night, she thought I was with Jay. She managed to find out where Jay was staying and called him and asked if I was with him. That's when she told him she was having me watched," Lacy explained.

"Was he mad?" asked Stephanie.

"Yes, and so was I. But he made me promise to let him take care of her. Then when I got home, I saw a car sitting down the street and went down and asked the man in the car why he was watching me. It seems he was only waiting for his daughter, who'd spent the night with her friend. I was so embarrassed. I tried to explain that I was being watched, told him I was sorry, and ran back to my house while he sat laughing at me. I felt like a big dope. Why don't I think before I leap?" Lacy asked, feeling the heat in her face again.

"That's my best friend, Dopey. Let's go take your puppy to the park for lunch." Then they both had a good laugh together.

Chapter 10

Lacy called Spence after she got back home and Stephanie had left, but he didn't answer his phone. She remembered what Lily Rose had said about not waiting too long to have a talk with Spence, because he may give up on her. She hoped that wasn't the case. But she decided to try not to worry, because she had other things she needed to get done. Jay had called after she got home to make sure she was safe. He said he'd had a talk with Lori and told her what he was going to do if she didn't stay away.

***

Lacy was in her office working on her assigned project for the day when her boss, Jason, came in. He told her that WWSP had contacted him that morning and was sending someone in after lunch to speak to them about plans for an appearance on the show. He also asked her to call Stacy, because they wanted to talk with her also. He then told her how very proud he was of the way she'd taken on the project and turned it into such a huge event, and hoped she'd be able to reach out to a large number of people to get them involved. Lacy thanked him and was feeling pleased with all of his praise. Maybe she wasn't such a dope after all.

For lunch, Lacy decided to run down to the deli on the first floor and grab something to eat so she wouldn't be late for the meeting. She had called to tell her Stacy about the meeting, and Stacy had been very excited that she'd been invited to attend the meeting and especially for all the coverage the shelters would get. She also informed Lacy that there'd been a large number of adoptions already, and that Facebook was being flooded with all of the advertising. There was one ad encouraging the public to report stray animals to help the shelters round them up and bring them in. They were being told not to touch the animals unless they were sure the animals were safe. Also, families no longer able to care for their pets were encouraged to bring them to the shelter. One of the shelters was planning a beauty show, and they would dress up the available pets and walk them down a runway as their history was read aloud. People interested in the pet could fill out the adoption paperwork right there and, if approved, could take the pet home.

While Lacy was paying for her lunch, she saw Lori walking past the deli. Her first instinct was to go after her and give her a piece of her mind, but she saw Jay stop in front of her.

"Worthless worm!" Lacy whispered to herself. Some words were exchanged between the two, and they walked off together. Lacy was shocked and then felt angry. She wasn't sure if she was angry at Lori or at Jay. Maybe she should be angry at both of them, and she might as well be angry at Spence also. But she couldn't waste any more time standing here, so she headed back up to her office to eat her lunch and calm down.

Stephanie was just coming in from lunch and rode the elevator up with Lacy. One look at Lacy and Stephanie knew she was upset about something.

"Okay, Lacy Rose, tell me before you explode."

Lacy told her what she'd just seen and that she was very angry and upset. "Jay told me he'd talked to Lori and told her what would happen if she didn't stay away, and then she meets with him today where I work. Yesterday Spence didn't answer his phone when I called him, and he hasn't called me today. Jay calls me every day, but he hasn't called me today either. Grandma told me that if I didn't talk to Spence soon, he might give up on me, and Jay may have just given up on me also. It's all Lori's fault for spreading lies about me. Oh, Stephanie, I had two boy toys, and now I don't have any."

Stephanie couldn't help laughing at Lacy. "I'm sorry. Did you hear what you just said? Don't get your gray matter in a bunch. Wait until you talk to them. I'm sure they'll tell you what's going on, and if it's something that makes you angry, then we can go out and find another boy toy, okay?" Stephanie replied.

"I guess I'm thinking too much again. Sorry for being a drama queen. But maybe I'll take you up on finding another man, because the two I have are making me crazy," Lacy said, laughing.

"You sure that's just acting?" asked Stephanie.

The meeting with Joe Sliver, a reporter for WWSP News, went very smoothly. After the introductions were made, Joe explained to Lacy, Jason, and Stacy that the news station would like to record two interviews with them. One interview would air next week, and one would air two days before the big event scheduled to be held at the Pebblestone County Fair Grounds. They'd run both interviews on the morning and afternoon shows the day before the event, to make sure more people would see the ads, and they would run them again on the morning of the event. Before Joe left, he set up a time that would work for all three of them to be there for both interviews.

When she got back to her office, Lacy called Spence, and this time he answered his phone. "Hi, Spence. How did your trip go? Sorry I missed your call, but I needed a break and went to the farm for the weekend."

"The trip was worth it. I went to find out for myself what was true and what was false on all the information that Lori was feeding me. Most of it was false, and I'm glad I didn't run the article before I found this out, because I may have found myself AND the newspaper with a lawsuit on our hands. I tried to call you several times and gave up. I forgot that your cell phone doesn't work on the farm, but I'm glad you called," Spence told her.

"I'm glad you answered this time, but it sounds like you needed a weekend away also. I guess by now you've found out that Lori has been playing us both. She wants Jay, but he doesn't want to have anything to do with her, and she thinks he wants me, so she's trying to go after you to get back at me and make him jealous. Too bad she couldn't keep her husband," Lacy blurted out.

"Is that right? What I found out is that her husband didn't have much time for her because of his responsibilities, so she found 'other ways' to amuse herself, which I cannot disclose. When he filed for divorce, she found out what was on the papers she signed and became enraged, so she was trying to ruin him with these lies, which is why I went to find out what was true and what was false. Needless to say, the article is being killed. What makes you think she's after me?" he asked, sounding frustrated.

"Well, she found out that Jay went out of town for the weekend, and she was having someone watch my house. When that person told her I'd left and hadn't come back home, and after finding out where Jay was staying, she called him the next day. She told him what she'd done and asked if I was with him. So he called me to warn me to stay away from her and that he'd take care of her. Then he told me to warn you about her," Lacy explained.

"Oh, that was nice of him to think about keeping your 'friend' safe from Lori," he said sweetly.

"Spence, I told you I was sorry for saying that. I was frustrated, because I didn't know what to say to him when he said he was staying. You *are* my friend—my *boy*friend. You're not my fiancé, because you've never asked me to marry you—I'm sorry, Spence, I didn't mean to say that. I've been so confused because you quit calling and coming around and Lori seems to get more of your attention than I do. I think it's time for me to shut up and get back to work. Glad you had a safe trip. Love you. Goodbye," she said, and she quickly hung up the phone. *I'm back to being a dope again.*

Lacy called Lily Rose and told her about the conversation she'd just had with Spence. Her grandmother told her she was sorry it had gone so badly and maybe she should've talked to him at her house or invited him out for dinner first, but maybe he'd think about what she'd said now that he knew a little about how she felt. What her grandmother said helped Lacy calm down and finish the work on her desk.

Lacy called Stephanie before she left her office and told her what happened. "I guess I've lost Spence. I just hope he finds out what Lori's up to before it's too late. Do you want to go out for dinner and help me find someone to replace him?" Lacy asked.

"Yes, I do. I'm tired of taking dinners to Lowe's and eating in a break room or in my car. I really like Andrew a lot, but I want someone who can spend time with me. I'll come to your office and we can decide where to go."

Lacy and Stephanie sat at a table at Bloom 'N' Steak House staring at each other across the table.

"Stephanie, why don't you start, because you've been listening to me for the past few weeks now?"

"Oh, Lacy. I really like Andrew, but he works two jobs, and we never get to spend time together. I know he's trying to pay off his student loans, and he's starting his new business, which I think is great, but he has no time to date. I feel so selfish when I try to tell him that it's hard for me to only see him when I take lunch to him sometimes, or for when he gets a day off, which only happens about twice a month. I don't want to quit seeing him, but I don't like staying home and not going out with him. So we decided to remain friends for now and see what happens when he gets more time off," she explained.

"I'm so sorry, Steph. I'm in the same boat as you. Since my parents' party, I've only gone out once with Spence—the night you joined us for dinner—and I had to call and tell him he was taking me out. Jay stops by my office to say hello when he has a meeting in our building and sometimes stops by my house to give me kisses, then he leaves. I only went out with him that night I got hit by the football. You made that happen. Oh, and that time they both took me out for pizza. Things haven't been the same since Jay accidently came into my life, with Lori right behind him," Lacy said sadly.

"You forgot Spence came by one evening when I was there," Stephanie reminded her.

"Yeah, and he left soon after you left. What's happened to us, girlfriend? I have two guys, and I find myself all alone. What do we have to do to get a guy to take us out on a date?"

"Hello, there. Excuse me, ladies, but my friend and I have been trying to figure out where we've seen you two before," a nice looking young man said, pointing to his friend sitting at a nearby table. "Did you attend school in Stoneybrooke?"

Both women glanced up to see a nice looking young man standing by their table, and they both turned their heads at the same time to look at the other nice looking man sitting at a table. Then they looked back at each other and smiled.

"Yes, we did, and graduated five years ago. We both graduated from university last year," Lacy answered, and then flashed her sweet smile. "And what year did you and your friend graduate?"

"We were in the class ahead of you," he explained, waving his hand at his friend to come join them. "We were on the football team."

"I remember you. You're Mark Williams and that's Scott Woods," Stephanie said when the other man reached their table. "You two led our team to victory in the playoffs. Long time no see. Where have you guys been?"

"You're Stephanie, and she's Lacy, right? I told you we knew them, Scott. How could we forget the prettiest cheerleaders on the squad?" Mark said to Scott. Then, turning to the women, he said,

"We both got scholarships to attend a college in California and stayed there for a while. We got back home a couple of months ago."

"Why don't you join me and Stephanie for dinner, so we can get caught up on what's been happening since we last cheered for you?" Lacy asked.

"We'd love to, Lacy. Right, Mark?" Scott replied, sitting down next to Stephanie.

"That's right, we'd love to," Mark said, and he sat down in the remaining chair.

For the next hour the conversation flowed easily among them, and they got caught up on each other's lives up to the present. The boys had decided to stay in California after graduation so they found jobs and an apartment to share, but they missed their families and friends back home. It was time to come home and start finding jobs and maybe settle down. Mark's father was a doctor, and Scott's dad was a dentist. But they both had become lawyers and might get into government work. Mark had been in a relationship, but decided it was time to take a break before coming home, while Scott had tried to keep his relationship going, but the miles between them made it impossible, and it ended. So they both were single.

After dinner, Lacy invited everyone back to her house. She knew Sammy would need attention, and no one seemed eager for the evening to end, so going back to her house made everyone happy. Stephanie followed Lacy, and the guys followed her in Mark's car. Since no one had dessert at the restaurant, Lacy offered them coffee with some cookies she'd made. While they were enjoying their treats Lacy's phone rang so she excused herself to answer it. It was Jay calling to tell her he'd missed her.

"Well, I guess that was because you're too busy with Lori. I saw her while I was in the deli getting lunch. I also saw you come up to her, and then you left together," she said in a sweet voice.

"Are we about to have our first fight? Yes, that all happened, but I walked her to the front door where I handed her a restraining order to stay away from my beautiful Rose Petal. I'm sorry you had to see that, and sorry even more that you got upset. Let me make it up to you and take you out to dinner tomorrow night," Jay said, sounding sincere.

"I'm not really mad at you, just confused and a little mad at Lori. I'm glad you called, because I did miss hearing from you. Listen, my friend Steph is here with some other friends, and I need to go. See you tomorrow. Good night, Jay," she said, and she hung up.

Stephanie came into the kitchen to get more coffee for the guys and saw Lacy smiling while shaking her head. "What's up? Did you just win the lottery?"

"That was Jay calling, because he missed me today and told me he'd been busy. I let him know that I saw him with Lori. He said he'd walked her to the door where he gave her a restraining order and told her to stay away from me. Then he asked me out for dinner tomorrow. Do you realize that all it took for us to get a date was for me to say 'What do we have to do to get a guy to take us out on a date?' Then two gorgeous guys show up at our table to share dinner with us, and Jay calls to ask me out to dinner. Wow! If I'd known that, we'd have had dates every day," Lacy exclaimed.

"Who knew you had such powers? We better get back to the guys before they get bored and leave. Oh, by the way, I think Mark is real cute, okay?" Stephanie said with a wink.

***

Lacy was getting ready for bed when her phone rang. Picking it up without looking to see who was calling, she said hello and was surprised to hear Spence return her greeting.

"Hi, Spence. Are you at home?" she asked.

"Yes I am. I picked up a pizza earlier and stopped by your house, but you were having a party that I wasn't invited to," he replied, sounding hurt.

"Why didn't come in? You know you're always invited, or did you forget? It wasn't really a party. I asked Steph to go out dinner with me, since we don't have boyfriends who ask us out anymore, and we ran into Mark Williams and Scott Woods. They were on the football team and a year ahead of us. You remember them, don't you? They just got back home from California. They joined us for dinner, and we asked them to come by my house to catch up on what's been happening. You should have come in and joined us. I think Stephanie likes Mark," Lacy explained.

"What happened to Andrew?"

"He doesn't have enough time to date right now. That sounds a little familiar, doesn't it? He's starting a business and working at Lowe's. So they decided to take a break and see what happens later. Was your pizza good?" Lacy had to ask.

"Yes, it was good, and hot, just the way you like it. I guess I should've called you first before I came by."

"Or you could have eaten your pizza with Lori. Oh, wait a minute, I saw her with Jay earlier, sorry."

"Is that why you think I came to your house?" he said, sounding shocked.

"I thought you came to my house because you loved me and wanted to be with me, but the last few months have made me think that you want to be with someone other than me. I know we've both been busy, but we've never let it come between us before. I know something has changed between us, because when you've been confused before, you could always talk it over with me. I think it's time to come clean with each other, but not tonight and not over the phone. I love you, Spence, and always will, but if you don't feel the same, I'll be hurt, but I will survive. Good night, Spence, and thanks for bringing me a pizza." Lacy hung up before Spence could break her heart.

***

It was Saturday, and Lacy was headed to the Pebblestone County Fair Grounds across the street for the first interview by WWSP News. The grounds were crowded with people setting up booths for all the events to take place for the animal shelters. This event had grown so large that it was going to be held for two days. There would be entertainment by local bands and some well-known names. Booths were being set up for games, arts and crafts, and food. A portion of the money made would be donated for the cause. Then there was going to be a fashion show of adoptable pets. The event was growing bigger every day.

Lacy had worked hard getting advertisements to all the outlets, like the newspapers, Facebook, Twitter, and even some billboards along the highways. The event also received much attention from the business community and spread by word of mouth. Everyone was talking about attending and inviting friends and families who didn't live in the area. It was turning out to be a huge affair, and Lacy hoped it would be successful. Stacy told her they wanted Sammy to be the poster dog for this occasion, and he would ride the car leading the parade that opened the event. "Oh, and of course, you will be honored and ride in the same car with Sammy," Stacy informed her.

After the filming was over—and it had gone very well—Spence approached and told Lacy how proud he was of her. She wondered how he knew she was going to be there, and he explained that he'd been asked to cover the event from beginning to end. Then he asked her to have lunch with him, and they went to one of their favorite fast-food restaurants to eat lunch. While eating, they caught up on what was going on with their jobs. Then Spence finally decided it was time to talk about what was causing so much trouble between them.

"Lacy, I'm so sorry about the past few months. I was angry when you told Jay that I was your friend, but until you explained to me the way you felt, it made me realize that I was only a friend, a boyfriend. I guess I got so caught up with my position on the newspaper and trying to make a name for myself that I neglected our relationship. Then Lori came to me with what I thought would was a huge story, one that would get everyone's attention, which turned out to be a bust. When I first met Lori, I felt sorry for her because she seemed depressed, needy, and so vulnerable. Her husband had promised her a wonderful life, but he left her alone while he continued with his own. She made a few mistakes, and he threw her out with a small settlement. She was hurt and wanted revenge. I felt sorry for her at first and wanted to help her feel better, but I started feeling more than pity. I felt close to her, and the more I was with her the more I felt myself being drawn in. She told me she was falling in love with me, and I thought I felt the same, but I also felt ashamed because I loved you too. Then I started to see through her little act. You confirmed it when you said that she wanted Jay and was using me to get at you. I'm sorry she was stalking you. I've been a fool."

"I don't know what to say except I wish that you'd told me what was happening sooner. I've been very confused. I tried to give you a chance to tell me, but I think I made it worse. I've been very busy myself but that's no excuse. I should have made it clear to Jay that you and I were a couple, but I never got a chance. I'm glad you decided to finally explain everything," Lacy returned.

"Well, I've enjoyed having lunch with you, but I have to go. I have a meeting with Lori at my office," Spence said, getting up from the table and bending over to kiss her cheek before going out the door without an explanation.

"Burning britches, you've got to be kidding me!" she said out loud. "Does that witch have a spell over him?"

Lacy got up slowly and walked to the door to go home, feeling like she'd won a prize and then lost it. Was that his way of telling her it was over between them? "Sorry for everything and sorry for the way Lori has treated you, but excuse me while I go see her."

Chapter 11

Lacy was getting ready for dinner with Jay, but she felt depressed after Spence had left, and her heart just wasn't in it. But she was determined to enjoy herself. *Life is too short to be depressed about something that you can't change*, she thought to herself. Maybe Jay was right when he told her that if she played her cards right she may get her bloom, whatever that meant. She didn't even know she had cards to play, but she was going to play them anyway.

Jay was on time to pick her up. He didn't tell her where he was taking her to dinner, so she decided to wear something that made her look and feel sexy. When she opened the door, Jay couldn't stop his eyes from traveling all the way down her slim but shapely body to her feet in high heels and back up to her face, on which she had applied just enough make-up to bring out her natural beauty.

"Lacy, I always thought you were a beautiful young woman, but you really *are* a beautiful young woman! And I'm the luckiest man in Pebblestone tonight." Then he took her in his arms and kissed her.

When he let her go, she was panting and trying to catch her breath, her heart was skipping beats, butterflies were doing flip flops in her tummy, and her hands shook a little. She didn't really know what to say. "Oh. Thank you. You're beautiful too. I mean . . . handsome. I mean, looking good yourself." *Just shut up, Lacy.*

"Are you ready to go?" Jay asked, laughing.

Her response was to close the door and let Jay lead her to his car, where he helped her in. They drove to an expensive restaurant on the other side of Stoneybrooke. Lacy had never been to this restaurant before, but had heard it was a place that everyone should put on their bucket list and visit at least once in their lifetime. She felt like Cinderella going to a ball with Prince Charming and hoped she didn't have to leave before midnight. Her high heels weren't made of glass, but they were expensive, and she didn't want to lose one.

They were seated in a beautiful dining room with lighted candles and vases filled with tiny colorful flowers on the tables. Crystal chandeliers hung from the ceiling, and paintings by local artists were hanging on the walls. The restaurant offered two other dining rooms for their busy times. Lacy was happy to let Jay order for her, because she was enjoying just sitting at their table soaking in the beauty of the room. The lights overhead were dimmed, which made the flickering candles glow on everything, making this moment feel like a fairy tale. "I am Cinderella!" Lacy whispered.

"Did you say something, sweetheart?" Jay asked, giving her all his attention now that the waitress had left with their order.

"I feel like Cinderella, and you're my Prince Charming," she said, without stopping to think how that sounded.

"I don't know if I'm Prince Charming, but I do know you're my precious, beautiful Rose Petal," he said, reaching across the table and gently rubbing her cheek with his right hand. Then he slowly moved his thumb across her lower lip, causing such a feeling of excitement inside that she had never experienced in her life before. Especially with what's his name. *Oh shoot, what's happening to me? Am I playing my cards?*

When the waitress brought the drinks Jay had ordered for them, he moved his hand from her cheek. Lacy was glad that he ordered non-alcoholic drinks, because she decided not to take up that habit herself and was getting the impression that he was on the same page. He asked her about the big event she was working on, and she became animated, talking about everything that was happening.

"It's grown into something so big that it almost overwhelms me. But it also makes me feel wonderful to be a part of it," Lacy explained with emotion in her voice.

"You're not just a part of it, you're the creator of it, and I'm so proud of you. This is going to be so inspirational to everyone, and just think about how the shelters are going to be able to help all the poor critters find someone who will share their homes and give them the love they need."

"Oh, I really want this to be successful and hope they do find goods homes for all of them. There also is a program being set up to stop animal abuse," Lacy added.

"It's already a success. I was told that the shelters have had adoptions taking place every day and donations are pouring in," he bragged.

"Yeah, I heard that also. Isn't that wonderful? I did a good thing, didn't I?"

"Yeah, you did a good thing, sweetheart, and I think you're wonderful." Jay got up and pulled Lacy into his arms. He gave her a hug and a kiss and then sat back down. This heartfelt act of showing how much he truly cared made Lacy feel so loved.

The first course was served, and they began to eat their delicious meal together. Lacy was impressed with Jay's choice for dinner and loved the way the meal was prepared. It was no wonder the restaurant was so popular. She wondered how Jay was able to get reservations as quickly as he had. She decided to ask him.

"Jay, you asked me to have dinner with you yesterday, so how did you get reservations for this evening?"

"Well, actually, I made them two weeks ago to give myself time to persuade you to join me. I thought I was going to have to do a lot more than just ask, but you surprised me. I'm so happy to be here enjoying our evening together," Jay explained. *I hope you're enjoying it as much as I am.*

"Really, or are you just pulling my leg?" she said with amusement.

"Maybe later, but yeah, I really made plans two weeks ago. I've been waiting to take you out for forever, but we've both been so busy with so little time off, and I was surprised and excited when you said yes to my invitation. Thank you for this evening."

"Thank you for asking me. I'm having a great time," Lacy returned, her smile radiant.

Dessert was offered after their plates were cleared, but Lacy told Jay she was full and didn't think she could eat another bite. But he ordered one rich dessert with two spoons and two cups of coffee. He wasn't ready to leave and was hoping she'd be tempted to help eat the dessert. He noticed that Lacy didn't seem to be in a big hurry to leave either.

Lacy decided that this was a good time to finally right the wrong she had caused at the party so Jay would know that she'd been in a relationship when she met him, although she wasn't so sure she was still in it.

"Jay, when you came to my party, I misled you about something.

I introduced Spence as my friend, but actually at that time he was my boyfriend. I met him when we were in kindergarten, and we've been together ever since. He got his feelings hurt and was angry at me, although I tried telling him how sorry I was many times." Lacy looked at Jay to see his reaction.

"I knew that already, because I saw his reaction when you introduced him. What I don't understand is why he didn't step up to the plate and let me know he was your man. I'd let him know if the situation was switched. What's his problem? You said he was your boyfriend at the time—have things changed?" Jay asked, hoping they had.

"Well, sort of. He met Lori a few months ago. She came into his office at the newspaper to have an article written about her ex-husband. She wanted to get revenge on him, and since he was well-known, the article would be huge. Spence wanted the credit for it. She'd heard about the way you and I met and thought we were becoming a couple and got very jealous. So she did a number on Spence. Poor, depressed, penniless, divorced, young lady who needed help. She poured on her charm because she wanted to tear us apart to get back at me, because she was jealous of you and me. He told me that she even went so far as to tell him she was falling in love with him, and he said that he was beginning to feel the same way. He felt ashamed because he still loved me. But when he checked out her story, he learned that most of it was lies, which made him begin to see through her little act. He killed the article, and now has started to have doubts about her. I confirmed it when I told him what you said—that he was being played. I thought he was done with her, but he met with her at his office today."

Jay could hear the pain in her voice. "I'm sorry meeting me has caused you so much pain. But I'd like to ask you something. Did you and Spence have plans to get married? Has he ever asked you to marry him?"

"No, he hasn't asked me yet, but I always thought one day we we'd get married. I don't know why it hasn't come up. We have our careers established now, and we're both doing great. We always enjoy doing things together and love the way our relationship has grown, but I just don't know what's going on anymore. We've pulled apart."

"Did you ever think that just being friends was all there was in your relationship? If he really loves you and wants to be your husband, he should go down on one knee and ask you to wear his ring. He should've already asked you to marry him after all this time, and the same goes for you. Most women in love will do anything to get their man to ask for their hand in marriage."

"I never thought about it that way. I was happy with our relationship the way it was going. But I do have to say that what he said caused me a lot of pain. But I also have to say that being here with you makes me feel happy," she said with a smile.

"Well, I'm glad I can make you happy," he returned.

While they were having their conversation, the dessert that was on the table had been eaten by both of them, and they washed it down with their coffee. Not wanting the night to end, Jay asked her if she would like to go with him to a little club where live music was played and where there was a dance floor to enjoy. Her answer was, "Let's go."

The last time Lacy was at a place that played music and had a dance floor was when she was still in school. She'd forgotten the excitement of listening to a live band and watching others dancing and having fun. She was glad that she'd decided to come here with Jay. They found a table and sat down to listen to the music.

"Okay, I've been talking about myself all night, so maybe it's time to change the subject, and you tell me all about you. Tell me what's been keeping you so busy," Lacy begged.

"I don't enjoy talking about myself, but since you asked so sweetly I'll try. My dad is retiring from the business he started years ago and has decided he wants me to replace him. I've spent a lot of time helping him with it through the years, but now he wants me to take over. My mom has opened her own restaurant and wants him to help her run it. She has always wanted to have her own place. So, being the great son that I am, I'm going to make my parents happy and take over. But let's not talk about business, because I want us to enjoy our time tonight," Jay said, then he took her hand and led her out on the dance floor where he took her in his arms and started moving to the music. Lacy couldn't believe how much she loved being held in his arms, his body very close, and their cheeks touching. They danced together for an hour before they decided it was time to leave, and Lacy asked him to come in when they reached her house. Sammy was very happy to see them, and when they took him out Jay threw the ball for him to chase.

"He really is a good dog, isn't he? You got lucky when he found you, didn't you?" Jay said, teasing her.

"Yes I did. I don't know what I'd do without him. He's my baby boy, but he's growing so fast. I signed him up for a dog obedience class because he's going to be a big dog, and I need to be able to control him, although he's very well behaved. I've been told that Labs make great pets," Lacy bragged.

"I'm happy that you have him in your life and that he brought you into my life," Jay said, taking her hand and raising it to his lips for a kiss.

Lacy was speechless, which didn't happen very often, but she had to say something so she said, "I'm happy that I made you happy. Let's go inside and have a cup of coffee and some of my cookies."

Jay stayed for a short time, and they shared cookies and coffee while Sammy sat close by and begged for a bite, which he got. Lacy walked Jay to the door where they hugged, kissed, and said good night to each other.

When Lacy was ready to go to bed, she called Stephanie to talk about the evening she'd just spent with Jay. "Hi, Steph. Bet you can't guess where I went to dinner this evening?"

"Well, I know it wasn't with Spence," Stephanie answered.

"How did you know that? I went out to lunch with him today, and we had a good talk, but then he met Lori at his office afterwards," Lacy added.

"Because he called me today and asked me to meet him in the park. He told me about the conversation you two had, and that he was glad that he finally told you about what was going on with Lori. He also told me that he met with her at his office to tell her he wasn't going to print her story. He had a good talk with her and convinced her that she needed to get help for her depression so she can move on with her life and that he'd still be her friend. He is very confused, and I think a little depressed. So I decided to ask him to have dinner with me, because he seemed so down. I think he felt better after dinner. I knew you'd want me to help him, because he's been my friend for so many years too," Stephanie confessed.

"I'm glad you were there for him. I don't know what he wants me to do anymore. He told me he was seeing Lori, but he didn't tell me why. Then he just got up and left," Lacy explained.

"Where did you go to dinner?"

"I went to a new restaurant. Steph, thanks for listening to Spence and taking him to dinner. I was about to go to bed, so I'll talk to you later," Lacy said, with mixed feelings.

Lacy climbed in bed and pulled the blankets up to her face while Sammy curled up next to her. Lacy wasn't sure if she was happy or sad about Spence, but she had to let him figure out what he wanted, or who he wanted, in his life. She couldn't stop the feelings that she was developing toward Jay—being with him made her feel things that she never experienced with Spence. She knew she shouldn't get any closer to him, but she couldn't stop herself. The cards had been dealt, and she'd played her first hand. She didn't know how the game would end, but she knew she must keep playing.

Lacy kept going over the evening she'd just spent with Jay until she finally went to sleep. She woke up feeling pretty good and decided she wasn't going to let her guilt make her feel bad. She was going to church, and if Spence was there, she'd enjoy being with him if he'd let her, and if not, she'd enjoy church anyway. Spence wasn't there, so her parents invited her to have lunch with them after the service, and then she decided she'd take Sammy to the farm.

Lily Rose was very happy to see Lacy and Sammy, as was Grandpa Robert. Sammy played with Oscar in the yard, while Lacy visited with her grandma and brought her up on what had been going on. Then she climbed onto the tractor with her grandpa and rode out into the fields with him to check on his crops. She once said to him when she was younger, "Look at me, Grandpa! I look just like that commercial for allergies." She'd always loved riding on the tractor with him since she had been little, and he loved it too. He always told her that you can take the girl away from the farm, but you can't take the farm away from the girl. That saying always made her giggle and still did. He was right about that, because she always felt at home here on the farm. After her tractor ride, she helped Lily

Rose work in her garden, and later they fixed dinner together. Then it was time to go home and get ready for the coming week. When she got home Jay called to tell her how much he'd enjoyed their evening together, and she agreed that she'd had a good time also. Then she called Spence to make sure he was well, since he wasn't at church, but she got his answering machine and left a message.

Lacy didn't have to go into her office that week, because she had meetings set up with Stacy and many of the people involved with the big event, and WWSP had decided to hold its second interview at the fairgrounds. She was planning to take Sammy to some of them, since he was going to be the top dog and get to ride in the first car. Everything seemed to be coming together and it looked like it was going to happen without too much trouble. Her boss had attended some of the meetings to lend a hand and let her know what a great job she was doing, and that, if she kept it up, he might have to give her a raise.

Although Lacy stayed busy all day, she had a lot more time since she didn't have to drive so far. She'd called Stephanie earlier and found out that she was home from work with a cold, so she thought she'd take her some hot soup and a sandwich for lunch. When she got there, she saw Spence's car parked in the driveway. She wasn't sure if she should go in, but since she'd brought lunch she decided to stay, and she wanted to make sure Spence was okay. So she knocked on the door and went in. "Steph, I brought you some lunch. How are you doing?"

Stephanie was sitting next to Spence on the couch with tissues in her hand, and her nose was red.

"Hi, Lacy. Thank you, but you didn't have to come back home to bring me lunch."

"I didn't go to the office today, because I have meetings here all week. Hi, Spence. How are you doing today? I missed you in church yesterday. Did you get my message?" she asked.

Spence turned his head to look at her when she spoke to him. His nose was red also. "I wasn't feeling so good, so I stayed home. I guess I caught a cold too. Yes, I got your message this morning when I got up. I went to bed early last night. I figured you'd be at work already. Thank you for asking," Spence returned.

"Sorry you're both under the weather. There's enough soup and sandwiches for both of you, so I think I'll leave before I catch whatever you two have and go back to work. Get better and enjoy your lunch. If you need me, call me."

Since she was close to her house, and she'd given her lunch away, she went home to get something else to eat. She'd taken Sammy home earlier, and he still was very happy to see her, but she wasn't so sure that Spence had been.

"But, my sweet little puppy, he did look sick and like he felt awful," Lacy said to Sammy while rubbing his head. "He didn't go to work because he's sick, but I can't think of any reason why he was there with Stephanie."

She'd been home about an hour and was getting ready to leave when her phone rang. It was Stephanie.

"Thank you for bringing us lunch. It was just what we needed. Spence told me to tell you thanks, and that he will call you later."

"Glad you enjoyed it, and I hope it made you feel better," she replied.

"I thought I should explain why Spence came by."

"Why? He's your friend too. I don't have any say about where he goes or who he sees," Lacy explained, trying hard not to let the emotion she was feeling come out in her voice.

"I went to Lowe's Saturday night to see Andrew and see how he was doing. What he was doing was having lunch with another girl. And it wasn't his sister, because he has no sister. He was holding her hand over the table. I left before he could see me. I guess he's already moved on. I didn't think I'd feel as depressed as I do, but I do. I went home and cried myself to sleep, and you know I didn't go to church either."

"I'm so sorry to hear that, Stephanie. Why didn't you call me?"

"I did call you yesterday afternoon, but you didn't answer your phone, so I figured you were at the farm. Then Spence called to say he was sick and wondered if I was too. When I had dinner with him on Friday, a family was there eating, and their daughter was coughing and sneezing the whole time, so we must have caught what she had. While I was talking to him, I broke down and started crying again.

He told me he was coming over to see what was wrong, and then you stopped by and brought us lunch. Thank you again. I hadn't eaten much before that." Stephanie's voice started to crack while she was talking.

"Listen, honey, I have a meeting to go to, but I'll stop by later, and you can cry on my shoulder, okay?"

"I'm sick, so maybe you should stay away so you don't get it too," Steph said, sounding sad.

"Let me worry about that, okay? See you later, and I'll bring dinner," Lacy promised.

Lacy felt sorry for her friend, and was glad that Spence had been there for her while she had been at the farm. Poor Stephanie; all she wanted to do was find the right man. Spence had always been Lacy's right man for most of her life, and he'd always been there for her. She couldn't imagine how she could live without him in her life. But since she met Jay, her relationship with Spence was changing and getting complicated. She was scared to death that she was losing him, but at the same time she felt like she'd grown up and was experiencing an adult relationship with Jay. She always thought that her life was moving along just the way it was supposed to, until she was rear-ended by Jay. She still wanted Spence and the life they were looking forward to, so she made a promise to herself that she was going to work very hard to get her relationship back on track and show Spence how much she really loved him.

Lacy took dinner to Stephanie, and, while they ate, Stephanie talked about how she was feeling. Stephanie told her there was one good thing that happened—Mark had called to see if she'd like to go out sometime for dinner and she told him yes. After all, she and Andrew had decided to cool it for a while, and since he had already moved on, she was going to let go of her disappointment and try to move forward too.

"That's my girl. Life is too short, and we need to laugh every day. Remember when we had to spend a week working with other people on a job that wasn't related to the class we took together, and we both chose to work at our old high school as janitors during the Christmas break? We laughed so much," Lacy stated.

"Yeah, and remember that day the custodian propped the back

door open when it was cold, and we all went outside to get some fresh air? You were the last one coming back inside, but you left the door open," Stephanie said, giggling.

"Yes I do," Lacy answered. "And you said 'What's the matter with you? Do you think you live in a barn?' And I said 'But I do.'"

"Then I answered 'Oh, I'm sorry, I forgot you do live in a barn,' and you're the only one I could say that to and it would be true." They had a hearty laugh about that incident.

"And remember the day I learned to strip wax off the floors, so they let me do that the rest of the day? At the end of the day we were in the main office gathering the secretary's garbage, and she asked me what I did all day," Lacy said, "and I told her 'I've been stripping all day.'"

"Yes, I remember, and when you turned around there stood the UPS man behind you with his jaw dropping. And I said 'The floors,' and he quickly turned around and left the office."

"The secretary said that was the first time she'd ever seen his face turn red and that we had made her day," Lacy finished. "We both got an A for our class."

Chapter 12

Lacy managed to get through her busy week and was able to get a lot of loose ends worked out. One more week and the big event was going to be held. She couldn't believe how it had grown and how many people were participating to help make it happen. Everyone told her that it was going to be a big success and it wouldn't have happened without her. She was so thankful that her boss had let her take on this project and pleased with herself that she was able to prove to him just how good she was at her job.

Spence called her when he said he would, and she went to his house every evening after work to take care of him. She also stopped to check in on Stephanie to make sure she was getting well. Since they were both feeling better, she invited them to her house Friday evening for a grill out. Stephanie asked Lacy if she could invite Mark and Scott and Scott's new girlfriend. It turned out to be a great evening. Everyone brought their favorite dishes to add to the steaks Lacy had bought. Spence and the guys talked about the things they had done when they were in high school, while the girls talked about the guys. Scott's girlfriend, Barbara Deaton, turned out to be another cheerleader at their school, but was a year behind Lacy and Stephanie. The whole evening turned out to be more of a school reunion, and everyone was having a blast. Spence stayed behind after everyone else left.

"Thanks for taking care of me and Stephanie after working so hard all week. I brought this movie, thinking you might like to watch it with me. I heard it's very good," Spence said, holding it up for her to see.

"I'd love to," she said.

They went into her living room, and she sat down while he put the movie in her DVD player. They sat together on the couch to watch it, with Sammy curled up at their feet. It was late when the movie ended, so Spence gave Lacy a kiss on her cheek, because he didn't want her to get sick from him, and went home. This was the first evening since the accident that she felt like things were getting back to normal between them, and he seemed to enjoy it as much as she had.

Lacy went back to her office on Monday and was working on the project she had been given for the day when Jay stopped by her office. Although he'd called her every day last week, he'd been busy, and since Lacy was away from the office, he couldn't stop by to see her. He told her he'd helped his parents all weekend with the new restaurant.

"I'm so happy to see you, honey. It's seems like a lifetime has passed since I saw you last. I'm glad you didn't catch what your friends had. Are they feeling better?" Jay asked.

"I'm fine, and they feel better now. How's your mom's restaurant doing?" she asked.

"It's starting to feed a lot of hungry customers, and Mom is going to have to hire a few more people. I heard that your project is going to be a big hit and that you're becoming a well-known celebrity and that everyone, including me, has fallen in love with you and your dog named Sammy." *There, I finally said it.*

"Thanks for saying that, but I was just doing my job, and I've fallen in love with everyone I've worked with," Lacy said. *Did I just dodge a bullet?*

"I've got to go because I have a job to do, but do you think you can spare some time to meet me in the deli in an hour to share lunch? Please?"

"Okay, see you in an hour." There's nothing wrong with having lunch with a friend.

Jason, Lacy's boss, had told her that WWSP was airing their first interview on the twelve o'clock news and again at 6 p.m. I can't wait to see what Jay says after he sees that, because he thinks I'm becoming a well-known celebrity, and he hasn't even seen me on television yet. She called her parents, her grandparents, Spence, and Stephanie to tell them to watch the news so they wouldn't miss seeing it. An hour later, she walked into the deli and saw Jay sitting at a table looking up at the television on the wall. She said hello to him and realized that she'd arrived just in time to see Stacy, Jason, and herself on the screen. The reporter had done a great job with the interview, and she was surprised at how well it went.

"You're just as beautiful on the screen as you are in person. I think everyone did a great job, and it's going to bring people from all over who will come and enjoy themselves and help the shelters find homes for all the homeless animals in the process. They're fortunate to have you helping them," Jay said, taking her hands and kissing her. "Now let's grab a bite to eat before we have to get back to work."

Jay's kiss left her breathless and wanting more. And the things he said to her made her feel very special.

As she walked into her office, the phone rang. Spence was calling to tell her how much he liked the interview. While she was talking to him, someone beeped in so she said goodbye to him to answer the other call. It was Stephanie calling to tell her how impressed and proud she was of her. As soon as she hung up with Stephanie, her mother called, and then Lily Rose called her. She was starting to feel like the well-known celebrity that Jay had called her earlier. She wondered if Stacy and Jason were getting as much attention as she was. She hoped so, because they deserved it too. She was so pleased with herself for all the hard work she'd put in and for the way this special event was turning out. It really was going to be a special event.

Lacy was very busy the rest of the week, and Jason told her she didn't have to come in Friday morning, since she was needed at the fairgrounds that morning to make sure everything was set up and ready to open on time. Everyone who was going to participate in the parade on Saturday morning was to meet at a certain place across town to line up to head back to the fairgrounds. She was allowed to have one person sit with her and Sammy—there was only room for five. Jason was going to drive the convertible while Stacy would sit in the passenger seat. Lacy would sit in back on top of the folded down top with Sammy and that would leave a spot on the other side. She'd asked Spence to share that spot, but he said since he'd be covering the event for the paper he was expected to ride on their own float with his boss and co-workers. She was going to ask Stephanie, but Spence told her that he'd invited her to ride on his float since he'd asked her to help them put it together. Stephanie hadn't mentioned that to her, but she was glad that her friend wasn't letting her breakup with Andrew keep her down and depressed, and she was glad that Spence was trying to cheer her up. She was going to have to find someone else. One name came into her mind, but she wasn't sure if that was a good idea because she'd be playing her cards again and she had promised herself that the game was over.

Before leaving her office, Stephanie called her. "Hey, Lacy Rose, I was just thinking about how much fun we had at your house when we grilled out with all our friends. What would you say if I invited everyone back to grill out again in your yard on Friday after work? But this time I'll buy the steaks. I promise you won't have to do anything but enjoy yourself. I know how tired you are and that you need to rest up for the big event."

"I think that's a great idea. It was loads of fun wasn't it?" Lacy said, looking forward to being with all her friends again. "How's it going with Mark? Did you two go out for dinner yet?"

"No, but we talked on the phone. He's busy with interviews for a job, and so is Scott. I've been busy too," Stephanie explained.

"I heard you've been keeping yourself very busy."

"You did? Who from? And what did they say?" Stephanie asked, sounding a little puzzled.

"I talked to Spence. He told me that he was going to ride on the newspaper's float and that, since you had helped him and his co-workers put it together, he invited you to ride with him."

"Yes, that's right. Do you have a problem with that?"

"I'm just feeling a little jealous, because I wanted you to ride with me, and he invited you first. Does that make you feel bad enough to change your mind and ride with me? We'll be riding in a convertible," Lacy begged.

"Lacy, you aren't down on your knees begging, are you? I'm sorry, but I did tell him I'd ride with him and his co-workers. I was invited to work on it, and they were nice enough to include me. I'm sorry. If you'd asked me to ride with you before he asked me, I would've told him I already had a ride. Sorry, Lacy. I'll see you after the parade, all right?"

"You better hang out with me, because it's going to be crazy all day and very crowded—I hope. Did you ever think your best friend could pull off something so big that it would bring so many people together for such a great cause?" Lacy sounded amazed with herself.

"Yes, that's why I became your friend all those years ago. I knew you'd show up on television one day and be famous. And then you'd introduce me as your best friend, and I'd become just as famous as you are. What are best friends for anyway?"

"That's right. I *was* on television, wasn't I? And I was good, so good," Lacy said, giggling.

"Okay, girl. It's time to let the air out of your enlarged head and get back to work. See you later. Oh, and thanks for agreeing to the grill out at your house Friday night." *Oh brother, I created a monster, didn't I?*

On her way home, Lacy thought about who she could ask to ride with her. She could ask one of her parents, but which one should she ask? And would the other one have hurt feelings? Or how about one of her grandparents? She knew her grandpa wouldn't mind if she asked her grandma, but she also knew her grandma would probably not like riding in an open convertible. Then there was Jay. He'd told her that he planned to be at the fairgrounds for all the action, but should she ask him? She'd ride in the first car, which would be up a couple of blocks ahead of the one that Spence would be riding in, because he said his float was closer to the end of the parade, which meant they'd not see each other before the parade started, and her part would be over before he got to the fairgrounds. So maybe it'd work out without causing any trouble. She decided to make that decision after she got home and had more time to think about it. Why was it so hard for her to find someone to ride with her? Maybe she should let Stacy ask one of *her* friends to do it. *When did my life become so complicated? It's because of Jay.*

Lacy was glad to be back home, and Sammy was very excited to see her. She was tired and still confused and decided a soak in a warm tub with lavender-scented crystals and some candles would be just the thing. She closed the bathroom door so Sammy wouldn't knock the candles off the tub, but had to open it again when his whimpering began. She gave him a doggie chew to keep him busy. Then she sank down into the tub and let the tension in her body melt away. After a short time, she got dressed and went down to the kitchen to find something for dinner.

When the doorbell rang, she went to see who it was. When the door opened, in walked Stephanie, with Spence right behind her.

"Hello, Lacy Rose. Spence called and said he was bringing you a pizza, and asked if I wanted to join you."

"Come on in and let's eat pizza," Lacy said, surprised. "I was just looking for something to eat."

"I was too when Spence called me."

"That was okay, wasn't it, Lacy? You've been so busy that we never get to spend time with you," Spence explained.

"Of course! You both know you're welcome here anytime. After this weekend, things should slow down again." Lacy really enjoyed working on her extra project, but was glad it was almost over.

"That's good, because we've been worried about you working so many hours every day for weeks now. I know you're worn out and glad you didn't get sick taking care of us. We both appreciate what you did for us, right, Spence?" Stephanie said, taking a big bite from a slice of pepperoni pizza.

"Yes, Lacy. You've always been there for all your friends. You have a big heart filled with love that overflows with caring. You should've been a nurse," Spence replied, his mouth full of pizza.

"Okay, what's going on? Why all the compliments? Are you guys trying to tell me something I might not want to hear?" Lacy said, laughing, and they laughed too.

"Nothing is going on, honey. We both love you and appreciate everything you do for us," Spence told her.

When the pizza was gone and the kitchen cleaned up, they all went outside. Lacy and Stephanie sat on the swing while Spence played fetch and retrieve with Sammy and his ball. Sammy was good at bringing the ball back, but he wanted you to take the ball from him. After he got tired of playing, Spence sat down in a lawn chair, and everyone caught up with each other's news.

Stephanie said she'd signed up for a night class to further her career, and Spence said that covering the big event this weekend was helping get his name out there and might include a promotion. Lacy told them that her boss said she might get a raise too, or a promotion, or both.

Then Stephanie told them her plans for the grill out on Friday. There was going to be lots of food and games to play. She asked Lacy if she would make her famous potato salad, but only if she felt like it, since she'd already told her she didn't have to lift a finger.

The friends spent the rest of the evening talking and laughing about things that happened to them. When the sun began to set, they went back inside. Both Spence and Stephanie said it was time to go home and told her good night. Spence gave Lacy a hug and quick kiss before he left.

On Friday morning, Lacy decided to drive her golf cart over to the fairgrounds. Her grandpa had given the golf cart to her when she was living on the farm. It was gas-powered, which made it easier to get around the farm. Over the past couple of years, she had added a windshield, a steering wheel with a matching dashboard, an overhead enclosure, lights, and a radio and speakers. She had bigger wheels put on with better shocks, making it sit higher off the ground, and added a black front fender with matching side foot rails on both sides. She had the body removed and replaced with a newer one in red. It had a back seat with a foot stand and hand rails and the seat folded down so she could use the platform to carry things. She had turn signals installed, so she could drive it in the dark, and a gadget to tell her how fast she was going, because she had a kit put on so she could go faster when she drove it on the streets. It had a regular horn, but she had a google horn put on and a radio gadget that played over fifty songs, animal sounds, and different sirens, and it had a microphone so she could speak to a crowd when she drove it in a parade. She had to put a "slow moving" sign on the back and had put two tall bicycle flags on each side behind the front seat and put red stick-on reflectors on the front, back, and sides to make it safer to drive.

She wasn't the only one who drove a golf cart to get around town. There were so many golf cart drivers that everyone decided to get their carts registered with the state so they could buy car tags and get them insured. The police only asked that those who drove on the streets pull over if they were holding up traffic. She'd had her cart registered and put a license plate on the front and back fenders, with a light installed underneath the back one, as required by law. The golf cart also had to have seat belts installed for the front and back seats. She planned to have lights installed under it that would shine on the road. She loved driving her golf cart, and it saved her a ton of money on gas. She took Sammy on many rides, and he really loved it.

Sammy got so excited when he saw Lacy get the cart out of the garage. "I'm so sorry, boy, but Mommy's got to go to work now, but I promise to take you for a ride when I come home for lunch." She checked to make sure the lock was on the gate so no one could open it and let Sammy out of the yard. She could lock him in his pen, but he didn't like to go potty while he was inside it. Her next door neighbor promised to keep an eye on him for her. When cold weather came, he'd go stay on the farm with his friend Oscar again.

Lacy parked the golf cart near the office building of the fairgrounds, put the lock and chain on it, locked the radio in the glove compartment, and then she met Stacy, who was with the fairground secretary, and some of the others. They went over the schedule of events—the times and where they would be held—and walked around to check in with people setting up booths, tents, and chairs for tomorrow's crowd. By the time they got back to the office, it was noon. Stacy asked Lacy if she wanted to join them for lunch, but Lacy said that she had someone waiting at home for her.

Lacy had unchained the golf cart and was about to take off when she heard someone call her name. She looked behind her and saw Jay.

"Where are you off to in such a big rush?" Jay asked her.

"I've got a male waiting for me to come home for lunch," she said in her sexy voice.

"Sammy's a lucky guy. Do you think he'd mind if I came home with you? I brought some lunch from Mom's restaurant, and I'd love to drive your fancy golf cart," he explained while holding up a big bag.

"Okay, climb on board. But be careful, this cart goes pretty fast, and I wouldn't like to see you get pulled over and get a ticket," she informed him, laughing.

"Wow! This cart is great. I'm going to have to get one." He pushed the gas pedal down and the cart took off like a shot being fired. "Oh, my goodness! Did I give you whiplash? Oh, this is great! Where did you get this? And where can I get one?" he asked excitedly.

Lacy filled him in on how she came about having it, and all the improvements she'd made, as they rode back to her house, which only took a couple of minutes. When they got there, Sammy was so excited to see them that they gave him a ride before going inside to eat lunch.

Sitting at the table eating the best bagged lunch she had ever tasted, she was trying to think of how to ask Jay to ride with her in the parade without giving him the wrong idea.

"This is really good food. Thank you for bringing me lunch, and tell your mom she's a great cook. Oh, by the way, Jay, how'd you like to ride with me and Sammy in the parade tomorrow?"

"I'd love to ride with my beautiful Rose Petal."

"And I'd love it if you would ride with me, my handsome Jay Bird. Oh no, I gave you a name! Does that mean you belong to me now?" Lacy said, shocked at herself.

"Yes, that's exactly what it means," Jay replied, giggling. *I'm finally making some progress.*

"Did I say that out loud?" Lacy groaned.

"Come on, sweetheart, I'm just as cute and cuddly as your puppy, and you gave *him* a name and brought him home to live with you. When can I move in?" he said, sounding serious.

"I'm just asking you to ride with me. I'm not asking for a roommate."

"Of course I'll ride with you. Are we going to ride in that awesome golf cart?"

"No, we'll be riding in Jason's convertible with Stacy. We'll be sitting on top of the backseat, with Sammy between us. We'll be leading the parade."

"You *should* be in the lead, because without you, there'd be no parade or anything else happening to help those little critters find families of their own. I'm so proud of you, sweetheart." Jay took her in his arms and showed her just how proud he was of her. In return, she put her arms around him, and, when his lips touched hers, she could feel her heart racing with the excitement he made her feel for him. Could this be love? If it was, she was really beginning to love the way he made her feel.

A few minutes later they cleaned up their mess and climbed into the golf cart and headed back to the fairgrounds. On the way back, he told her he had planned to walk behind his parents' car advertising their restaurant, but he was happy that he'd be riding with her and not having to walk. She almost asked him if he wanted to come to the grill out later that night, but decided that'd be like striking a match to start a fire, and lately she'd started too many of those.

The rest of the day flew by, and everything seemed to be ready for the next morning. She jumped on the golf cart and drove home. Stephanie was already there setting up the games, and Spence was getting the grill ready for the steaks. As she pulled into her driveway, she could hear them laughing as they worked. She walked into the backyard and greeted them.

"Hello, sweetheart," Spence said. "You look tired. Why don't you go take a bath, and we'll get everything ready," he said, giving her a quick kiss.

"Okay. Thank you, honey, my sweet and handsome man."

Lacy ran inside, patting Sammy on the head as she passed him. She took a quick shower and got dressed. Then she went back outside to see what needed to be done. But, true to her word, Lacy didn't have to lift a finger to help Stephanie. Lacy had made the potato salad the night before, so it'd be good and cold. It wasn't long before Mark and Scott and his girlfriend Barbara arrived.

Spence put the steaks on the grill and everyone sat around talking. After the steaks were grilled to perfection, the rest of the food was brought out, placed on the table that was set, and they all sat down to a delicious meal. Mark brought a chocolate cake his mom had baked, and Scott brought ice cream. When everything was cleaned up, they began playing games. The evening was a big success, and everyone seemed to enjoy it, including Sammy, who was very playful and loved all the attention. Everyone decided to leave a little early because they knew tomorrow was going to be a big day for Lacy and they wanted her to get some rest.

Lacy got ready for bed after they left, but it took her a while to fall asleep. Sammy fell asleep as soon as he curled up next to her. She was so excited about tomorrow, and a little worried, although everyone assured her that, no matter what happened, it was already a huge success. She decided to read her book for a while until she was able to relax enough to fall asleep.

Chapter 13

The big event started the following morning at 10:30. All the floats were lined up and ready, waiting on the side roads leading to the main route to the fairgrounds. All the participants were ready to follow the convertible that would lead the parade. Jay decided to meet Lacy at her house to park his car, because her parents were picking them up and taking them to the convertible to lead the parade. Lacy was so excited about the whole day, and so was Sammy. He thought everyone came to play with him. Jay also was excited just to be able to be next to Lacy in the car, although Sammy rode between them. Stacy couldn't believe how big the parade had grown, and Jason was speechless at what Lacy had accomplished with this project. He wasn't sure if he could've done as good a job as she had and was surprised at how much she had learned in the short time she worked for J.S. Bloom Advertising Agency.

Jason got the signal that it was time to take off. As they moved along the route, they waved to all the people who had lined both sides of the street to watch and wave back. Some were sitting in lawn chairs and folding chairs they had set up earlier to get a good spot. Others were standing. The shelters had put together some floats that carried a number of pets looking for homes. Many businesses had made floats to advertise their products or services to the public. There were school bands, people running for office, fire engines, church representatives, horses, daycare centers, and a variety of other entries participating. There was even an old steam-engine train that had real steam coming out and a whistle that had been restored. It had tires installed so it could be driven on a street. It was a very big parade. It only took fifteen minutes for the first car to reach the fairgrounds, but the whole parade lasted an hour as the police car that followed the parade finally got there. The parade went past the stadium full of more people waiting to see it. When the parade broke up, everyone could decide to stay for the events or leave. Buses had been provided for the band members to ride back to their schools. After they passed the stadium and got out of the car, Jay and Lacy found a place to sit and watch the rest of the parade. She was surprised to see Grandpa Robert and her Grandma Lily Rose go by on Grandpa's tractor, and it made her laugh. He was always trying to get her to ride with him, but she'd shake her head no. *I wonder what Grandpa promised to do for her to get her to ride with him?*

The first event after the parade ended was the "Crowning of the Kings and Queens of the Festival for Pets Finding Forever Homes." There was a big platform set up in the middle of the oval horse-race track. While the rest of the seats were filling up Stacy, the secretary of the fairgrounds, and the workers from the other pounds were bringing pets nominated for the crowning onto the platform. There were six dogs competing in the first round: three males and three females. The dogs were led across the stage in front of the crowd, and the amount of the clapping each dog received would determine which one would be selected to be king and queen. The second round was done in the same way, except the contestants were cats. Everyone cheered for the four winners as little hats with colorful crowns were placed on the animals' heads, held on by a stretchy band. All twelve of the pets were up for adoption, and anyone interested could come up to the platform and fill out an adoption application, while everyone else could go enjoy the rest of the events and attractions.

Lacy told Jay she had to take Sammy home before she could walk around to see everything, and Jay went with them.

She couldn't wait to get back to the event because she planned to enjoy herself. There was so much to see, lots of food to taste, arts and crafts to buy, rides to have fun on, and music to listen and dance to. Since she'd forgotten to make plans on where to meet Spence and Stephanie, she walked around with Jay, who was happy to be spending all day with her, and, to be honest, she was happy to be spending time with him. She was surprised at how much fun he was, because when she'd first met him she thought he was a mean, weird person, but the more time she spent with him, the more she began to realize what a really nice man he was, and so lovable. He seldom got angry with her, but when he did, he let her know he didn't like something and then he moved on. He always had lots of patience with her, even when she gave him a hard time, which she did, because of the feelings she was developing for him and the guilt she felt about that.

Jay talked her into going on one of the rides with him. She realized too late that, as the ride twirled around, she was sitting on the outside, making her slide across the seat and press against Jay's body the whole ride. Jay put his arm around her as they turned, and they both laughed the whole ride. When they got off the ride they both felt a little dizzy, so they walked together holding hands. He bought ice cream cones, and they sat on a bench to enjoy them.

They heard a band playing close by so they went into the tent to watch and listen. They were really enjoying the music when Jay asked her to get up and dance with him, which she did. She'd almost forgotten how much she'd loved dancing with him, remembering the time he took her to dinner. Dancing with him made her feel like she was right where she belonged, in his arms and floating in air. After they sat back down, she thought she saw Stephanie and Spence walk by with his camera around his neck—he was taking pictures for the paper—but when she got up to go look, she didn't see either one.

It was one o'clock and time for the beauty show, so they walked to the building where it was to be held. Stacy had asked Lacy to introduce all the pets, giving their history as they walked across the stage, hoping that would give them a better chance of finding a home. All the animals walked down a path, dressed up to impress everyone who came to watch and to make everyone fall in love with them so they'd take them home. There were dogs, cats, two pigs, and one goat that made them all laugh as he strutted down the walkway. One of the pigs was wearing a black vest and top hat that kept sliding sideways, and the other one was dressed as a bride. The dogs and cats were dressed as cartoon characters, but most of the cats had wiggled out of their costumes. After the show, all the animals were brought back on stage so people could meet them and get to know them and maybe adopt them.

During the show, Lacy had seen Spence taking pictures, but, as the show was ending, he left before she could catch him. She hadn't see Stephanie in the crowd. Jay was waiting for her, and they both decided to go find something to eat.

A tractor crash-up derby was being held in front of the stadium, and it drew a big crowd. Jay and Lacy watched for a short time before moving on to the arts and crafts building, and then on to watch they baby pig races, which made everyone laugh. She told Jay she needed to go to the building where the shelters had set up with their pets to see how things were going. When they entered the building, everyone treated her like a famous celebrity—coming up to her and telling her how grateful they were for all she'd done for the shelters. There were many, many people checking out the animals and playing with them, but the most important thing of all was that many of them were being adopted. Veterinarian booths had been set up and the vets were offering free check-ups and shots for the adopters' new pets. All the adult dogs and cats had been spayed and neutered already. Donation cans and boxes were located all around the fairgrounds so money and supplies could be collected. They were secured and watched so they couldn't be tampered with or be stolen. Lacy was told that many people were putting in donations.

As Lacy and Jay were nearing the door to exit the building, Lacy saw a little white Chihuahua puppy with beige spots. She was sitting in a box on a baby blanket. "Oh, look at this precious, tiny little puppy."

"It's a puppy? It looks like a kitten to me!" Jay said.

She carefully picked up the puppy up and saw that it was a female. The puppy was really shaking and seemed to be afraid, so she cuddled her in her arms. "I love you, and I'm going to take you home so you can play with Sammy," she said to the puppy.

"I don't think that's a good idea. Sammy would squash it if he stepped on it," Jay replied.

Amber, a shelter worker, overheard their conversation and came over them. "What breed is Sammy?" she inquired.

"He's a black Lab puppy, but he is very gentle and well behaved," Lacy told her.

"Yes, Labs are gentle and make great family dogs. They're good with children. But you'd have to be really careful with the puppy around him," she explained to Lacy, taking the puppy.

"I know she's just a baby, but she'll get bigger. I want to take her home with me. I'll be a great mommy for her, and Sammy will make a great big brother," Lacy begged.

"Yes, she'll get a little bigger, but not much bigger. She'll still be half the size of an adult cat."

Amber took them to a table where Lacy could fill out all the necessary paperwork to adopt the puppy. Lacy also wrote a check to cover the small fee that included the puppy's first shots. Then Amber handed Lacy the flyer with the puppy's history. Amber wrapped the blanket around the puppy and handed her back to Lacy. "A young couple bought her online when she was two and a half months old. But they couldn't take care of her, so they brought her to the shelter. We had to give her a little care before putting her up for adoption. She's four months old now. They brought her wrapped in this blanket, and it helps calm her down, so please take it with you," explained Amber. Then she reminded Lacy to stop by one of the vet booths and to get a coupon for a free check-up and a set of shots.

"Thank you so much for all your help, Amber," Lacy said.

"Thank you for giving her a good home. Here's my card. If you have any questions, feel free to call me any time," Amber told her.

Lacy and Jay walked to the vet booths and saw Sammy's vet standing in one. Lacy went over to his booth and introduced him to her new puppy. He petted the new puppy on the head. Then she made an appointment for both dogs to get their second set of shots free.

"What are we going to do now?" Jay asked, taking the puppy, still wrapped in the blanket, and snuggling her into his arm.

"Well, it's six now, and the fairground closes at eight. I've done all my duties for the day, so why don't we take our new baby home and have dinner?" Lacy said, without realizing what she'd just said to him.

"Let's go. That really sounds so good to me."

On the way home Lacy asked Jay, "What are we going to name her?"

"How about we call her Alley?"

"No, she doesn't look like an Alley," Lacy said, shaking her head.

"How about calling her Squirt? Tiny? Spot? Monkey? Molly?" Jay said, laughing.

"Molly sounds good. Let's call her Molly, and see how she likes it."

It only took Jay and Lacy five minutes to reach her house. They went to the backyard to introduce Molly to Sammy. Jay put Molly on the ground and Sammy came up to sniff her. Molly got scared and growled, so Sammy backed up, sat down, cocked his head, and looked at her. Then he began to get very excited and wanted to play with her. He went down on his front feet and wagged his tail. Molly barked at him, which seemed to confuse him, so he stood behind Lacy, which made Lacy and Jay laugh. Molly ran over to Jay and put her front paws on his legs to be picked up, so he bent over to get her, and they all went into the house.

Jay sat Molly down on the floor, where she squatted and made a boo-boo. Lacy picked her up and rushed her outside. When she brought her back inside, she said to Jay, "I've got my hands full now, don't I?"

"What are you going to do with her when you go to work?" Jay asked.

"I hate the thought of being away from her while she's so young. I guess I'll take that week of vacation Jason told me I could have next week and figure it out," Lacy said, shaking her head. "What do you want for dinner?" Lacy said, turning to look at Jay, who was sitting at the table holding his stomach.

"I don't know," he replied.

"What's the matter? Is your stomach hurting?" she asked, walking over to where he sat.

"Yeah, I ate something that was in my fridge last night that I shouldn't have, and my stomach has bothered me all day," he explained.

"I can fix you some chicken noodle soup and crackers. Maybe that will help," she returned.

Jay tried to eat some soup, but it wasn't helping. He did manage to eat some of the crackers. After Lacy finished her dinner, she cleaned up the kitchen and took the puppies back outside. When she came back inside, Jay was in bathroom vomiting. She put Molly and her blanket inside the crate and hurried to the bathroom. Jay was down on his knees in front of the toilet groaning. She grabbed a wash cloth, ran cold water over it, and got down on her knees to bathe his face. After a short time, she helped him get on his feet and into the living room to sit on the couch. He rested his head against the back.

"Do you want me to take you to the hospital?" she asked him.

"No, I'll be alright. I'll go home soon," he said weakly.

A little time went by before he got up and headed for the bathroom. She stood by the door to make sure he was all right. "Do you want me to call your parents to come help you?"

"No, they're both at the restaurant. I don't want to be any trouble for you, so I'll leave." But he sat back down on the couch.

"You're going to stay here with me until you start feeling better," she told him.

Lacy went into her bedroom and found her extra-large, pink flannel pants and a large white T-shirt that she kept in a drawer and wore when she was sick. She laid them on her bed and went to get Jay. He got up when she asked him to and followed her into her bedroom. He even put on the pants and shirt she'd laid out for him. She'd left the room while he changed. He was already lying on her bed when she came back into the bedroom. She could hear him groaning again, so she got a heating pad for him and brought him a bottle of water. He drank a little of the water and took some meds for an upset stomach that she gave him. She let him lie there while she took care of the puppies.

It was getting late by now and it was dark outside. She'd have to figure out where she was going to sleep. She was tired and needed to get some rest, because she had to be back at the fairgrounds by noon the next day.

Lacy locked up the house and put the puppies in the crate before she went back into her bedroom to get ready for bed. Jay opened his eyes when she walked into the room.

"Are you feeling any better?" she asked him. When he shook his head no she asked, "What can I do to make you feel better?"

"Would you wear that red sexy nightgown for me, please? I know that will help me feel a whole lot better," Jay begged weakly.

"Jay, I can't wear that," she shot back.

"Please, I'm sick, and you asked me what would make me better and that would do it. Put it on for me, please."

"Okay, I will, but only because you're sick. But no funny business, buster." She was too tired to fuss with him.

She got the red nightgown out with the matching robe and went into the bathroom to get ready for bed. When Stephanie had given her the gown as a gift, she never thought she'd wear it for anyone so soon or so often, and she thought that she'd be wearing it for Spence. But lately, it seemed, she was finding out that things in real life don't always happen the way you think they are going to. After she was dressed, she went back in to see Jay.

"I can't see the gown with the robe over it," he said.

"Okay, I'll open my robe, but only for a couple of seconds, and only because you're sick," she replied, untying the belt and pulling the robe open.

"Oh, you look so sexy, my sweet Rose Petal. Thank you for wearing it for me again," he told her.

"You're welcome. It's time to go to bed now. Good night, Jay Bird." She gave him a quick kiss on the cheek, turned off the lamp, went into the living room, lay down on the couch, and covered up with a blanket.

Lacy had just drifted off to sleep when she heard Jay in the bathroom again. She jumped up off the couch and went in to help him. This time when he lay back down, she decided to lie on the other side of the bed, on top of the covers, with her own blanket. She hadn't planned to fall asleep, but after he had quit groaning and she knew he was finally resting, she fell asleep, which didn't last long, because Molly started whimpering. She got up and took her outside with Sammy, and then, when she came back inside, she put Molly under the cover with her on the couch. Molly settled down, and they both went to sleep, with Sammy curled up at her feet.

Lacy woke up about nine the next morning and took the puppies outside before she used the bathroom in the hallway. Then she went to the kitchen and made herself a cup of coffee and was sitting at the table drinking it when Jay walked in, still wearing her clothes and looking so cute. She picked her phone up off the table and quickly took a picture of him.

"Oh, no. You didn't just do that, did you?" Jay asked, sitting down at the table.

"Do what? Do you feel well enough to drink some coffee?" she asked, placing Molly in his lap.

"My stomach feels a little better, so I'll try some." The tie on her robe was not tied so Jay knew that when she turned around to bring him a cup of coffee, he'd be able to see her red sexy nightgown. While her back was turned, Jay picked up her phone, and, as she turned, he took a picture of her. Before she could set the cup of coffee down and take the phone out of his hands, he had sent the picture to his own phone.

"Jay, did you just take my picture? I look awful this morning," Lacy said, her voice rising.

"Yes, I agree you look *awful sexy* this morning. We're even now, because you took one of me wearing your clothes," he shot back.

"We're not going to stay even, because I'm going to post it on Facebook and Twitter," she told him, sticking her tongue out at him.

"You know you won't do that, because you're too nice to embarrass me like that." *I hope she doesn't post it.*

"I won't, because you've been sick, and that'd be awful mean of me," she promised him.

"Do me a favor. Don't delete your picture. Send it to your computer to be saved in the picture file," he begged.

"Okay, I will, but I'm sending yours there also. So just remember that."

"I'll remember. We can look at them later and have a good laugh."

Lacy fixed some scrambled eggs and toast for breakfast, and they ate. Jay still looked weak but told her his stomach had stopped hurting. He got up to help her clean up the kitchen, but she told him to rest while she did the dishes. She fed the puppies and took them back outside. Molly seemed to be getting the idea of what was expected of her when Lacy put her down in the grass. She also expected to get a treat, just like Sammy always did, when she came back inside—after all, her big brother was showing her the ropes.

It was too late for Lacy to go to church, so she went to clean her bathroom and change the sheets on her bed. Jay had followed her and helped with the bed. He seemed tired after they got it made, so he sat down on the couch. Lacy told him that she had to go back to the fairgrounds at noon and told him that he could stay at her house and rest. She asked if he'd take care of the puppies while she was gone, which would help her a lot, and that she'd bring a late lunch back for both of them. He was very pleased with her plans and told her he'd do something nice for her sometime to pay her back.

"You've already done something nice for me when you took me to the hospital and spent the night. You even fixed my breakfast. I'd say we're even now," she reminded him.

"Oh, I didn't count that because you were very nice to me by letting me have dinner with you and going to see a movie afterward, even if we didn't get to see how it ended. I know what we should do. We can rent the movie and watch it here sometime."

"That sounds like a good plan. I've got to get ready now and get going. Is there something that sounds good to you that I can bring back? I know your stomach is still a little touchy."

"I'll leave that up to you to figure out because I trust your decision."

Chapter 14

Lacy walked to the fairgrounds, but before she left she told Jay to call her if he needed her to come back. She reminded him to drink plenty of water, which would help clear out his system and make his tummy feel better. She met Stacy and the others at the platform in front of the stadium where a ceremony was being held to let everyone know what events were scheduled for the day and to tell everyone how successful yesterday had been. They called Lacy up on the stage and presented her with a plaque congratulating her hard work in bringing this whole event together and for all the wonderful contributions and forever homes found for their animals. They hadn't figured out the total number of adoptions made since the whole thing started, but more than half the animals in all the shelters had been adopted. They told the crowd how Lacy had adopted Molly for herself. They even had managed to talk the one shelter that still euthanized animals to become a no-kill shelter.

After the ceremony, Lacy walked around to enjoy the events and see what she could find that Jay could eat. She hadn't gone far when she ran into Stephanie.

"Hello my hard-to-find best friend."

"Hi, Lacy. Did you see the paper this morning?" Stephanie asked. When Lacy shook her head no, Stephanie said, "Yesterday Spence took a picture of you and that goat that was making everyone at the beauty show laugh, and it made the front page. He wrote the best article about all the hard work you put into this and all the time you spent making this special event happen. You have to read it. Some of his other pictures and stories are in another section of the paper. His editor was so impressed with Spence that he was assigned to write stories with his pictures and post them in the paper for the rest of the week. Isn't that great news?"

"Yes, that's wonderful news. I'm so proud of him. I'm going to have to read the paper when I get back home," Lacy said, feeling excited for Spence. "How's it going with Mark?"

"It's not going anywhere. He told me last week that he ran into Lori a little while back and that they'd been friends when they were in school. They just decided to start seeing each other. She told him everything that had happened to her since they both graduated and that she was in counseling and had joined a weekly group where everyone helps each other learn how to cope with the problems in their lives. So, I'm back on the market again."

"I'm so sorry to hear that, Stephanie."

"It's okay. I'm just glad this happened before I started having feelings for him. I'm trying to be careful about letting myself fall for someone who will break my heart again. I need to know someone for a long time before falling in love. That way, I'll really know him and what kind of person he is," Stephanie said, with feelings in her voice.

"You'll find someone you can love. Someone who'll love you the way you should be loved. Don't give up. Who knows, it might be someone you already know, just like what happened to Mark. Remember, you are very special to me, and I love you, Steph," Lacy said.

"Back at you, girlfriend, and I love you too."

"Busy bees! I've got to go grab some lunch and get back home to Jay Bird and the puppies," Lacy said, racing off.

"Wait, what do you mean jaybird? When did you get a bird?" Stephanie yelled as Lacy hurried away. "She's acting a little weird again, but I guess that's okay, because she looks so tired."

As Lacy was waiting in line to get some soup and grilled cheese sandwiches that she thought would be easy on Jay's tummy, she realized what she'd said to Stephanie. *Goodness gracious*, she thought, *I've got to start filtering what I say out loud.* She was pretty sure she hadn't told Stephanie about the Jay Bird nickname that she'd given Jay. She'd only just made it up recently, and this was the first time she'd seen or talked to her friend for a while. Maybe she hadn't heard what she said, and if she had, maybe she'd forget it. Anyway, she didn't have time to dwell on *what ifs* at the moment.

When Lacy got home, she found Jay stretched out on the couch napping with Molly, still wrapped in her blanket, lying next to him. He'd taken off Lacy's clothes and put on his own. She put the plaque down and took the bag of food into the kitchen and, while it was warming in the microwave, went to wake up Jay. Sammy was lying down in front of the couch when she came back. Jay looked so sweet laying there with the puppies that she couldn't stop herself from reaching into the pocket of her jeans to pull out her phone to take a picture. He opened his eyes as she pushed the button.

"You took another picture? If I weren't sick, you wouldn't get away with that," he warned her, sitting up.

"At least you weren't wearing my flannel pants," she said, giggling. "Are you hungry? I brought you some soup and a grilled cheese sandwich."

"Yes, I'm starving. Thank you, Miss Sweet Pea." He couldn't keep from giggling himself.

Jay took the puppies out while she finished getting their lunch ready to eat. After giving the dogs their treats, he sat down with Lacy, and they ate lunch. Lacy told him about the ceremony that was held and all that was said about her. She got up to get the plaque for him to see.

"That is great, Lacy. You deserve it, and you should put that beautiful plaque on your wall," he told her.

The colorful plaque featured different types of pets that were positioned around the outside edges, and in the middle was written "Thank You, Lacy, for Finding Forever Homes for Our Pets." She was so surprised when she saw it and had felt so honored when they handed it to her. She hadn't expected it because, after all, she was just doing her job the best way she knew how. She also didn't expect all the attention she was getting since the WWSP News coverage and interviews on television. She hoped she wasn't getting a big head from all of it. The best thing that came from this whole thing was Molly. *And she got a Jay Bird?*

After lunch they went outside and sat in the swing and watched the two puppies play together. Actually, Sammy was trying to play with Molly while Molly was trying to show him she was the boss and he'd better listen to her when she barked at him. They were so funny to watch. Sammy sat down and kept turning his head to look at her whenever she barked at him. When she got up to walk around, he followed after her, but she flipped around and barked, which scared Sammy, and he ran to Lacy. They were both surprised, with her being so small and him being so much bigger, at how she could scare him.

"And that, my Jay Bird, is how it's done," she said, laughing.

"I'm scared, so scared," he returned, and he laughed with her.

Lacy needed to go back to the fairgrounds around four to help Stacy with the closing events that ended at six. She asked Jay if he felt strong enough to go with her, and he said that he did. So, after putting Molly in the bedroom crate, they walked over. They were surprised at the number of people still there enjoying themselves. Their first stop was the building where the adoptable pets were. Lacy was surprised to see that only two dogs and three cats were left looking for homes. Stacy came up to her very excited and told her that all their animals had found homes—even the ones still here were waiting to go home with their families after the fairgrounds closed. Some of the shelters still had a few animals at their facilities that hadn't been cleared yet for adoption, but now they had enough funds and supplies to take care of all their problems. Lacy was very pleased at the outcome, because she believed that every pet deserved a forever home and someone to love and care for it and give back that love and caring in return.

Next they went to watch the talent show, which was winding down and which had been open to anyone who wanted to participate. They enjoyed watching the talented people performing on stage. Then they moved on to play some of the games and look at some of the arts and crafts again. Lacy found a booth that had just about anything you needed for pets. She bought a little dog sweater, a collar, a leash, some small doggie chews, and a couple of small toys for Molly, and a big pull toy and some bigger doggie chews for Sammy. She didn't want him to feel jealous of Molly, because he was still her baby bear cub.

It was getting closer to six, and they noticed that some booths were closing up, and they were both getting tired. Lacy told Stacy that she was going to call it a big event and go home. Stacy told her how much she appreciated all she had done for the shelters and how much she enjoyed working with her, and that she wanted her to keep in touch. She also agreed that she was about ready to close up and go home too. All the pets had by now left the building, so there was nothing keeping her there.

Jay told Lacy that he wanted to take her out to dinner, but somewhere quick and easy on the tummy. After giving the puppies some attention, they went out and grabbed a quick meal. They talked about some of the things they had done and seen over the weekend. They also talked about how cute Molly was and how funny she acted around Sammy, who seemed to be happy with her although she confused him. Jay thanked her again for taking care of him while he was so sick. Lacy told him that he didn't have to thank her for that because wearing her pants and making her laugh was thanks enough.

Jay came in when they got back to the house to make sure he hadn't left anything lying around. He pulled her into his arms and kissed her to show her how much he cared for her and told her how much he appreciated all she'd done for him.

"Thank you for letting me wear your pretty pink night shirt and pants," Jay said.

"My pleasure. It sure made a pretty picture."

"I guess it was less embarrassing than my sleeping in my birthday suit."

"Yes it was. It sure was," Lacy said, flushing.

"And thank you for being there for me when I was feeling so sick. I'm glad you didn't send me home alone."

"I wouldn't do that to you, Jay. You needed someone, and I'm glad it was me."

Jay said it was time for him to go home, and Lacy walked with him to the door where he gave her another kiss, told her goodbye, and then he turned and walked to his car. She had to admit that she was going to miss him not being here. It felt like they belonged together and even with him being so sick she enjoyed him sharing her home.

She picked up Molly and sat on the couch, putting Molly her on her lap, while Sammy curled up next to them, and she pulled out her phone to look at the two pictures she had taken of Jay. She knew she'd have to delete them at some point, but not right now. She smiled as she looked at them. "Oh, Jay Bird, why are you trying to make me fall in love with you?" she said out loud and looked at Sammy to see if he had an answer for her. He just turned his head like he always did when she talked to him.

It was too early to go to bed, and too late to go out, but she was too tired anyway. Then she remembered that she hadn't read the paper yet. She went out and found it lying on the porch. She picked it up and sat back down on the couch. When she opened it, she was shocked to see a big picture of her at the fashion show with the goat looking so cute. Normally she didn't like to see pictures of herself, but Spence had captured her true self, and she loved it. She began to read the article, and, as she read, she could feel the love Spence felt for her through his writing as he described how hard she had worked on the event for the shelters and how much compassion she had for the pets she was helping. The article went on for a while talking about her before it finally explained the situation that the shelters were facing and why this event was held. Then it told about how successful the first day had been. It ended by telling everyone what a great job she had done bringing everyone together to enjoy themselves and how it had helped out such a great cause. She had tears rolling down her face when she finished. He had done a wonderful job writing this article, but not because it was about her. The way he wrote touched her heart, and it explained so clearly why this event needed to take place and what it meant for all the shelters. He also wrote about how it brought so many people together to join in and enjoy the weekend and what a great fund-raiser it turned out to be, not only for the shelters, but for everyone who participated. It showed everyone who read the article what a great news reporter and writer he'd become. No wonder Stephanie had been so excited when she had talked about it.

She folded the newspaper carefully because she didn't feel like reading anymore at the moment and laid it down on the table. She'd read the rest of it later. She'd seen Jason at the ceremony this morning and told him she was going to take a week's vacation, so she'd have plenty of time to read it tomorrow. He told her again how proud he was of her, and he was going to give her a bonus with her week of vacation. She was about to tell him he didn't have to, but if that was what he wanted to do, she wasn't going to turn it down. Maybe she could get the lights installed under her golf cart sooner than planned.

What was she going to do with herself this week with no office to go to and no special project to work on? She'd work on getting

Molly potty trained and maybe take her out to meet her new grandparents and Oscar the bulldog. But right now she was going to call her mom to catch up on things, and then she was going to take a nice warm bubble bath. She really loved bubble baths. She also wanted to call Spence to tell him what a great job he had done, but she figured he'd be as tired as she was and probably working on his articles. Plus, she was feeling a little confused and needed to have time to figure things out and get her feelings under control. But other than that, she'd had a great weekend.

Lacy was lying back in a tub of warm water filled with bubble bath while Sammy lay on the bath mat with Molly curled up next to him. She looked down at them and smiled. *My little family*, she thought. She'd only had Molly for a little over twenty-four hours, but she loved her so much already and knew that Sammy did also. He'd become very protective of her. She couldn't wait to take them to the farm and show Molly to Lily Rose and her grandpa. She finally climbed out of the tub and put on her red sexy nightgown since it was still lying where she had taken it off this morning. The phone was ringing as she pulled on the matching robe, and she went into the bedroom to answer it.

It was Stephanie. "Hello, Lacy Rose. Have you had time to read the article Spence wrote about you yet?"

"Yes, I read it about an hour ago. Spence did a great job, didn't he? It made me cry when I read it and it showed me how much he really loves me. He's really a great writer. I'm going to read the rest tomorrow, because I'm so tired and the bubble bath I just took has made me even more tired."

"Yes, he's a wonderful writer, and he did a great job. I'm so proud of him. Oh, I'm a little proud of you also," she kidded.

"Only a little bit?" Lacy asked with a smile on her face.

"Okay, I lied. I'm *real* proud of you and a little jealous because you are getting so much more attention than I am," Stephanie said in a baby voice.

"Yeah, I am, ain't I? Don't worry, my sweet friend, someday you'll do something important and then you'll get all the attention."

"Thanks, that makes me feel so much better. How about having lunch with me tomorrow?"

"Sorry, I'm going to be on vacation all week, and I'm getting a bonus to go with it. Maybe we can have dinner together. I'm planning on going to the farm tomorrow morning to introduce Molly to my grandparents," she apologized.

"Molly? Is that the name of your new jaybird?" *Now she's got a jaybird named Molly.*

"No, silly! Molly is my new Chihuahua puppy that I saw at the fairgrounds yesterday. I fell in love with her and adopted her. She's four months old and so tiny." Lacy was trying not to laugh at what she'd said but was having a lot of trouble. *She did hear me say Jay Bird. And just how am I going to explain that?*

"You got a new puppy? But I thought you said something about a jaybird."

"You're just being silly now. Listen, I'm worn out, so I think I'll just say good night. Sleep tight, and I'll see you tomorrow when you come for dinner." *I'm starting to get good at covering things up, but shouldn't I feel bad about it?*

Lacy decided that she wasn't going to let things like that bother her. Her friend probably had some things going on in her private life that she hadn't shared with her. Didn't everyone? She let Sammy out the door and watched as Molly followed him. She watched them do what they were supposed to do, run back inside, sit down, and wait for the treat they both expected now. "Sammy, you're teaching Molly all your tricks, aren't you, big boy? You're even helping me potty train her, good boy. Let's go to bed now."

Lacy got in bed with Sammy curled at her feet with his blanket and teddy bear, since he was getting bigger, and Molly pressed up against her side under the cover. "Sammy, I'm going to buy you a doggie bed so you can stretch out and not take up so much room, and I'll have room to move my feet." She picked up her book and propped her head up with a couple of extra pillows and began to read. The romance suspense novel was getting really exciting now. It wasn't long before she realized she was very hungry and decided to put the book down and go find something to eat to hold her over until breakfast. She was planning on sleeping in, but she knew she'd have to get up for the dogs at their normal time, but she'd go back to bed after their trip to the backyard and giving them their treat.

Lacy picked Molly up and headed to the kitchen, with Sammy following on her heels, to find something she didn't have to spend much time fixing. There were cookies she'd baked, the leftover cake that Mark's mom had made, and the ice cream Scott had brought to the cook out, but she wasn't hungry for something sweet. She wanted food. She found a frozen pot pie, put it in the microwave, and got a root beer out of the fridge. When the pot pie was ready, she sat down with Molly on her lap. Sammy sat under the table waiting for a bite. It didn't take long to finish eating, since she had a little help. Then she ate a piece of the chocolate cake with some ice cream on top.

"Remind me to take you both on a big walk tomorrow while we're visiting the farm, because I'm going to need it after eating all of this," she said to Sammy.

He cocked his head and wagged his tail, like he knew what she was saying. "Hey, boy, you're going to see Oscar tomorrow, and you can play together." He became excited, and she knew he was aware of who Oscar was—every time she mentioned Oscar, Sammy got really excited.

Lacy cleaned up the kitchen and headed back to the bedroom, got back in bed, and picked up her book. It wasn't very long before she began to get sleepy, so she laid her book down, turned off her lamp, and went to sleep. She slept well, and she'd earned it.

Chapter 15

Lacy only had to get up once to take the puppies out, but she didn't mind because it didn't take long before they were back in the bed. It was nine before she woke up again. After seeing to all their needs, she went into the kitchen to eat breakfast. She filled both the puppies' dishes with their food and sat at the table to eat her own breakfast. She hoped it'd keep them busy so they wouldn't beg for hers. She picked up the paper she wanted to finish reading, along with today's edition, and took them into the kitchen with her. She opened it up and found the rest of the pictures Spence had taken and read the little stories he'd written under each one. They were worth reading and the pictures were really good. He could list photography as one of his assets. Each picture told a story without using words. She was going to call him after breakfast to tell him how proud she was of him and thank him for the beautiful picture he'd taken of her and the wonderful words he'd written about her.

After cleaning the kitchen and reading the papers, Lacy called Spence's office, and he answered after two rings.

"Hi, Spence. I loved the picture you took of me, and you know that's saying something big, because I hate to have my picture taken, and the things you wrote about me made me cry. I always knew you were good at what you did, but I never knew how great you really were. Well, yes, I did, but thank you for all you said about me," Lacy said with emotion.

"I'm glad you loved it, and what I wrote was all true, and it was easy for me to write. You deserve a lot of praise for what you were able to accomplish this weekend. You brought so many people in the surrounding communities together to participate and help all the shelters. Everyone I talked to was very thankful for all you did to help their pets and for the donations they got. All the money that was raised will go a long way toward helping them with the problems they are facing. Now everyone knows what I've known forever, that you're a special person, Lacy," Spence told her, and he meant every word.

"Thank you so much, Spence, but I better hang up now so you can get back to what you were working on. Stephanie said you have articles to write all week. I'm on vacation this week, and I'm going to the farm this morning. Have a great day, Spence."

"You, too, honey."

Lacy called Lily Rose next to tell her she was on vacation and coming to the farm and that she was bringing a surprise to show them. Lily Rose told her that they had a surprise to show her also. She got the puppies ready and off they went to the farm. Lily Rose came out to meet her as she was getting out of the car. She put Sammy down on the ground, and he ran to Lily Rose to get petted, and then he ran off to find Oscar. Then she picked Molly up, who was still sitting in the car, and turned around to hand her to Lily Rose.

"Meet Molly. I adopted her two days ago at the fairgrounds. Ain't she precious?"

"Yes, she is, and so tiny. How old is she?" Lily Rose asked her.

"Four months. So she'll get a tiny bit bigger than she is now, but not much bigger, and Sammy loves her and is so careful of her. Do you like my surprise?" Lacy asked, smiling.

"I love it. Do I get to keep her while you're working?" Lily Rose asked, cuddling Molly in her arms.

"If you don't mind, that would be very helpful. She's already learning to go potty. Sammy is teaching her," Lacy said like a proud mommy.

"Okay, where's your surprise?" Lacy asked.

"Follow me," Lily Rose replied, walking toward one of the barns, still holding Molly.

When they walked in, she saw Grandpa Robert with a goat eating hay out of his hand. Lacy went closer to get a better look at the goat and thought it looked a little familiar. "Oh, my goodness, you have a goat? When and where did you get it?"

"We got Jack a couple of days ago. Do you remember that goat that made everyone laugh at the beauty show? Well, meet Jack. Robert saw him and didn't want to leave without adopting him," Lily Rose explained.

"Now, Lily Rose, you tell the truth. You fell in love with him too, and we both decided to bring him home to the farm," Robert exclaimed. "Jack is a good little goat. He's about a year old and has a silly personality. He likes a lot of attention and follows us around the yard. Oscar hasn't figured him out yet."

"We couldn't help it because he's so cute. Look, Lacy adopted a pet also." Lily Rose handed Molly over to Robert.

"You got yourself a little Chihuahua, how cute. What does Sammy think about her?" he asked.

Sammy came running into the barn when he heard his name, and Oscar came running in with him. Sammy wagged his tail to get Robert to pet him. "Well, hello, big boy. I see you have yourself a little sister. Come here and meet your cousin, Jack," Robert said, laughing.

Sammy walked up close to Jack, but when the goat starting making the sound that all goats make, Sammy shied away and stood behind Lacy, which made them all laugh. Jack walked over to Sammy to get a better look at him. Sammy got down on his front legs and wagged his tail in the air and the goat started running round in circles, which made Sammy start chasing him. They played like that until Lacy and her grandparents left the barn. Sammy and Jack followed after them. Oscar came out with them, but he was still keeping some space between himself and Jack.

Lacy and Lily Rose sat on the porch swing for a while with Molly sitting on Lacy's lap. Robert had climbed on the tractor with Sammy to go check his crops. Lacy told her grandma everything that had gone on since she'd had a talk with her the first time.

"Why is this happening? I was so happy and made so many plans with Spence, then *bang*, along comes Jay and everything started to change. I'm not so sure what I want anymore. The time I spent taking care of Jay this weekend felt so right, and I missed him when he left. Then I read what Spence wrote about me and realized that I still care so much about him. His words made me cry." She laid all her feelings out for Lily Rose.

"Sweetheart, all things happen for a reason. You met Jay for a reason, but what you choose to do about it is up to you. You have to follow your heart and don't let your head cause you to make the wrong decision. I'm not telling you to pick Jay, but don't let him get away if you really think he's the one you love. Let me tell you something that I don't tell everyone. Before I married your Grandpa

Robert, for a long time I had a huge crush on Martin, your grandpa's big brother. I thought I was falling in love with him and that he was falling in love with me. But one day I met Robert. He made me feel nervous and excited when he was around me. He also gave me a lot of attention, made me laugh, and made me feel special. Martin always treated me nice, but he didn't do all the things Robert did or make me feel as special. It didn't take too long before I knew I loved Robert. But, just like you, I felt a little guilty because of my feelings for Martin. But my feelings grew so strong for Robert that I decided to become his wife. Later I found out that Martin was relieved that I chose his brother, because he loved me, but he only wanted to be my friend. You're still young, and I know you will know what to do when the time comes. Don't worry, because things will work out just fine, but you need to ask God to help you make the right decision. Remember, He is always there for you, and He will never let you down. Always keep Him in in your prayers," Lily Rose said. She hoped that what she had told Lacy would help her relax and enjoy every day without worrying about things.

"Thank you, Grandma. You always know just what to say to make me feel good. I'm going to let things happen and enjoy what comes my way. You're right, I'm still young, and I have a lot to learn, and I do believe in prayers," she returned.

Lacy helped Lily Rose fix lunch and then left shortly afterward to go home. Sammy was excited about getting back in the car, and when she put Molly in, she curled up next to him. When she got home she decided that she was going to get some house cleaning done and do the laundry. She was running the sweeper when the puppies started barking. She turned it off to quiet them down and realized the door bell was ringing. She opened the door and there stood a woman with a big bouquet of roses and a box of chocolates and a card. Before she could thank her, the woman turned and started back toward the van parked in the driveway. Lacy closed the door and set the vase down on the table with the candy. Before she could pick up the card to see who it was from, the doorbell rang again. She opened the door and the delivery woman was standing there again, but this time she held two vases of flowers. Lacy took the flowers from her hand and said, "Thank you so much."

"You're welcome," the woman said, smiling, and she walked

back to her van. This time Lacy waited until the delivery woman climbed into her van and drove off.

"Well, how about that? I got flowers and chocolates," she said to Sammy, who sat looking up at her. "And you can't have any because chocolate is so bad for you. It'd be bad for me, too, if I ate them all at once. Let's see who sent them."

Lacy picked up the card from the roses with the box of candy and read it. It was from Jay, thanking her for all she'd done for him and telling her how much he'd enjoyed being with her, especially after he started feeling better. She was going to call him later and thank him for them. The second vase of beautiful flowers was from Stacy and the card stated that there weren't enough words for her to thank Lacy for what she'd done to help her and all the others. The third vase of colorful lilies was from her boss, Jason. His card praised her for her for doing such a great job, and then it said he hoped that she'd enjoy her week of vacation.

She'd have three calls to make later, but right now she wanted to finish her cleaning, so she turned her sweeper back on and the barking began again. She turned it off and, sure enough, the doorbell was ringing again. She opened the door and there stood a man with two more vases of flowers and two more boxes of chocolates. One was from Stephanie and the other from Spence. She thanked the delivery man, and he left. Stephanie's card read "For my best friend forever," while Spence had written, "For my special lady," and his card was signed, "Love you, Spence."

"Gee whiz, when I finish eating all this candy I'm going to have go to the gym and work out all week," she said to herself, because the puppies had decided to go hang out in the bedroom. She put away the sweeper and went to get them—she wasn't sure what Molly might do behind her back—and took them both outside. She sat on the swing and watched as the puppies played. So far her week was starting great. She'd had such an enjoyable morning visiting with her grandparents and having lunch with them, then all the flowers and candy started rolling in, and tonight she was having dinner with Stephanie. She was having such a nice day and she hoped that the rest of her week would continue to be as good. It felt good to be able do what she wanted without having a million other people asking her to do something for them, although she liked her job and didn't mind helping other people. But it felt so good to be off work for a week and getting paid for it, plus a bonus check. Jason hadn't told her how much, but she didn't care how much because she hadn't expected it in the first place.

Instead of going to the gym, Lacy decided to take the puppies to the doggie park. She took a ball for Sammy to chase and some doggie treats. Sammy ran around having a great time while Molly followed Lacy, wanting to be picked up.

"I guess if I were as little as you I'd want to be carried too," she said to Molly, hugging her close. She put the leash on Sammy, and they took a long walk, because Lacy was planning on opening Jay's box of chocolates when they got back home, and she was going to eat a bunch. She'd worked hard for that chocolate, and she was going to enjoy it. She might save some to share with Jay if he came by before they were gone.

When Lacy got back home, she decided it was time to make some calls. She called Stephanie first and told her thanks, and they finalized their dinner plans. Then she called Spence and told him that she really loved the flowers and the candy. He told her he was proud of her and that she deserved a lot more than that. She had to leave a message for her boss thanking him because he was out of his office. Stacy seemed pleased that Lacy had loved her flowers and the two of them made a date to have lunch that week. She wasn't sure if she should call Jay or wait until he called her. But he'd done something good for her, so the least she could do was call and thank him. So she dialed his number, and he answered his phone on the first ring. "Hello, Lacy, is everything okay?" he asked, sounding alarmed.

"Yes, I'm fine, Jay. I'm just calling to tell you I got your beautiful roses, the box of chocolates, and the nice card you sent me, and to let you know I loved them. Thank you so much, but you didn't have to do that."

"Oh, I'd forgotten about that. You never call me, so I thought something was wrong. I'm very happy to hear that you loved them. Just do me a favor, and save me a piece of your candy, okay?" he begged.

"Okay. I was going to open the box and eat all of it, but since you begged so sweetly, I'll wait and open it when you're with me. I've got to go now, because I have to get ready for my date tonight."

"Did I ask you out tonight?" he asked, sounding a little confused, thinking he might have asked her in the card.

"No, silly. I have plans with Stephanie. She asked me to go to lunch today, but I told her I was on vacation this week, so we decided to have dinner instead."

"Oh, that sounds nice. Have fun. Tell Stephanie I said hi, and let me know when you get home— maybe I'll stop by to get my piece of chocolate." He giggled.

"Goodbye, Jay. Talk to you later." She hung up, giggling herself.

The two women decided to go to their favorite restaurant in Pebblestone, so Lacy wouldn't have to drive so far, and Stephanie already had to make the drive home. Lacy decided to pick her friend up and drive them to the restaurant. Stephanie told her about the busy day she'd had, and after they'd been seated, Lacy filled her in the day she'd enjoyed.

"Oh thanks, Lacy. That really makes me feel a lot better about my day. Just kidding. I'm glad you're finally getting some time to relax and take it easy, because you've worked so hard for weeks. It's great you have some time to spend with me and your family. How's Sammy and Molly doing—that is her name, right?"

"Yes, and they're doing great. You'll never guess what my grandparents did," Lacy said.

"What did Robert and Lily Rose do now? They never cease to amaze me," she said, shaking her head.

"Do you remember that goat in the beauty show? They adopted him and took him home to the farm. They named him Jack. He's very cute and follows them around like a dog."

"You've got to be kidding me! Well, they do own a farm, so I guess that's a great home for Jack. He was so cute. I'm happy he found a good home. We'll have to go out and visit him someday soon."

"Yeah, let me know when you want to go for a visit, and we'll go so you can meet Jack. He thinks he's a dog, and Sammy loves playing with him."

When they got back to Lacy's house, Stephanie told her that she wasn't coming in, because she was tired and had some things to do. She said she wanted to walk home and told her she really enjoyed having dinner with her and that she'd call her tomorrow. Lacy forgot to tell her that Jay said hello—or maybe she didn't forget. Lacy went inside to get the puppies and take them out. She was sitting on the swing when Jay came walking down the driveway and into the backyard. He sat down beside her on the swing and gave her a quick kiss. "Hello, Lacy. I'm here to eat my candy." He looked at her, and she just sat there with a big smile on her face.

The sun had set before they got up to go inside. Lacy had figured that Jay would stop by, so she put all the other flowers and candy in one of the other bedrooms, because she didn't want him to think that his gifts weren't special to her. If he saw all the others, he might think that what he got for her just fit in with all the others. She let him open the box, and he picked out a piece for her to eat and one for himself. It was the expensive kind and very delicious. It was so good that they shared a couple more pieces with a cup of coffee. They sat and talked for a short time before Jay told her he had to leave. He kissed her at the door and told her to have a good night and left. What a good ending to a great first vacation day.

Lacy went into the bedroom to bring out the other flowers and the two boxes of candy. She put the candy in a bottom drawer in the refrigerator, but she had marked the box that Spence had given her, so she wouldn't forget. She planned to share his box with him too, and would do the same with Stephanie's box of candy—or she'd eat it all herself, whichever came first.

While Lacy was getting ready for bed, she realized that she hadn't felt guilty about sharing her candy with Jay. In fact, she had enjoyed it very much. She thought about her grandmother having a crush on one man, thinking she loved him, and then meeting and marrying another man—his brother. She was glad Robert was her grandpa and that Lily Rose had followed her heart, because if she hadn't, Robert would be her uncle. Lacy loved her Uncle Martin, but she loved Robert with her whole heart and was glad she'd grown up calling him Grandpa. Lily Rose had made her realize that you have to let things happen and enjoy yourself. God has a plan for your life, and He will help guide you through it.

Molly walked to the door to let Lacy know she wanted to go

outside. "You're such sweet little thing and so smart. How come you're so smart? You hear that, Sammy? I think you could learn a thing or two from her." Sammy wagged his tail and followed them out the door.

Lacy was used to working on her computer while propped up in bed at night, but now that her extra assignment was complete, she felt a little lost. She decided to finish reading the book she'd been trying to read. She got everyone settled in their places in the bed and picked up her book. She read a couple of chapters until she became too sleepy to read anymore. She turned off the lamp and went to sleep.

Chapter 16

The next morning went like clockwork. Lacy finally got a schedule worked out for her and the puppies for their morning routine, which would change next week, because she'd be taking them to the farm when she went back to work. But for the rest of the week, it should work out fine. After breakfast she took the puppies to the park for a nice walk and to get some fresh air. It wasn't as big as the park in Stoneybrooke, but it was really nice just the same. They walked for a short time, or at least she and Sammy did—Molly kept hitching a ride. She took them back home before lunch time because she was meeting Stacy for lunch.

Stacy made plans to meet Lacy at a nice family restaurant close by. Lacy parked her car and pushed her keys into the little pocket on the outside of her purse where she always kept them as she entered the door. Stacy was sitting at a table near a front window, so she went over and sat down and told her hello. A couple just coming in walked past their table laughing, and Lacy heard the woman say to the man, "I wonder whose car is making all that noise?"

Lacy looked out the window to where her car was parked, and sure enough the lights on her car were blinking, and, although she couldn't hear the horn blowing, she knew it was, and knew her car was the one the couple was laughing about. While Stacy was looking at the menu the waitress had brought them, Lacy reached down and got her keys out of the little pocket in her purse and pushed the panic button. She prayed that she was close enough for it to work. Thank goodness it worked. The lights quit blinking, and she put her keys away, looking around to see if anyone else was laughing. Then she picked up the menu to pick out what she wanted to eat, trying not to laugh.

After they ordered their lunch, Stacy told her about all the improvements that she and the other shelter owners were going to be able to make to their facilities and how many of the pets had found homes. One shelter had actually adopted out all of their animals. The small number left at the other shelters were ones that were either being treated for an illness or were too young to be adopted. The shelter that no longer had pets decided to take this opportunity to remodel their building and to add an outside play area. Sadly, she told Lacy, the numbers would soon increase again. But they could handle it better now, and they were starting a new program to help round up strays and unwanted pets.

At the end of the meal, and after passing along all the praise and thanks from everyone for her help, Stacy handed Lacy a card. Lacy opened it and read what it said and felt honored to have been able to help them. Then Stacy handed Lacy an envelope with a check written for a large amount.

"Stacy, this is more than we agreed on. You don't have to do this," she said, surprised.

"It isn't as much as you deserve for all you did, but we hoped you'd be pleased with it." Stacy smiled and patted her hand.

"I'm thrilled! Thank you, and tell all the others I said thanks. If I can ever help again, I'm in," Lacy exclaimed.

"I'll pass that on. I heard from Amber that you adopted the little Chihuahua. How's she doing?"

"Yes, I did, and Molly's doing great. Tell her that Sammy is so good with her, and that she's already going to the door when she needs to go outside."

"That's wonderful, and I'll tell Amber. You should take Molly by so Amber can see her sometime. She got very close to her."

Lacy told her she would. They agreed to keep in touch and left the restaurant.

What am I going to do now? Lacy thought as she sat in her car. *Might as well head to the grocery store and buy some groceries.* Lacy wasn't in the store long before she saw her parents pushing a cart. She stopped and chatted with them. They asked if she wanted to have dinner with them that night. Lacy told them she would rather they came to her house, because she wanted to introduce them to her new puppy. She was happy that she'd decided to go get groceries and told her parents she'd buy hamburger and hot dogs and make some potato salad. Her mother said they'd bring the other dishes and asked if they could invite Lily Rose and Robert. Lacy agreed heartily and pulled out her cell phone to call and ask them. They told her that they'd love to come and were looking forward to it. Lacy told her parents she'd see them later and went to get what she needed.

While Lacy was looking at the hamburger, she heard a voice close by that sounded a lot like Stephanie. When she looked up, she saw a young woman rush around the corner of the aisle. She heard a man's voice say something, and then heard them laugh. She push her cart quickly to the aisle to see two people rushing around the other end of the aisle and out of sight. If this wasn't a week day, she'd swear that the woman looked like Stephanie and the man looked like Spence, but it was a week day, and they'd be at work. Besides, they were moving so fast she'd only got a quick glimpse of the couple. "I've got too much time on my hands," she said out loud, and went back to her grocery shopping.

On a whim, as she was driving home, Lacy decided to go past Spence's house. She didn't see his car, but it could be in his garage. She pulled over and called his office, but he didn't answer, and she decided not to leave a message. Then she thought, just for the heck of it, she'd drive past Stephanie's house. Stephanie's car was there, and Spence's car was parked behind it. She drove a little farther up the street, pulled over, and called Stephanie's cell phone.

"Hello, Lacy. What's up? Did you run out of things to do?" Stephanie asked.

"Yeah, I did, so I went to get groceries, and a funny thing happened at the store. I thought I heard your voice, and when I looked up I saw a woman who looked like you run around the corner of the aisle. Then I heard a man's voice, and the man and woman were laughing together. Then I saw the woman turn the corner at the end of the aisle with a man. I could've sworn it looked like you and Spence. Don't you think that's funny and a little strange, since you two are supposed to be in Stoneybrooke at work? You're at work, aren't you?" Lacy asked, hoping she wouldn't lie to her.

"No, I'm not at work. I took off half a day today. You're right, Lacy, it was me and Spence you saw. He was working on a story, and we ran into each other in the store. He went in to get something to fix for lunch and so did I. We saw you talking to your parents and didn't want you to think we were plotting something together, so we tried sneaking away to avoid running into you. Sorry, Lacy. I guess we should've just stopped when we saw you, and I might as well tell you the rest while I'm talking to you now. I invited him to have lunch at my house. He has to go back to work after he eats. Do you want to talk to him?" Stephanie asked.

"No, that's okay. I've got to go home to get things ready for a cookout this evening. My parents and grandparents are coming over. I planned it with my parents while we were at the store. That's one of the reasons I was calling. To ask you and Spence to come if you want to. There will be plenty of food. You can ask him for me, okay? I've got to go for now," she said, and then put her car in drive and drove off.

As she was driving home, she looked at her gas gauge and saw that it indicated almost empty. Since she wasn't far from a gas station, she decided to fill up and not risk running out. As she was pumping gas, a car pulled up and a woman got out of the driver's side and ran into the station. When the woman came rushing back out with a drink, she went to the passenger's side and opened the door only to realize that her friend was sitting there. Lacy could hear someone yell "Hey!" and then laughter coming from inside the car. The woman quickly walked around to the driver's side to get in, laughing at what she'd done. Lacy couldn't stop herself from laughing, because she'd done that once before.

When Lacy got home, she put all the groceries away, gave her puppies the time they needed, and started fixing her part of the meal. She was looking forward to having her family come to her house tonight. But she wasn't so sure if she felt the same about her best friend and her boyfriend. Lacy was glad that Stephanie hadn't lied to her, but she wasn't sure why Stephanie and Spence seemed to be running into each other so often lately. Maybe she was just feeling guilty for seeing Jay so much and a little jealous because Spence wasn't spending enough time with her, but he seemed to be hanging out a lot more with Stephanie. Oh, well. She needed to quit worrying and start getting things ready for this evening.

Lacy decided she'd let her dad get the grill out of the shed and get it ready for the meat. Since she had finished everything inside the house, she took the dogs outside with her to play while she straightened and cleaned up the yard. Then she put out enough chairs for everyone. She was still outside when her parents arrived. They saw her in the backyard, so her dad went to the shed that she'd unlocked earlier to get the grill out while she went to help her mother bring the food inside. She told her mother about how Spence and Stephanie had been in the store and how weird they had acted. Then she told her mom about driving past both of their houses and the conversation she'd had with Stephanie. She also told her that she'd invited them to come eat dinner with them.

"I really thought that something was going on with them behind my back, but she didn't lie about anything. I feel bad about spying on them, but they were running away from me," Lacy said.

"Well, she just proved to you that you can trust her, because she told you the truth, and if something were going on, I think she'd come and talk to you about it first. She's been your friend forever," her mother told her.

"I know, but I just have a feeling that something I won't like is going to happen, and I don't want to lose either one of them because they're my best friends," Lacy tried to explain.

"Then don't let it. Try to find a solution for whatever you're afraid is going to happen and work it out."

"I'll have to try to do just that, Mom. How did you get to be so smart? Oh, wait, you've always been that smart," Lacy said, laughing and making her mom laugh also.

It wasn't long before Lily Rose and Robert arrived. The hamburgers and hot dogs were sizzling on the grill and Lacy and her mom were setting out the rest of the food.

"Hi, everyone," Lily Rose greeted the group as she came into the backyard. "Thanks for inviting us." She and Grandpa Robert both carried a dish in their arms.

"Grandma, you didn't have to bring anything, but I can't wait to see what you brought," Lacy said, taking the dish from her grandpa. Robert went over to the grill to talk with his son, William, Lacy's dad, while Lily Rose put what she was holding on the table.

Stephanie came walking into the backyard holding up a bag of chips. "Thanks for inviting me, Lacy. It smells so good, and everything looks so delicious. I brought chips. If I'd had more time, I would have baked a cake."

"Sorry, we just decided to have this cookout at the last minute today. I'm glad you came. Is Spence planning on coming too?" Samantha asked her.

"He said if he finished the story he was working on he'd try to come," Stephanie answered, glancing at Lacy to see how she reacted to what she said.

"I hope he can, because William and I haven't seen him for a while."

As soon as she said that, Spence came walking into the backyard, carrying a chocolate cake. "Hi Lacy, Stephanie, everyone else. I didn't have time to bake a cake so I bought one."

Stephanie smiled at Spence as she walked over to take the cake from his hands. She set the cake on the table and then sat down in one of the chairs. Spence walked over to Lacy and gave her a quick kiss before sitting in a chair next to Stephanie. Lacy thought that what had just transpired seemed a little fishy. They both talked about baking a cake. It sounded to her like they had rehearsed it and had a discussion about what to bring and came up with the idea that one would bring chips while one would buy a cake. She decided to ask them. She walked over to where they were and sat down beside them.

"Okay, the cake thing was rehearsed, wasn't it? Did you come up with that when you were having lunch at my best friend's house today?" she asked Spence while she looked into Stephanie's eyes.

"You caught us. Guilty as charged. Is there anything else that needs to be explained while we're telling all our little secrets?" Spence returned, sounding a little upset and looking at Lacy.

"What are you asking me, Spence?"

"Well, the first night of the event, I came by to tell you how great everything had gone, and I saw Jay's car parked in the grass across the street in front of your house, and it was getting late. So I decided to go on home," he explained.

"Why didn't you come in? Because if you had I could've told you why Jay was here. Jay asked me if he could park his car there that morning because he'd planned to join his parents who had their float in the parade. My parents stopped by to take me to where it started, and we invited him to ride with us. When I got to the fairgrounds, I couldn't find either one of you anywhere, so we walked around together while I did my duties. I know you were very busy doing your job, and I never saw Stephanie. When we got back to my house he wasn't feeling good, so I asked him to come in and sit down for a while, and while he was here he started to get really sick from something he'd eaten the night before. I offered to take him to the hospital but he said no. Then I told him I'd call his parents, but he said that they were both at his mom's new restaurant. He was too sick to drive home, so I told him he could stay here. It was almost one in the morning before his stomach settled down enough for him to able to rest and go to sleep. I finally was able to go to bed, and when I got up it was too late to go to church. He was still feeling very weak the next morning, so he stayed here while I went to the fairgrounds to finish the event. He rested and took care of the puppies while I was gone, and it wasn't until I got home that he was feeling strong enough to drive himself home." Lacy hadn't told them the whole story but they didn't need to hear all of it.

"I saw you the next day at the event, and you said you were in a hurry to take lunch home for—" Stephanie started to say when Lacy chimed in.

"Yes, I took Jay something to eat for lunch because he was feeling weak and needed to eat, and I was in a hurry because I had to get back to the event," Lacy told them. "What would you two have done in my place? I would've done the same for both of you."

"I'm sorry, Lacy. I thought you were keeping something from me."

"Why didn't you take a little time to call and ask me? You should've come in that night because you know you're always welcome anytime, and you wouldn't have had to go home thinking bad things about me and Jay. You never call me anymore, so I wasn't able tell you about anything until now," Lacy said, sounding upset.

"You haven't called me either," Spence said in a low voice.

"I did call you to thank you for the flowers, but you were at work and I didn't want to take up all of your time because you are so busy right now writing stories about this weekend. I'm on vacation, so you could've called me whenever you had some free time, but so far you haven't had any time for me. I called you at work today, but you were in a store running around with my best friend and then at her house having lunch. Were you going to tell me this? If I hadn't called Stephanie today I wouldn't have known that you guys were hiding from me. Remember how long it took you to tell me about what was going on with you and Lori? Do you still love me, Spence?"

Stephanie got up and left to join Lily Rose, who was putting dishes around the table. Stephanie didn't want to hear Spence's answer and wanted to stay out of the conversation. She hated to hear her best friends having a disagreement, especially since she seemed to be part of the problem that they were disagreeing about.

Before Spence had time to answer Lacy's question, Lily Rose called everyone over to the table for the prayer. After it had been given, the plates were handed out and everyone filled them up with all the delicious food. Spence jumped up to go get his plate, and after it was filled he went to sit with Robert. Lacy excused herself to go inside the house. She picked up her cell phone and called Jay. He answered quickly, and she told him that she had a grilled steak with his name on it and to get here before it got cold. She also told him that her family was there. He told her he was in his car and driving very close to her house and would be there soon. She took out the steak that was in the refrigerator and went back outside to put it on the hot grill. She no longer cared what Spence thought about Jay coming to see her.

Jay came walking into the backyard while Lacy was standing by the grill making sure his steak was not getting too brown. When she saw him, she put his steak on a plate. When he walked over to her, she handed him the plate, whispered, "Just act like my friend today," and gave him a wink. Everyone told him hello, including Spence. Lacy grabbed a hot dog from the top rack of the grill, and she and Jay went to fill up their plates together. They sat at the picnic table with her mom and Lily Rose, while Stephanie sat close to Lacy's dad, who was sitting close to the swing.

When Jay got up to refill his plate, Lily Rose turned to Lacy and said, "What's wrong, sweetheart? I know you're upset about something."

"Yes, honey, did that thing you were talking about happen between you and your friends? Earlier she told me she was afraid something was going to happen that she was sure she wouldn't like," Samantha explained to Lily Rose.

"We had a little talk and were able to clear up some misunderstandings, but we haven't made any decisions yet. I'll talk to you both later and let you know what's going on when we do," she told them, and smiled as Jay came back.

"I want to thank you for asking me to share this with you today," Jay told them.

"You don't have to thank us. We love having you join us," Samantha replied. "Any friend of Lacy's is a friend of her family."

"Thanks so much. She must get her sweetness from you and Lily Rose. This is so delicious, especially your potato salad, Lacy. You two have taught her well," Jay said, taking a big bite.

"His mom opened up a new restaurant in town," Lacy said as she stood to go let Molly out of the pen, because she was barking. She would let Jay tell them about it.

Lacy was finished eating, although she hadn't eaten very much, but she'd make up for it later when she wasn't so upset. She picked Molly up and introduced her to Stephanie and Spence. This was their first time meeting her; Lacy's mom and dad had met her earlier.

"This is my new puppy, Molly. I adopted her the first day of the event. Don't you think she is cute?" Lacy asked, holding her out so Spence could hold her.

"Oh, Lacy, she's precious. How old is she?" Stephanie asked, taking her out of Spence's arms.

"She's four months old. Sammy loves her, and they're learning tricks from each other," she answered. "I was walking out of the building when I saw her lying on a blanket in a box and fell in love with her at first sight."

"I can't blame you. I might've adopted her myself if I'd seen her," Stephanie said.

"She's very cute and so little. Sammy is so much bigger," Spence said.

"Yeah, but he is so very careful when she's around, and he lets her eat out of his dish first. He's her big brother," Lacy bragged.

She left Molly with Stephanie and went to help her mom and Lily Rose put away the food and to clear the table, which didn't take very long with all of them helping. Her dad cleaned up the grill and then, with Robert's help, put it away. Spence came up to her when she was alone and told her he had to leave, and that he was sorry for what he had said earlier. He also told her that he did love her and that he'd always love her. But he didn't give her a kiss before he left. He must be upset at her for asking Jay to come. Stephanie was talking to Lily Rose when she went back outside. It wasn't long before she came to Lacy to tell her thanks for inviting her, that she enjoyed being there, and that she was going to go home. Lacy didn't know if she should be happy she was going home, or if she should be sad. She knew things had changed between her and her friends today and that it was going to be up to her to fix everything as soon as she got all the facts. But she was afraid the facts were going to be the end of her and Spence as a couple.

Jay stayed until everyone left, and Lacy was happy about that. She needed to be with someone for the rest of the evening— someone who wasn't afraid to show her that he really liked being with her. Before they left, Lily Rose and her mom told her to call if she needed to talk about what had upset her, and she promised she would and thanked them.

Jay sensed that Lacy was upset about something and wondered why she had invited him after everyone else was already there. What she'd said to him when she handed him his steak confused him too, but the look on Spence's face gave him a clue that something had happened before he got there that had made him angry. He also noticed that Stephanie was acting nervous and upset about something as well and wondered if he should ask Lacy or wait until she decided to tell him about it. He hoped that it wasn't something that he'd done to cause all the tension. The last thing he wanted to be was a problem for Lacy, because he loved her.

After Lacy and Jay had waved to her parents, who were the last to leave, Lacy went through the gate in the backyard with Jay and picked up Molly. She took Jay's hand in hers, and they went inside the back door with Sammy following behind them. When they were standing in the kitchen, she set Molly down on the floor and turned and leaned her face against Jay's chest and began to cry. He put his arms around her and held her close until her sobs began to subside. Then he guided her into the living room, sat down with her by his side on the couch, put his arm around her shoulders, and handed her a tissue.

"Are you ready to tell me what's making you so upset, my sweet Rose Petal? Did I do something wrong?" Jay asked.

"Yes you did, and it's all your fault, because before you came crashing into my life, all the plans I'd made for my life were going so well, or so I thought. Then you kept coming around for more and using your charm and good looks to make me care about you. Now I think my relationship with Spence is in trouble, and there may be some trouble with my best friend Stephanie too. The only thing I can't blame on you is the fling that he had with Lori," she told him, knowing that he wasn't responsible for all the problems she had.

"I'm so sorry I made you cry. Do you want me to leave you alone?" he replied with his heart sinking, thinking she didn't want to see him anymore.

"No, my silly Jay Bird. That's the real problem. I don't ever want you to leave," she said, and she kissed him.

Chapter 17

It was the middle of the week, and Lacy didn't have any plans for the day. Jay had stayed with her for a short time trying to cheer her up by making her laugh. It worked because she relaxed and enjoyed her time with him. He finally said he had to leave, kissed her goodbye, and left. She decided she wasn't going to feel guilty about it because when Spence had told her he thought he was falling in love with Lori there must've been some kissing going on, and she decided it was time for him to let her know just what had gone on between them. She picked up the phone and dialed his office.

"Hi Spence, how are you feeling today?" Lacy asked sweetly. *Guilty I hope.*

"Hi Lacy, I'm feeling confused but other than that I'm fine," he answered truthfully.

"Confused about you and Stephanie, you and Lori, or you and me? I'm confused also. I'd like to clear up a few things if you're not too busy to talk to me. When you said that you thought you were falling in love with Lori, how far did those feelings go? Were there lots of hugs and kisses and sometimes ending up in a bedroom or wherever?" she asked, feeling afraid of what he was going to tell her, but hoping he'd tell her the truth.

"Lacy, that's over now so we need to move on," he said, hoping she'd let it go.

"Spence, I need to know," she shot back.

"Yes, I kissed her and hugged her, but I wouldn't let it go any further because I didn't want to hurt you. I would've told you about Lori first before deciding to let it go that far," he explained to her, sounding guilty.

"Oh, I'm glad you would've dumped me first before going to bed with her. It's also good to know that I'm your girlfriend when you aren't kissing another girl. Are you kissing Stephanie now?" she asked, hoping he'd say no because she didn't want to lose her friend.

"No, I haven't kissed her, at least not that in that way, but as a friend I've known all my life and you were usually there," he confessed.

"Are you trying to tell me not yet?" Lacy asked, determined to find out.

"Lacy, I'm sorry to make you feel like you can't trust me, but when I saw Jay's car at your house the other night I thought you were..." Spence didn't finish what he was saying.

"You thought I was cheating on you with Jay, didn't you? No, I wasn't. I hope that answer didn't disappoint you because now you can't use it anymore to make yourself feel better about the situation you are in yet again. Although I do admit that Jay has kissed me, but not that night, and yes, I did clear up the misunderstanding with Jay that you were my boyfriend. I told him that you were more than a friend to me. Do you want to know what he said about that? He asked me why you didn't step up to the plate and tell him I was your girl. Then he said that if you really loved me you should go down on one knee and ask me to marry you and to wear your ring, especially after all the time we've been together. What do you think about that? Is he right? You don't have to answer that right now," Lacy informed him, and then she told him she had to go. "I don't think I want to hear your answer right now," she whispered to herself after hanging up the phone.

Lacy wasn't sure that if he asked her to marry him today that she'd say yes. He'd already had a short relationship with Lori and with whatever was going on with Stephanie right now, it made her think that he didn't want to be married to her anymore. If Spence really loved her in the way a man was supposed to love a woman, with all his heart, he wouldn't be having feelings for other women. But she couldn't blame it all on Spence because she wasn't innocent herself. She let herself develop feelings for Jay. But the whole thing started when he pulled away from her and he started giving his attention to Lori, and she feared it was starting all over again with her best friend. Lacy knew that introducing him to Jay as her friend may have hurt his feelings, but she knew it didn't cause him to have feelings for Lori. That was a mistake he made on his own. But two wrongs never make a right, and it was up to her to come up with a way to fix everything before it went too far, if it wasn't already too late.

Lacy decided since she didn't get all the answers she wanted from Spence that she'd try getting them from her best friend

Stephanie, so she picked up the phone for the second time and called her. Stephanie answered and seemed surprised that she was calling her.

"Hi Steph, my best friend in the whole wide world, how's your day going? Hope I didn't catch you at a bad time. I just talked to Spence, and I thought I'd call to see what you had to add to what he's already told me today. Can you tell me your side of what's really going on?" Lacy asked, hoping to catch her off guard, hoping maybe she'd tell her something he hadn't.

"I'm sorry, Lacy, but we didn't mean to do anything to upset you. When I asked Spence to have dinner with me I was trying to help him feel better because he was so confused and upset, and I was upset too because of my breakup. He told me he felt a lot better after being able to talk to a friend, and so did I, and we did enjoy having dinner together that evening. Then when he came by my house to check on me that day you brought us lunch, we talked about old times and that's when we started feeling closer to each other. Lacy, to be honest, I can't explain why I'm having these feelings for him, and he can't explain his feelings for me either, but I swear to you that we haven't done anything to break your trust. But it does make both of us feel so guilty. He was so angry when he saw Jay's car parked at your house that night, but I told him that there had to be a good reason because you wouldn't do anything to hurt him. Then he got very angry again when you went inside to call Jay to invite him to come join us. He still loves you, and that proved it to me, so I'm going to cool it for now. I was feeling so lost, but having Spence to talk to has made me feel better. I'm so sorry, Lacy," Stephanie said, almost in tears.

"Stephanie, I have to go now," Lacy told her, and hung up.

Lacy had decided that the best thing for her to do was hang up and think about everything that Spence and Stephanie had told her. She didn't want to say something in anger and have to apologize for it later knowing that it was said while she was angry and confused. She didn't want to lose her friends. After all, Lacy had to admit to herself that she knew a little about what Stephanie was experiencing with her feelings for Spence, because she was experiencing some of the same feelings with Jay. The one thing that was different was that Jay wasn't Stephanie's long-time boyfriend/possible husband-to-be.

But that still wasn't an excuse for Lacy to act the way she was acting, or for Stephanie either. She felt bad that she didn't realize how lost her friend had felt over her break up and that she hadn't had time to be there for her.

Lacy couldn't stop everything that she'd been told by her friends that morning from floating around and around in her head, and it was driving her crazy. She called Lily Rose and told her she was coming out to the farm. She was ready to have a talk with her to help her sort through all of it. She got the puppies ready and drove to the farm to spend the rest of the afternoon. Lacy always felt at home there and knew she could relax and enjoy herself. Sammy always loved going, and Molly loved it too. When she pulled into the driveway, Sammy got all excited. While she was getting him out of the car, Oscar came running up to see him with Jack running behind him. The three of them went running off together with Jack jumping up and down around them. Lacy took Molly out of the car and went into the house to see Lily Rose, who was sitting at the kitchen table breaking green beans for dinner. Lily Rose got up and hugged her, telling her that she was always there for her. Lacy grabbed herself a bowl to help her.

"What's going on between your two best friends? I could see that both of them were upset and acting very nervous around you the other day. They aren't falling for each other, are they?"

"Bingo! You won the jackpot. They had dinner together one evening to talk about each other's feelings. Spence was confused and upset over me, and Stephanie was broken-hearted because she was dumped, or maybe a better word would be was replaced, by Andrew. They made each other feel better and enjoyed their dinner date. A couple of days later, they'd both picked up a bad cold from a little girl at the restaurant and stayed home from work. I went to take Stephanie some soup for lunch, and Spence was there to check on her. I left the soup, told them both to get better, and left. Stephanie told me they'd talked about old times and got closer. They were together at the weekend event, and when they saw me in the store yesterday, they ran away and hid so I wouldn't suspect them of something. I wasn't sure it was them so I called Spence, and he wasn't in his office. I decided to drive past both of their houses and Spence's car was parked at Stephanie's house. I called her, and she said that it had been them I saw in the store. Spence was working on a story in the area, and she'd taken half the day off when they both ran into each other in the store to get something to fix for their lunch. After hiding from me, she asked him to have lunch with her at her house. That's where the 'I'd have baked a cake if had more time' line was rehearsed when they got to my house yesterday. I called both of them this morning. Spence didn't really want to give me too much information, but Stephanie admitted that there were some feelings developing between them. But they hadn't cheated on me yet. But she saw how mad Spence got when I invited Jay to come join us and realized he still loved me. And she is going to cool it for now." Lacy took a breath and looked to see how Lily Rose was responding.

"Okay, just why was Spence upset about you?"

"We'd met for lunch one day, and he finally told me about his fling with Lori. He said he was angry at me for the 'friend' thing, but realized that he was only a friend to me because he's not engaged to me. Then he told me about how he felt sorry for Lori at first, then as it went on he thought he was falling in love with her until he found out she was using him, and he was sorry for letting it all happen. He was confused, hurt, and sorry, and then he told me he had to go to his office to meet with Lori. Stephanie told me later that the meeting was to talk her into getting help for all her depression from her divorce. Then he went out to dinner to talk with Stephanie about his depression."

"You should write a book about all this. You poor thing, all of this was going on while you were working so hard on both jobs. You're one strong young lady, Lacy Rose. So Stephanie said she was going to cool it?"

"Yes, she did, but I don't know what Spence wants to do because he didn't want to talk about it. Stephanie told me she was sorry and didn't want to upset me, but she couldn't explain why she started having feelings for him, or why he did for her. I'm angry at both of them, but I also know how she feels because I'm going through the same problem with my feelings for Jay. Why is this happening to me?"

"Things happen for a reason, Lacy. Stephanie was looking for someone to take Andrew's place because she misses being with him, and Spence just happened to be there for her. Spence was a little upset with you, and when Lori threw herself at him, she did that because she was angry at Jay because he fell for you. Lori is just pitiful and needs counseling. Jay is just as cute as a button and has made it clear to you that he's falling for you, and I can't blame you for falling for him. He didn't know about your relationship with Spence until after his feelings for you grew stronger. He's a handsome man—I'm not trying to take anything away from Spence, who's handsome too—but I can tell that Jay really loves you. But you are the one who has to decide who you want as your husband and who will spend the rest of their life with you. You have to decide who makes you feel like you cannot live without them—who makes you feel loved and special, someone who gives you butterflies in you tummy, makes your hands sweat, knows how to make you laugh, makes you miss them when they are not with you, and someone who just flat out makes you feel good when you're with them. Do either one of them make you feel that way? You've only dated Spence in your whole lifetime so far. It's no wonder that when another man literally came crashing into your life you found him exciting and so different from Spence. And did I tell you how cute he is? Sorry, I can't help myself. He's been showing you what you've missed by not dating anyone else. I know some relationships like the one you have with Spence can last a lifetime, but it is rare and doesn't happen that often. You have to decide who you want before they choose someone else, and if you and Spence decide to move on—and I'm not saying that's going to happen—you have to respect his decision whoever he chooses, or you will lose him forever, and maybe your best friend as well. I hope I haven't confused you with all the things I said to you." Lily Rose decided she'd said enough for now.

"Well, you made it clear that you really do like Jay, but no, I understood what you're saying, and I think you're right about everything. I need to have a serious talk with both Jay and Spence, and I need to do it ASAP. Then I may take a little time away from them to make up my mind. But I'm determined to stay friends with both of them. Thanks, Grandma, I love you so much," Lacy told her, and she decided it was time to round up Sammy and go back home. She told Lily Rose that she was ready to have a talk with Stephanie and tell her that she wasn't upset with her and that she would always be her best friend no matter what happened.

"That's a great idea. Do it as soon as you can because she's probably feeling very bad about what she told you today and is worried about losing her best friend," Lily Rose advised her.

When she put the puppies in the car Jack kept jumping up until he managed to get in the car with them. Her grandpa had come up from the fields in time to tell her goodbye, and he told her she should take Jack home with her to play with Sammy for the evening. He'd become fast friends with Sammy. He told her that Oscar was starting to accept him a little more. Lacy told him she'd take Jack home with her and the puppies if he promised to come get him before their bed time. They took off for home.

Jack was so excited he wouldn't stay still, so she pulled over and figured out a way to strap him in with the seat belt. Lacy laughed at the sounds coming from Jack while Molly sat in her lap and barked at him. Sammy sat between them turning his head from side to side looking at Jack and then at Molly.

"I'm not sure this was a good idea. Sammy, what do you think?" Lacy asked him. His answer was to bark one time.

When Lacy got home she took Sammy and Molly into the house first then came out with a leash to put on Jack before getting him out of the car. Jack was used to running around free, but she was afraid he'd run out into the street and get hit by a car. She turned all three loose in the backyard, but had to bring Molly back in the house because Jack wasn't as careful of her as Sammy was. She enjoyed looking out and watching them playing together and wondering where they got all their energy. Molly was happy to be in her little doggie bed wrapped up in her blanket, watching Lacy. She was always cold and shivering.

Jay called her when she got home, asking her how her grandparents were because that was the only place he knew she usually was when she didn't answer her cell phone. He said he was calling to make sure she wasn't upset and crying again. Lacy assured him that she was fine now because she'd had a good talk with her grandma, which made her feel a lot better about things. He was pleased that she was feeling better and told her he'd like to see her some time tomorrow.

Lacy decided to call Stephanie and invite her to come to her house for dinner so she could tell her everything was going to be fine and that she wasn't angry or upset at her.

"Hey Stephanie, I'm just calling to ask you to come have dinner with me at my house tonight, and I'll introduce you to Jack," Lacy teased her.

"Okay, that sounds like fun. But who the heck is Jack?" Stephanie asked, a little puzzled.

"You can meet him when you get here. See you later," Lacy said as she hung up, laughing and wondering if Stephanie thought that she'd found another guy for her to date so she'd stay away from Spence, which might solve a few of their problems if it was true.

Lacy went into her kitchen to see what she had to fix for dinner. She found everything that was needed to make lasagna with garlic bread, and a salad. She got out the noodles to boil on the stove and turned the oven on. It didn't take long before she had it made and placed in the oven. Then she decided to straighten up the house that was already clean and took Molly outside to watch Sammy playing with his new friend. Jack looked like he belonged here in her backyard, but she didn't need another pet, and she didn't think living here in the city that she'd be allowed to keep a goat in her backyard anyway.

Lacy was in her kitchen setting the table when she heard the doorbell ring and went to open the door. Stephanie was standing there looking a little nervous.

"Come on in, Steph. I fixed us a great dinner."

"It smells so delicious in here. Is that garlic bread I smell?"

"Yes it is. You've always had a good nose. I made some lasagna and salad to go with it."

"Where is Jack? Is he coming to eat with us?"

"Jack is already here. He's out in the backyard playing with Sammy right now. Would you like to go meet him before we eat?" Lacy was having trouble keeping a straight face.

"Of course I would. Let's go outside," she said, sounding a little excited.

When they both got outside, Sammy came running up to her to

be petted with Jack right behind him. Stephanie bent down to say hi and rub Sammy's head as Jack came over to her.

"Well hello there, you little goat. Lacy, when did you get him, and where is Jack?"

Lacy couldn't keep herself from laughing at her. "You're looking at him right now," she told her, laughing even harder.

"Wait a minute. Is Jack the goat your grandpa adopted the other day?" Stephanie asked. She started laughing when she saw Lacy shaking her head yes. "What's he doing here?"

"I went to the farm to visit them today, and he jumped up into the car, so Grandpa asked me to bring him home to play with Sammy for a while, but he's coming to get him later."

"Cute, Lacy, very cute, and Jack is cute too. That wasn't funny, but it really was, wasn't it? Thanks Lacy. You really got me, didn't you?"

"What do you mean, Steph? Oh, did you think that Jack was a guy I was going to introduce to you?" Lacy asked innocently. "Oh, I'm so sorry about that, but I really got your goat didn't I, Steph?"

"No, you aren't sorry, and you knew that's what I thought," she shot back, cracking up.

"I told you last week that Grandpa had adopted a goat, and I told you his name was Jack, don't you remember? Then you said you wanted to go with me to meet him. Well, you've just met Jack. Ain't he cute?"

"Yes, he's adorable," she replied, rubbing Jack's ears. "Now let's go inside and eat your great smelling dinner."

After they filled their plates with food and said a prayer, Lacy decided to have her little talk with her. They were getting along so good that she hated to spoil it.

"Stephanie, I just wanted to tell you that I'm so relieved and thankful that you've been truthful about what's been going on. I'm not angry at you or Spence, but it did upset me when I realized that you two were acting strange—well, in your case, a little stranger than usual, and that the two of you were developing feelings for each other. I'm sorry that I wasn't there for you when you had your heart broken. It just hurts to know that Spence has been interested in two other girls in the last six months. I guess he's outgrown our relationship. I haven't been so innocent myself with the feelings that I have for Jay. But I still love Spence and I really thought we'd be together for the rest of our lives, even though he's hasn't ask me to marry him yet. I'm going to have a serious talk with him and see if we still have a chance to move forward, and if not, then I'll have to move on," Lacy said with a heavy heart.

"Lacy, don't break-up because of me. I told you I'd cool it. You two belong together."

"It's not all your fault, because there are a lot of other things that needs to be worked out to fix the problems. But the one thing I want to make clear to you is whatever happens or whoever Spence chooses to share his life with, I'll always be your best friend. I won't let any man come between us. Is that clear?" Lacy said with a lot of emotion in her voice and tears in her eyes.

"Ditto," was all Stephanie could say, because she was so touched by what she heard that she was about to cry.

Chapter 18

Lacy had two more days of vacation before the weekend arrived. She decided to call Spence early this morning and ask him to have lunch with her. Stephanie had told her that he'd been working in town all week because of the stories he was writing, and she hoped that he'd still be here again today—she didn't want to make that drive until she had to next week. She was going to have that serious talk with him. She decided to call his cell phone to make sure he'd answer, and to catch him before he made other plans. She was starting to feel like she'd have to get in line to get attention from him.

"Hello, Spence. I was calling to see where you'll be around lunch time, because I'd like to invite you to have lunch with me today," Lacy said calmly.

"I'll be interviewing Grandpa Robert today, because he adopted the only goat from one of the shelters," he said, like he was proud of him. "I get to meet Jack today. I'll be free to meet you for lunch after I get done with that. Where and what time?"

"You can come to my house when you're done. I made lasagna yesterday, so it won't take long to warm it up with some garlic bread. I'll also make a salad," she told him. "I might even bake a chocolate cake for you." *And I'm going to save a piece of it for Jay.*

Lacy didn't want to take the chance of not being home when Spence got there, but she wanted to take the puppies out, so she decided to take them on a ride on the golf cart. Sammy started jumping up and down when he saw her bringing it out of the garage. She put his leash on for safety and put Molly in the doggie-carry for small dogs that fastened around her waist, and off they went. They'd only gone a few blocks when her sun visor flew off her head. Since no cars were coming, she stopped the cart, jumped off, and quickly went to pick it up. When she turned around, she saw the cart moving down the street.

"Goofy golf cart!" she yelled, and she took off running to catch up to it. She reached it just in time to get back on and stop it before it went through a stop sign. Looking down at the floor, she could see what had made it start moving. She had tied Sammy's leash short enough to keep him from jumping off the cart, but long enough for him to jump down on the floor, which he'd done to follow her. When his front paws had touched the floor, his left one had landed on the gas pedal, and off he went, driving the golf cart down the street.

"Okay, boy, I'm taking your license away until you're older, and you're going to ride in the backseat if you pull that trick again," she told him, laughing at the way he looked at her, and she could swear he knew what she was talking about as they went on with the rest of their ride before going back to her house to park the cart.

Lacy baked a cake before they went on their ride and she let it cool before putting the icing on it. She placed the lasagna in the oven to warm and got out the ingredients for the salad. She was setting the table when she heard a knock on the door. Seconds later Spence came into the kitchen.

"It smells really good, Lacy."

"It is good. I made it for dinner yesterday for me and Steph. Sit down while I get the lasagna out of the oven."

Lacy wanted to wait until they'd finished lunch before having her talk with Spence. So far it was going pretty good, and there didn't seem to be the tension she expected between them. Then she brought the chocolate cake and placed it on the table. When she looked at Spence, she could see that a change had come over him. She cut a piece for each of them and sat back down. Spence picked up his fork and took a bite.

"Spence, I think it's time for us to discuss what it is we both want and what we need to do to make it happen. I've loved you since we met in kindergarten. Although we've had a few ups and downs, we've always been together, except for the little break we took from each other in high school, which only lasted for a couple of months. We got back together because we couldn't stand being apart and after all these years we've always been there for each other. But I'm afraid that I may have become like an old glove to you. It still fits you well, but you want to try on something new," Lacy said honestly.

"No, Lacy. I still love you, and I never want to lose you. I'm so sorry that I've caused you so much grief. It won't happen again," Spence pleaded.

"Until you really decide what it is you want, and who you want to be with, it's going to keep on happening. I'm not putting all the blame on you, because I'm in this relationship too, and I admit I haven't always been there for you lately when you've needed me. I need to figure out what I want. Do you realize that we haven't talked about getting married since we were in our second year of college? I think it's time for us to take a break from each other and give each other some space. I'm not saying that we have to give up our relationship, unless that's what we both choose to do, but I never want to give up our friendship, because I'll always want you as my best friend forever, no matter who you decide to be with. But I'm giving you space to go out and make your own decision without feeling guilty." Lacy could see tears forming in his eyes. As they both stood up, they wrapped their arms around each other and cried together.

Spence was quiet, but this time when he left he hugged and kissed her. Lacy wanted to tell him to call her if he needed her, but she thought she should give him time to figure out what he wanted before telling him that. She felt like she'd just lost the most important thing in her life, but it had to be done. Just like Spence, she had to decide who or what was the most important thing in her life, and either way, she wasn't really going to lose Spence completely. She'd never let that happen to them.

Lacy called Stephanie to tell her that she'd just had a serious talk with Spence and asked that she please give him some time to think about what they had discussed. If he called her, she should talk to him as a friend, but not encourage him to lay all of his problems on her. He needed this time to make up his own mind about what he wanted to do and not think about what anyone else wanted. That way, when he did make up his mind, it would be his own decision.

"This is very important to me, and it will decide my own life," Lacy pleaded.

"Yes, Lacy. I'll do as you ask. I love both you and Spence," Stephanie told her.

"We love you too. Thanks, my best friend ever."

Then Lacy called Mitch and told him that Spence was going to need his friendship to rely on for the next few weeks, because he had to make some decisions for himself. Then she went into her bedroom with her puppies and curled up with them and had a good cry.

Jay told her he wanted to see her today, and when he got there, Lacy was going to have a talk with him too, but she still didn't know what she was going to say to him. She couldn't believe how complicated her life had become since her little accident, which she still blamed on Jay. Lacy must have cried herself to sleep, because the phone woke her up. She picked it up and it was Jay.

"Hello there, my pretty little Rose. I'm in your neighborhood and wanted to know if it was a good time for me to come see you."

"I bet you're sitting in your car in my driveway right now, aren't you?" she asked him.

"Yes, I am, but I'll drive around the corner and come right back if you want me to," he promised her.

"You don't have to do that because you told me yesterday you'd be here today. Come on in."

Lacy jumped out of bed and went into her bathroom to make sure she looked okay and combed her hair. When she went into the living room, Jay was standing by the door waiting for her. He could tell just from looking at her that something wasn't right.

"Did I do something to make you cry again?" he asked, sounding very concerned.

"No, you didn't do anything wrong, and it wasn't you who made me cry the first time. I just needed someone to blame it on, and you were the only person left. I was kidding you the other night. It's just that I had to straighten some things out with Stephanie last night and let her know that we were always going to be best friends no matter what happens. Then today I had a talk with Spence and told him that I thought it was time to take a break, because we've both been confused and we need time to figure out what's important and what we each need in our lives. That was very hard for me, because we've been together since kindergarten."

"I'm so sorry you're going through all of this. Do you want me to leave?" Jay asked, feeling badly for her.

"No, I'd like you to stay if you don't have anywhere else to be," she returned, and she meant it. "I have something I want to show you that I think you might get a kick out of."

Lacy went to the end table by the sofa and picked up a framed picture. She'd put it there after Spence left. Lacy had taken the two pictures that were taken when Jay was sick—the one with him in her flannel pants and the one he'd taken of her in her sexy red nightgown—and had them Photoshopped so they were together in one picture, and had it printed on photo paper. She handed it to Jay, and he was really surprised.

"This is great, Lacy. I love it, but please don't let anyone else see it. Please," he said, laughing with her.

"I'm glad it made you laugh. It's good and funny too, but it's for your eyes only. And, Jay, I need to have a long talk with you too. Oh, don't look so scared. I just need to talk to you about a few things, and maybe it will help clear up all my confusion. But first I want to ask you a personal question. Do you have a girlfriend? Or have you been seeing anyone else since we met? I want the truth."

"No, absolutely not. I haven't had a girlfriend in years, because I've been too busy learning the ropes to take over my dad's business. That's the whole truth, Lacy."

"Thanks for answering that for me, Jay, because I really needed to know. I have another surprise for you. I have lasagna with garlic bread and a salad to feed you for dinner and a chocolate cake for dessert." *I'll be so glad when it's all gone, because I don't think I can eat anymore lasagna.*

Jay seemed glad she was going to feed him, but a little nervous about what she was going to talk to him about. Lacy filled his plate, handed it to him, and put the small amount of lasagna that was left on her plate. When she sat down at the table to eat with him, he noticed the small portion on her plate and offered to give her some of his. She was quick to tell him that this was going to be the third time in two days that she'd be eating lasagna, so no thanks.

After Jay finished his dinner, he told her how good the meal was and how much he enjoyed having dinner with her. As she put a piece of cake in front of him, she felt like she was reliving her lunch all over again, but this time with another man. He started eating his cake, and Lacy knew the time had come for her to have her talk with him. She took a deep breath and began her speech.

195

"Jay, you came crashing into my life one day when I least expected it. In the beginning you really irritated me, but at the same time you made my hands sweat, my heart skip a beat, and you gave me butterflies in my tummy. The more I came in contact with you, the more contact I wanted, and needed. I've grown to love you and all of your irritating, sweet, and loving ways, but I have to make sure this love will be enough to last forever. I just don't know right now, and I'm so confused. I love both you and Spence in different ways and, in some ways, the same. That's why I need to take some time to figure out what I need to do to make the right decisions. I never want to lose you or your friendship, but I want to be sure I choose the right thing to do before I make a big change in my life. Do you understand what I'm trying to tell you?"

"Yes, I do. I know how important it is for you to be sure before making a mistake that could cause pain for everyone, including yourself. Lacy, I hope you don't think I was trying to rush you into this love we share for each other—because I'm in love with you too—but if you don't have the same love for me, I'll be hurt very deeply, but I'll live, and I'll move on. I'll be here to support you while you're making up your mind, and we'll always be friends," Jay answered, getting up and pulling Lacy into his arms as she stood up. "Do you understand that?"

Sammy came running into the kitchen to let Lacy know he wanted to go outside, so they took the puppies out. After Molly did her business, she came running back to Jay and put her front paws on his legs to be picked up. Jay bent over and picked her up, and she licked him on the cheek.

"Molly girl, you're such a sweet little thing," Jay told her. She started squirming in his arms to get back down to go see what Sammy was doing in the kennel.

"I'm glad you like Sammy and Molly, because they're a part of my family, and I'm a packaged deal now," Lacy said, laughing.

"I love packaged deals, especially yours, Lacy," Jay said, laughing with her.

Lacy was standing close to the back door with her back toward it, and Jay was standing in front of her, when Sammy came running toward them with Molly chasing him. Sammy couldn't stop in time to avoid a collision into the back of Jay's legs, which caused him to lunge forward into Lacy, who could see what was happening and threw her arms up to keep him from falling. Jay grabbed hold of Lacy, and they found themselves wrapped up in each other's arms. Lacy looked up into Jay's eyes and could see his lips slowly moving to meet hers. Jay's kiss was so passionate that it took her breath away, and it made her fingers and toes curl. No one in her life had ever kissed her like that, and she wasn't in a big hurry for it to end. A few minutes later they came up for air.

Jay looked at her with the love he felt for her glowing in his eyes, and said, "I love you, Lacy Rose Gardenia, but I want you to remember this—don't go after what you know you can never have from someone, but let what you have for someone come to you." Then he told her it was time for him to go home, but he asked if he could call her every day just to make sure she was all right—not to sway her decision. That was something she had to do on her own, and she told him that she didn't mind.

Lacy felt like she'd worked all week and it wasn't even Friday yet. She was emotionally drained from all the serious talks she'd had with her three closest friends, and she was feeling like her whole life was about to change forever. She felt like what she needed now was a vacation away from her vacation. She decided to call Jason in the morning to see if he could do without her for another week. If not, maybe he could send her something that she could work on at home, so she'd have something to help keep her mind from driving her crazy while she was trying to decide what she really wanted.

While she was getting ready for bed, another idea came to her. She was going to call Lily Rose and ask if she could stay there all next week, starting tomorrow. Even if she couldn't get off work, she was going to have to take the puppies there every morning anyway. That way she'd be away from her house and her three friends, and they wouldn't be able to call her cell phone. If there was a real problem, and they really needed to reach her, they could call her on her grandparents' house phone. She'd tell Jay so he could still call her, because she knew he already had their number.

It was getting late so Lacy got ready for bed. With the puppies all settled in bed, she picked up her book and decided to finish reading it that night. She was surprised at the ending of the book, but was pleased with the outcome. Maybe this would help her to make up her own mind about what she should do. She turned out the light, pulled up the covers, and went to sleep.

Friday morning after breakfast, Lacy called Jason and asked for one more week off. He said she could take it off, but there was some work he needed her to check out to see what could be done. He said he could bring it to her house in about an hour, because he had some business in the area. Then she called Lily Rose and told her what she had planned. While she waited for Jason to come by, she got everything ready to pack. If she forgot anything she could always come back when she needed and get it. While she was packing, her phone rang. It was Jay.

"Hello, Lacy. Is it okay that I called? I hope you're all right."

"Yes, it's okay, and I'm just fine. I'm glad you called, because I wanted to let you know that I'm taking next week off, and in about an hour I'm leaving to stay at the farm all next week through the weekend, so you'll have to call my grandparents' phone to reach me, or leave a message for me to call you back. And, yes, I will take your calls, or call you back if you leave a message. I just thought this would help me get away from everyone. And I'll have some time alone and a nice place to think about everything. I'm taking some work with me that needs to be done. Maybe, if you behave, I'll see if I can get you an invitation to come for dinner one evening."

"That sounds like a great plan to me. Call you tomorrow, honey."

After Jason dropped off the work he had for her, Lacy drove to the farm with her little family.

Chapter 19

Lacy was happy that she'd decided to get away from her house and have a real vacation, even if she did have to work a little bit. She loved being on the farm and spending time with her grandparents, and Sammy was more than happy to play with Oscar and Jack. Molly loved the attention she got from Lily Rose and Robert. After taking all her stuff up to her old room in the barn, she joined Lily Rose in her garden and helped her weed and gather vegetables. Her grandpa took Sammy out in his big enclosed tractor to check on his crops, while Molly stayed on her blanket in the sun near the garden. Jack was having fun following Oscar around.

While they were working in the garden, Lacy told Lily Rose all about the talks she'd had with her friends and what she'd said to each one, hoping her grandma would agree that what she'd told them were the right things.

"Sounds like you covered everything to me and did a great job. None of them told you they didn't want to be your friend anymore, so I'd say you handled it very well."

"Thanks. I have a good teacher. Well, I'd better go get Molly. Looks like she thinks she can be Jack's boss," Lacy said, leaving the garden to go get Molly, who was barking and running after Jack. "She tries acting so tough to make up for being so tiny. She's so funny and lovable."

Lunch was very good. There were lots of fresh vegetables. Robert ate like he was starved to death, but being out in the sun and fresh air and working on the farm gives everyone a big appetite and enough exercise to keep the weight off.

The rest of the day was very enjoyable, and Lacy was finally feeling like she really was on a vacation. She went into her grandpa's grain and seed business on the farm and said hello to all the people she used to work with while she was going to school. Everyone was excited to see her, so she decided to stay and help for a little while. Then she went back to the house to help Lily Rose fix dinner.

A couple of hours after dinner, Lacy said good night to her grandparents and then took her puppies and headed to her room upstairs in the barn. She got out the envelopes containing the accounts her boss had dropped off and started looking them over. She was excited to be working on them. Then she turned on the television and watched a movie until she was tired, took the puppies out for their last call, and then got ready for bed. Molly was finally able to make it through the night.

The next morning, Lacy woke up refreshed and rested. She felt happy for the first time in quite a long while. She heard her cell phone ringing, and was surprised. She picked it up and saw that it was Jay.

"Hello, Lacy. Did you go home?" he asked, sounding surprised that she'd answered.

"No, I'm standing in the middle of my room in the barn."

"I was just calling your cell phone first to see if I'd be able to reach you, because it's too early to call your grandparents' phone. I just wanted to tell you that I'm going out of town this morning to visit some of our other offices. I should be back the middle of next week. I'll call every day to let you know where I am and to check on you. Maybe you can get that invite to dinner for me when I get back."

"Okay, Jay. Thanks for telling me. Let me know when you get back so I can make plans for dinner," she replied, but as she started to walk toward the door she lost his connection.

She walked back to the middle of the room and called him back, "Jay, are you there?"

"Yes, what happened?"

"I moved toward the door. Apparently, I only have service in the middle of the room. I was saying to let me know when you get back so I can make plans to have you come for dinner," she repeated.

"Okay, but do me a favor. Keep your phone in that spot when you're in your room so I can reach you easier."

"I'll try to remember that, but I'll probably only be here early morning or in the evening, okay? But keep trying my cell phone first, because I think there may be some more spots on the farm."

On her way down the stairs to take the puppies out, she was

surprised to realize that she was starting to miss Jay already. She wasn't planning on seeing him while she stayed on the farm, except for dinner one evening, but now that she wouldn't be able to see him, she was missing him. She'd have to think about it later, because right now she had to take care of the puppies and go help Lily Rose make breakfast. While she was stirring the gravy to go with the scrambled eggs, bacon, biscuits with honey, and orange juice and coffee, she told Lily Rose about the call from Jay, the dinner invitation, and feeling that she was missing him already.

"I want you to remember that when making your decision. You need to write down everything you like and dislike about both of them and all the advantages or disadvantages you get with both, and then maybe that will help you see things more clearly. You have two great 'boy toys,' as Stephanie calls them, to choose from. But I want you to remember one thing, Lacy: you're still young, and you don't have to make a quick decision. If it doesn't come easy for you then don't make one right now. Promise me you won't do that, because you might lose your soulmate for life."

"I promise I'll take the time to consider everything and all my feelings before I choose one . . . or maybe neither one. But right now I'm going to set the table while you get Grandpa so we can enjoy this great breakfast."

After breakfast Lacy helped Lily Rose with some cleaning and laundry before working for a while in the garden. Then she climbed onto one of the riding lawn mowers to help her grandpa mow the yard. She put Molly in the doggie pouch to keep her safe. After they were finished, she showered, changed her clothes, and gave Molly a bath because of all the grass on both of them. Then she went out on the porch and sat at the patio table to go over some paperwork before dinner.

Her parents joined them for dinner that evening. Lacy told them that this was turning out to be a very enjoyable vacation. She filled her mom in on what was going with her friends, and her mom agreed with Lily Rose and said she thought Lacy was handling things the right way. After her parents went home, Lacy excused herself and headed for the barn with the puppies. She was planning on doing some more work, but first she wanted to call Jay to make sure he'd had a safe trip. For some reason, she couldn't feel at ease until she talked to him and he assured her that he had arrived safely and was glad she'd called.

Lacy attended church on Sunday with her grandparents and was a little relieved that Spence was not there. But then she felt badly thinking he might be at home depressed and all alone. Stephanie hadn't been there either so he might be with her. Lacy knew she had to stop thinking about them and pay more attention to what the preacher was saying.

After they got back to the farm and ate lunch, she decided it was time to sit down and make the list. She got out two sheets of paper. On the top of one she wrote *Spence*, and at the top of the other one she wrote *Jay*. She wrote for an hour, pouring her heart out and racking her brain, trying to remember everything so she wouldn't forget to write it all down for both of them.

For Spence, she had written that he had been her boyfriend since kindergarten. He was cute, smart, funny, and loved making her laugh.

For Jay, she wrote that he was handsome, sexy, romantic, sensitive, caring, dependable, lovable, and vulnerable, and he loved her dogs.

After she was done she handed the two papers to Lily Rose to read.

Lacy watched as Lily Rose read them and saw her nod her head yes at times and smile at other times. Then she handed the papers back to Lacy.

"Lacy, I think you did a great job writing these papers. You really know a lot about each one of them. Especially Jay. And you've haven't known him nearly as long as you've known Spence."

"Jay kind of grows on a person, but he really seems to be a good man, and I think he loves me. He told me he hasn't dated anyone for a long time and hasn't been seeing anyone but me. I wish I could say the same thing about Spence. Do you think if Jay hadn't rear-ended me, and if I hadn't introduced him to Spence as my friend, that this would be happening?"

"No, I don't. Spence had already decided to write an article for Lori before the accident, so things were already in motion, but it may have made it easier for him to let it go further than he should have. Then he turned to Stephanie for comfort instead of you. What was his excuse for that?" she asked, hoping this would help her sort it out.

"Spence didn't really want to discuss his feelings for Stephanie and didn't give any excuses for anything he'd done. He did tell me he was sorry about all of it. He must think I wasn't smart enough to know what was going on, or hoping I wouldn't find out. When I talked to him he told me he still loved me and he was sorry."

"Do you believe him?"

"I really want to, but he's seen two other women in the past six months. I feel like I'm that old glove I told him about. I still fit and feel good to him, but he's been looking for a new glove to replace me."

"How does that make you feel?"

"I feel hurt, a little angry, and like I'm losing a part of me, but I do have to admit that I haven't missed him since I had the talk with him. Do you want to know something funny about this whole thing? When Jay told me he was going out of town, I immediately started to miss him."

"Well, I think that you finally have a break in some of the things you've been confused about. Remember, you need someone who wants to be there for you, through the good times as well as the bad times, and who will not let something or someone else come between the two of you."

"I'll remember that. Thanks, Grandma. I love you."

"I love you too, Lacy. Now, I'm going inside to figure out what to fix for dinner. Do you have any special requests?"

"No, everything you cook is delicious. I'll be in soon to help you," she returned.

"Take your time. I'm in no big hurry."

Lacy went over the conversation she had with Lily Rose, and it helped open her eyes to a few things that were causing her some confusion. She hadn't known Jay long, but every time she was with him, she'd really loved and enjoyed herself. She'd only gone out with him because she saw Spence with Lori, which she knew wasn't the right way to handle it, but, then, she did get her brain damaged from the football, didn't she? Lacy knew that whatever she didn't know about him, she would learn with more time. She knew almost everything about Spence, but it didn't stop him from falling for two other girls. Was this the way it was going to be from now on? *I must not be the right person for Spence*, she thought. She knew Spence was a good man. He always treated her with respect. She knew he'd make a good husband one day whenever he found the right woman. But ever since knowing him, Jay had always been there for her. He'd called her every day since they met. He wasn't trying to rush her or influence her decision. And he made her feel things she'd never felt with Spence. She finally made a decision about what she wanted and what she had to do now. Lacy took her puppies up to her room to call Jay. She found the spot in the middle of the room and punched in his number. He answered on the second ring.

"Hello, my sweet Rose Petal. How's your vacation going?" he asked, sounding very happy.

"I'm having a great time. I've been cooking, cleaning house, doing laundry, working in the garden, mowing grass, and making a list of all the good things and not so good things about two guys I know. I've made up my mind on who to keep as a friend and who I want to spend the rest of my life with," she teased him.

"Should I be afraid to ask you who you picked to be your friend?" Jay asked, sounding a little scared.

"I've been doing so much thinking that I think my brain needs a vacation," Lacy said, dragging out her answer. "Jay, I want you to be the one I spend the rest of my life with. Spence is always going to be my friend, and I hope you can respect him enough to accept him as your friend too."

"Lacy, you have made me the happiest man in the world! I already like Spence, and I hope he'll accept my friendship," Jay replied, sounding thrilled.

"I'm going to tell Grandma my decision, because she's given me so much good advice and support, but I want you to keep it between the two of us until I have a chance to talk to Spence and Stephanie. They need to hear this from me."

"I think that's the best thing to do. I love you, Lacy."

"I love you too, Jay," she replied before she lost the connection.

Lacy went back to the house to tell Lily Rose what she had finally decided to do.

"Lacy, you look so happy. What have you decided?" Lily Rose asked with a big smile on her face.

"Yes, I decided that Jay is the man I want to be with. I called him to let him know. He was so excited, and so am I. I told him I'd ask you to invite him for dinner when he gets back home. I'd like my parents to come too."

"Oh, Lacy. I'm so happy for the two of you. I think Jay is wonderful man, and I know he loves you too. I think having dinner together is a great idea, so just let me know when he comes home. Just one more question: how were you able to call him?"

"I found a spot in the middle of my room where I can get service, but I have to stay in that one spot or it disconnects," Lacy explained, laughing before giving her grandmother for a big hug.

The rest of her vacation was great, and she was able to rest and enjoy herself.

Chapter 20

Six months later, the big day arrived for Lacy and Jay: their wedding day. It was exactly one year prior that Jay had entered her life. Meeting him had changed her whole life, and she felt like the luckiest girl in the whole world. But that meeting had brought some problems that had to be solved, and had caused some pain for her and her friends.

She had waited until she went back to work before telling Spence and Stephanie what she decided to do. Spence was upset, but he accepted her decision.

Lily Rose had told Lacy that they should invite Jay's parents to come to the dinner they were planning for Jay and her parents. That way they could all meet each other and could start planning the wedding. Lacy had laughed at the last part and told her she was going to wait until Jay asked her to marry him, but they told Jay to invite his parents, and they accepted.

On the night of the dinner, Jay surprised everyone, including Lacy, when he went down on one knee in front of all of them and asked Lacy to marry him. She told him yes. He stood up and put a beautiful ring on her finger and took her in his arms and kissed her. After everyone gave them their congratulations, the plans for their wedding began.

Lacy spent every evening with Jay during the rest of her time off and after she went back to work. She often went with him to eat at his parents' restaurant and got to know his parents very well, which made her realize why Jay had become the man she loved so much and was marrying soon. He was just like his parents, who were wonderful, and she was beginning to love them both. Jan, Jay's mom, was sweet and told Lacy that she was happy that her son had found such a beautiful young lady who was so loving and kind. She had read all the articles written about Lacy and heard about all the hard work she had done for the shelters. But Jan had no idea that she was going to meet Lacy and that she would become her daughter-in-law. Jan was thrilled. So was her husband, James.

It had been a couple of weeks before she called Spence to see how he was doing, and he told her he missed her very much, but he was ready to move forward. Stephanie was excited for Lacy and was enjoying helping everyone make plans for the wedding. She told Lacy that her feelings for Spence had grown stronger, and that Spence said he felt the same way about her. Lacy gave Stephanie her blessing and told her to go get her man. Then she invited Stephanie and Spence to have dinner with her and Jay at his parents' restaurant. After their dinner, the two couples were able to be best friends. Lacy knew that she had made the right decision, one from which everyone benefited.

Jay's father, James, owned two large farms: one had belonged to James's father and the other had belonged to James's grandfather. When his grandfather passed away, James inherited that farm, which he gave to Jay—Jay was their only child and would get it someday anyway, along with the one James owned.

Since Lacy owned a house in town, they had to decide where they were going live. Neither one wanted to leave their homes, so they decided to live at both places. During the week they could live at Lacy's house and go to Jay's farm on the weekends—or whatever felt right at the moment. They could even ride to work together to Stoneybrooke. All their plans were coming together so quickly and without anyone having to give up anything.

Finally the big day had arrived. Lacy and Jay wanted a small wedding for close friends and family. The ceremony would take place at Lacy's grandparents' farm in the gazebo in the backyard. They rolled out a carpet for the bride and her wedding party to walk on and set up chairs on both sides for the guests.

After the ceremony and pictures had been taken, everyone headed to "Lacy's barn" for the reception. It was a large working barn and had been decorated beautifully. Tables were set up to hold the food catered by Jan's restaurant and others were set up with place settings for the guests to sit down and eat. A local band would play music for the bride and groom's first dance after dinner. The cake would be cut and shared by the wedded couple, the bride's bouquet would be thrown, the toast given with grape juice, and then the couple would climb on the decorated golf cart with a sign that read "Just Married," pop cans tied to the bumper, while sunflower seeds were tossed in the air. From there they would head to Jay's farm with the puppies to start their honeymoon. They would wait until the puppies were older to go on a big trip. During the wedding proceedings, Sammy and Molly stayed upstairs in Lacy's apartment and were brought down when most of the activities were over.

The time had come for the wedding to begin. Lacy was wearing Lily Rose's wedding gown with her mother's sapphire necklace and a new veil—"Something old, something new, something borrowed, something blue." Her three bridesmaids wore pastel-colored spring dresses. When the band began playing the wedding march, Lacy and her father waited for the wedding party to head to the gazebo, where the preacher and Jay stood waiting. Stephanie and Spence went first, followed by Scott and Barbara, and then Mark with Lori, who had become their friend and had been accepted by the others.

Then Lacy and her father went out the door and walked down the aisle to the gazebo where she would become Jay's wife.

Lacy's dad gave her hand to Jay and sat down next to her mom. Stephanie walked over and stood next to Lacy, while Mark came up to stand next to Jay as his best man. The preacher began the ceremony with, "We are here to join this couple in wedded matrimony," and asked if anyone had any objections. Since no one answered, he continued.

"Lacy Rose Gardenia, will you take this man to be your lawfully wedded husband, to have and to hold, to love and to cherish, in sickness and in health, until death do you part?"

"I will," Lacy replied, placing the ring on Jay's finger.

"Jay Samuel Bloom, will you take this woman to be your lawfully wedded wife, to have and to hold, to love and to cherish, in sickness and in health, until death do you part?"

"I will," Jay said, and he placed the ring on Lacy's finger.

When the preacher announced that they were now husband and wife, Jay took Lacy in his arms and kissed his wife.

Jay had become her husband and was also her boss at J.S. Bloom Advertising Agency.

Lacy had finally played her cards right, and that's how Lacy Rose Gardenia got her Bloom.